One Love

THE FIRST NOVEL

TAMARA REEVES

iUniverse LLC
Bloomington

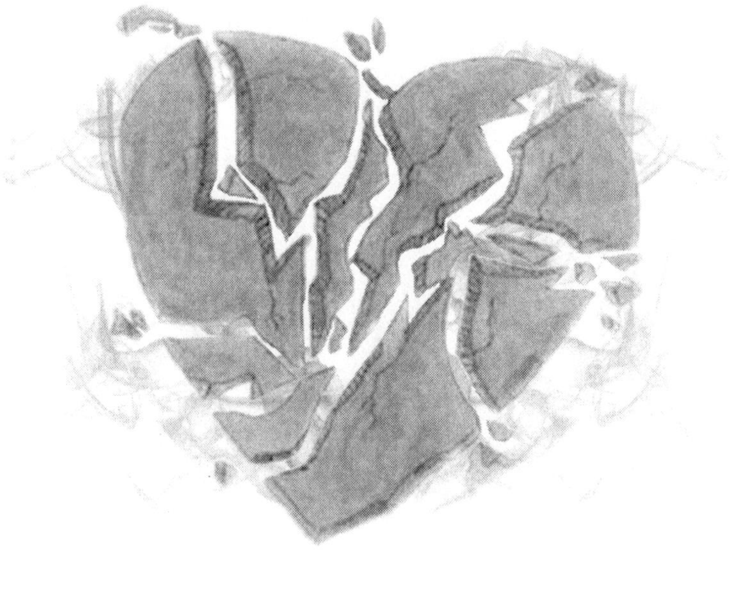

My love for you runs deep
In unseen places
Dark and secret
Singing in my blood and bone

My love for you brings me anguish,
Brings me joy
There is no other who can find
My dark and secret places

Your voice, your smile
Are all you need
To bring me crumbling to my knees
To pull forth from me longing and desire,

My body aches, my body burns
Touch me, hold me, cool my passion
My love for you runs deep
In unseen places
An untamed passion.

CHAPTER ONE

Breathless

It was dark, hot and cramped in the little enclosure. Everyone was sitting shoulder to shoulder two rows deep. Lynn was in the back against the tarp wall, pinned between two very large men who seemed to take up all of the available space. She felt hot and uncomfortable even before the hot rocks were brought in. Once the grandfather stones, as their leader referred to them, were all in place the helper stepped back and pulled the tarp over the entrance leaving the group sitting in absolute darkness, listening to each other breathe. The leader began praying,

"We pray to the four directions, north, south, east and west; to our ancestors and to grandfather sun. Guide us and keep us safe on our journey. Help us to heal and become one race, one people." as he began to chant the group joined in as they had practised the day before.

The smell of the hot rocks and the feel of the heat that flowed over her made Lynn feel weak and dizzy. As the leader poured water over the grandfather stones the heat just kept coming in waves, more intense with each one. Lynn could hear the voice of her Métis friend that had given her advice on surviving the sweat;

"Pray to Mother Earth to help you, ask her to keep you safe and cool you down." so Lynn knelt forward and placed her forehead against the cool ground and said a silent prayer to Mother Earth. The heat intensified as it rolled over her back and seemed to build up against the tarp wall, but Lynn began to feel cooler as Mother Earth drew away the heat from her head. As long as she kept in contact with Mother Earth she felt stronger, cooler and grounded. Sweat poured off her body and soaked her towel as she knelt and prayed. The chanting from the group grew louder and more intense as someone played a drum and began to sing. The darkness seemed to swallow all light as everything and everyone become disembodied. In that moment there was no time, no person, nothing that existed other than the heat and the voices that seemed to come from nowhere and from everywhere at once.

Then Lynn heard his voice as everyone sat quiet and listened to him play the drum and sing. She knew it was Owen, she would recognize his voice anywhere. She had been watching him all week long during their Native Awareness Workshop. Lifting her head, she tried to peer into the darkness but there was an utter absence of light. She could not even see her own hands in her lap. So Lynn sat quietly, entranced by the raw beauty, sadness and power of his song. Something deep inside of her longed to answer, even though this was all foreign to her she felt as if something inside her had just been roused from a long slumber; something that she could no longer ignore.

They stayed in the sweat lodge for what seemed like hours, days. It was if time had stood still. They did four rounds, stopping after each ceremony to open up the entrance to allow some air in and to let everyone cool down for a moment before sealing it up and adding new grandfather stones to the pit for the next round.

When it was over Lynn was one of the last to crawl out of the sweat lodge on her hands and knees. Too weak to stand, two of the men in the group helped her to her feet and propped her up as she staggered to stand in line so each person from the sweat lodge could greet her and give her a hug. As Lynn stood in line beside one of the older women in the group, she asked her if she could lean on her for a moment; just until the dizziness passed. Standing there squinting in the hot August sun Lynn looked up to see Owen standing in front of her draped in a towel and smiling. He was a prairie native man in his mid forties and he stood over six feet five inches; Lynn was almost six feet tall herself but Owen's size was daunting. He was a heavy set with an imposing presence and the most striking brown eyes Lynn had ever seen.

"May I give you a hug?" he asked.

Nodding Lynn stood up straight and gave Owen a weak hug as he encircled her in a large embrace and pulled her into his broad chest. Smiling he stepped back and gave her the traditional greeting,

"Oki, hello." smiling Lynn responded,

"Hello."

After the group had finished greeting everyone Lynn managed to find a small shady spot underneath a tree where she sat, soaked in sweat and exhausted. One of the men in the group that had sat beside her in the sweat lodge walked over and offered her a bottle of water. Too weak to talk she took it and smiling faintly at him she drank the whole bottle before taking a breath.

"Thank you," she gasped, "I really needed that." he smiled back at her as he said,

"That was quite an experience wasn't it?" Lynn was too weak to respond so she just nodded vaguely. Gesturing up the trail he added;

"The others are heading down to the river to cool off; do you feel up to walking there with us?"

"Okay" was all she could manage, as she struggled to her feet and headed down to the river. Lynn picked her way down the trail tripping over the larger stones and trying to avoid anything sharp or jagged with her bare feet. Emerging from the brush at the rocky shore of the river Lynn could see most of the group standing up to their knees in the Old Man River. Some were splashing themselves, trying to get as cool as possible, while a couple of the men had decided to sit or lie down in the slow moving river. Lynn waded out, hiking her skirt up around her knees trying to keep it from getting soaked. The cool, murky water swirled around her legs, cooling her off and making her long to take a swim even though the river was too low and shallow for that. So she scooped up the water and splashed her face as she sighed with the sheer pleasure of the moment. Conscious of the fact she was wearing a white tee shirt without a bra Lynn carefully lifted her long, blonde hair up from the back of her neck and tried to cool off with a couple of splashes of water against her neck before dropping her hair and sweeping it back. Everything seemed sharper, clearer and more vivid to her. The sound of the river was a joyous chorus and the birds singing, the sighing of the wind; even the stones on the shore seemed to be alive in that moment.

Cool and refreshed Lynn headed for the shore, picking her way through the stony ground not really noticing anyone else until she looked up at the crest of the trail to see Owen standing there in just his shorts, with a large crucifix on a gold chain resting on his broad chest. My God what a gorgeous man she thought as she looked up. He smiled quietly at her as she made her way to where he stood, dripping wet from his swim in the river. As Lynn stood in front of him she eyed the gold crucifix around his neck and tilted her head slightly to the side.

"How do you do it?" she asked, "Balance them."

"What do you mean?" he replied as he towel dried his short, jet black hair.

"Balance the two worlds, Christianity and what we just experienced".

"Oh" he replied with a shy smile, "it's not easy."

"No kidding." Lynn responded while she walked away,

"I have never met anyone so striking in my life."

She headed back to the group's bus where she had some dry clothes packed in a bag. There was nowhere for them to change but a couple of the women managed a makeshift change room with towels and at least they got some dry Tee shirts and bras on for the ride back to the hotel.

They all piled back onto the bus and headed back to their hotel at the top of the hill. Lynn noticed that Owen was not on the bus, he hadn't been on the bus on the way their either. She figured he must have stayed behind to help with the sweat lodge after the rest of the group headed back. Once everyone got back to the hotel everyone headed back to their room to have a quick shower and change. A buffet had been arranged for them that evening so Lynn headed back downstairs to the conference room to get something to eat. She was starving; after all they had eaten next to nothing early that morning before heading out. So she was looking forward to dinner.

Once in the conference room she scanned the group to see if Owen was there. She had been thinking about him all the way back to the hotel. He intrigued her; he seemed so interesting and he had such an imposing persona. She really wanted to talk to him again before she had to leave in the morning. Owen was standing at the back of the room talking to a couple of people so Lynn decided to stand in line and get her dinner before finding a place to sit down. As she stood in line Owen walked up behind her and introduced her to the friend that was with him.

"Lynn Thompson this is Jeff Brokenarrow." Jeff smiled and extended his hand. Lynn was intrigued by his beaded vest and long braided ponytail.

"Jeff?" Lynn replied, "I like your vest, it is very unique. Where did you get it?"

"Thank you, my sister made it for me." he answered.

"Very nice work," Lynn shook Jeff's hand. "Were you at the sweat lodge today, you look familiar."

"Yes I was there helping and I was inside with the group." They continued talking as they filled their plates and found a table to sit together and eat.

One of the other group members at the table was listening to their conversation when Owen asked Lynn what she did for the federal government.

"I am a Fishery Officer" she replied.

"What is that?" he asked. The young man listening to the conversation snorted with laughter as he turned to Owen and exclaimed,

"She's an RCMP officer in sheep's clothing! She may wear a different colour uniform, but she carries a gun and trains with the RCMP!" Lynn just smiled and looked down at her plate.

"You got me," she laughed. "It's true. I do carry a gun and wear a uniform." Owen just looked at her in surprise.

"You carry a gun for a living? How do you like your job?" smiling sheepishly Lynn replied,

"I love my job, even though I carry a gun it is not really the most important part of the job."

Lynn and Owen continued on with their conversation as she asked him what he did for a living. He frowned slightly as he tried to explain his role with the provincial government in the education department.

"I am the Director for Native Education in Alberta, he hesitated before continuing. "I have been doing it for about two years now." He seemed like he was not quite comfortable with what he is doing, as if he wanted to do something else, but he was not quite sure what it was that he wanted to do. Lynn nodded as she listened. She was still very curious about the sweat lodge she had experienced earlier that day in the park, so she decided to ask Owen and Jeff if they knew anything about it,

"Do either of you know anything about the history of the park that we were in today?" she asked. They both laughed as Jeff answered,

"Indian Battle Park is its real name; it was the site of a huge battle that took place around 1830 between the Blackfoot and the Cree. The Blackfoot won." He added with a grin, "We kicked their butts and sent them back north where they belong." looking triumphant Jeff turned to Owen and said, "Right cousin? The Blackfoot were strong then and we still are today." Owen grunted and nodded his head in agreement. Lynn smiled faintly at them as she remembered the feeling of the heat and darkness in the sweat lodge. Changing the subject Owen turned to Lynn and asked,

"Are you planning to attend the Pow Wow this evening with the rest of the group?"

"Yes," she replied," I understand that it is traditional for women to wear a dress to the event."

"That's right" he replied. "The dress you are wearing is very nice."

"Do you think so," Lynn asked, "it isn't too much? I wasn't sure what to wear to be honest." Lynn had worn her favourite summer dress that she loved because of the rose colour that complimented her blonde hair with a flirty diagonal cut just below the knee.

"No I like it." he replied smiling at her as he looked into her eyes.

"Thanks," blushing Lynn looked down and brushed away imaginary crumbs from her lap. "Well, I guess we are leaving pretty soon for the bus."

"Yes" Owen answered "I will see you there." Puzzled by his response, Lynn walked down to the lobby and waited for the rest of the group to join her. As she was standing in the lobby admiring the indoor garden that was growing under the central skylight her cell phone rang. Digging through her purse, Lynn managed to find it and answered it just before it went to voicemail.

"Hello?"

"Hello Lynn" answered her husband "Why do you sound surprised? Were you expecting someone else?" frustrated and feeling mildly guilty for the attraction she had been feeling for Owen she flushed and responded,

"No, of course not." still feeling guilty she looked around to be sure no one was listening to her conversation.

"Huh" Steve grunted on the other end of the phone. "Not sure I believe you but what can I do about it right now anyways? I just wanted to know when you would be coming back home."

"Tomorrow night." she replied tersely; hating the idea of going back home to him.

"Okay, what time?" he pressed, with an edge in his voice. Lynn could tell where this conversation was going. They were about to start another argument, again. God, being married to Steve was like being in hell on earth.

"I don't know, late. If my flights are all on time I should be home around midnight. If not then I'll call you and let you know." Lynn wanted to hang up the phone as soon as possible. She did not want to continue this conversation with any one from the group listening.

"I have to go Steve. I'll call you later tonight with my flight details. Okay?" she paused as she waited for Steve to agree.

"Okay, make sure you call me later and I don't want you screwing around with one of those guys from work while you are out there."

"Christ Steve. You know that is not even remotely true. I have to go now. Bye." she hung up without even waiting for his response. Maybe it was time to end her marriage. It had been on a steady decline for the past couple of years. Each year seemed to be getting worse than the last. Nothing she could do about it right now; so she decided to shrug it off and try to enjoy the rest of the evening.

The summer heat was fading as the evening began to settle in. The evening breeze was warm but it was refreshing after the stifling heat of the afternoon in the sweat lodge. Shivering ever so slightly Lynn pulled her light rose coloured sweater closer to her as she stood waiting for everyone else. The group piled back onto the bus and they headed out to the Lethbridge community centre for a Pow Wow that was being hosted by the Blackfoot. Curious to see what a Pow Wow was like Lynn stepped off the bus while talking with the older woman from the group had been kind enough earlier to help her stand in line for the welcoming ceremony after the sweat lodge. She was from the Northwest Territories and had attended a Pow Wow and other traditional ceremonies up north. She was trying to describe what they were like and what Lynn could expect. It sounded interesting to Lynn; she really loved the sound of the drum and was looking forward to hearing more drumming.

As she walked into the recreation centre with the other members of her group it became immediately apparent to her that they were the only non natives at the event. Now Lynn had been in situations where she was the minority before, it always made her a little uncomfortable but it was usually worth it in the end. She loved to push her boundaries and experience new things, so if it meant being a little uncomfortable she was okay with that. Owen and Jeff appeared as they walked into the arena and waved them over to a section of bleacher seats that they had reserved for the group. Lynn hadn't planned on sitting on a bleacher in a dress with a short skirt; in fact it was downright uncomfortable having her dress ride up half way past her knees. Squirming on the bench and trying to pull her dress down to cover her knees Lynn finally decided to take off her sweater and drape it over her lap. Sighing with relief she tried to settle in and relax until the beginning of the Grand Entrance. Owen had sat down beside her and had watched her squirming on the bleacher out of the corner of his eye. He tried to hide a smile as she settled down and arranged her sweater over her lap. Glancing at her long blonde curls sweeping across her bare shoulders Owen asked,

"Are you comfortable? The Grand Entrance should be starting soon. Have you ever been to a Pow Wow before?"

"No" Lynn answered, "I haven't. I'm not sure what to expect."

"Oh, you'll be in for a surprise then." smiling Owen pointed towards the front doors and said "Here they come." With that the drummers began pounding as the dancers began the procession into the building and around the arena. Lynn had never seen costumes like that before. The women were beautiful in their long dresses and the rows and rows of bells on the jingle dancers were amazing! As they walked past Owen tried to explain what each type of costume, or regalia was for and what the dance represented. Fascinated Lynn watched in awe as they paraded past her and around the centre before heading back out. Her eyes sparkled with delight as she took in the sights and sounds of everything going on around her. It was like she was a child again at the circus for the first time. Everything was new and interesting to her.

The night progressed as the men danced first and then the women. Lynn could not believe how magnificent the men were in their traditional regalia. She had never seen men that were so proud of their own heritage and so comfortable with themselves. The drumming was amazing; Lynn could feel the vibration of the drums in her bones. The sound of the singing and drumming made her soul yearn to answer, the same feeling that she had had earlier that day listening to Owen sing in the sweat lodge. Lynn was impressed to see Jeff compete in the Prairie Chicken Dance. He wore his traditional regalia and danced with the younger men. His headdress and tail piece were handmade with grouse feathers and as he whirled and leapt across the floor Lynn couldn't believe that he was almost fifty years old. During the event the announcer stopped to make a few presentations, including presenting a plaque to Owen for his contributions to their community. Blushing and mumbling something about it not meaning anything Lynn smiled at him when he sat down again and asked to see the plaque that he had been presented with.

"What is it that you did for your community?" she asked

"I was the principal for the elementary school on the reserve a couple of years ago," he replied. "Nothing, really."

"No that is something; you must be a role model for the children in your community. That is amazing, something you should be proud of."

"Thanks" he replied. "I like what I do, but sometimes it feels like it is not enough." Lynn looked at Owen sideways, confused as to why she felt a sadness or darkness surrounding him all the time; even though he seemed to be such a professional, successful man.

"Do you have any children Owen?" she asked, curious.

"Yes", he replied hesitating. As if he didn't want to talk about them.

"Oh, that is interesting."

"What do you mean by that?" Owen said turning to look directly at her.

"Nothing really, I just had the impression from you that there were no children in your life."

"No I have two daughters" he answered, "why would you say that?"

"I don't know it just seems that they are not part of your immediate life. Do they live with you?"

"No," he replied," they live with their mother."

"Ah, that explains it."

"Explains what?"

"Nothing, just the impression I get from you."

"Oh, I see."

"Have they lived with their mother for long?"

Glancing downward Owen responded, "Yes, we have been separated for a long time now."

"Hmm", that would explain some of the sadness that she sensed in him. Feeling like Owen was getting uncomfortable with the conversation Lynn decided to change the topic.

"So do you dance too?"

"No," he replied, looking embarrassed. "I never learned how."

"Really? That is a shame. It seems like such an amazing skill, certainly not something to be ashamed of doing."

"No, that's not the reason. We weren't allowed to dance when I was a kid. It was illegal."

"Oh, I didn't know that." Shifting his weight, Owen glanced up at Lynn and asked if she were thirsty.

"Yes, come to think of it I am."

"Do you want something to drink?"

"Yes, I think I would like a bottle of water."

"Here is a couple of dollars, would you mind getting me a bottle of water too?" Owen said as he handed Lynn a five dollar bill. Surprised, Lynn said,

"Okay," and headed over to the concession stand. She had never met a man before that had asked her to buy him his drink without first offering to do it for her; it really threw her off guard.

Walking back to the bleachers with the water bottles Lynn started to feel very self conscious. She was being noticed by everyone as she walked by, as if they were surprised to see someone that wasn't native attending the Pow Wow. When she got back to her seat and handed Owen his bottle of water and his change she mentioned the reaction she was getting from people in the arena.

"Don't worry about it," he replied, "We just don't see many non native people attending our Pow Wows, they are just surprised to see you and they are probably wondering why you are here."

"What do you mean?" she asked but before Owen could answer the announcer interrupted their conversation.

"We would like everyone to join in with us as we pray to our ancestors to help us through this difficult time. I am sure everyone here knows about the tragic loss of the three young men in our community recently. We would like their families to come up with their photos while we all remember them. Their deaths were tragic and senseless. All three were murdered due to gang violence on the reserve. Even the Grand Chief's own grandson was killed, but only after he was tortured and mutilated. Witnesses say he refused to agree to join the gang, even after they tortured him. So as a warning to all other young men in the community they castrated him and left his body his parents' doorstep. We cannot allow this type of violence to continue in our community. We must stand up and help our youth say no to this violence, before it's too late."

Shocked by the brutality of the deaths of the three young men Lynn sat speechless as she listened to the description of the violence that was raging through the reserve. It astounded her that so much violence could occur so close to such a beautiful community as Lethbridge. Turning to Lynn's group the announcer asked them to stand and be greeted by the rest of the people in the arena, as special guests visiting from the government. Lynn could hear whispers from the crowd,

"They must be social workers." confused by this response Lynn sat down and looked around at the crowd, that certainly would explain the blank stares. Everyone there thought they were social workers spying on the community. It was at that moment that Lynn started to understand the conflicted relationship Owen had with his reserve. His family was from there, he loved southern Alberta and Lethbridge, but he hated the violence and dysfunction that went on in his reserve.

Sitting on the bleachers Lynn thought about the day before when her group had been given a tour of the Blackfoot reserve. It had been shocking for all them to see the dirt roads that meandered through the downtown core of the reserve. The homes were in poor repair, many of them missing windows and looking like they had not been repaired or kept up for years. Old, broken down cars sat on the front lawns of many of the houses as children and stray dogs ran between them and crawled through them while playing. As their bus pulled up in front of the community centre they were greeted by the sight of locals standing around smoking and talking. One of the older men walked up to the group and asked if anyone had any spare change. The tour guide for the group, a band member himself was embarrassed and annoyed with him; turning to him he commented,

"Ah, come on man, what's wrong with you?"

Feeling uncomfortable and awkward the group headed into the community centre for a tour of the newly built facility. It was beautifully designed with large timber rafters and an open concept that allowed natural light to flow in from all directions. There were guided into a small meeting room where two of the reserves elders met them to talk briefly about the Blackfoot and their own beliefs and traditions. Leaving the centre Lynn was struck by the number of stray dogs running past them as they walked up to the council office. One of the younger women in the group was distressed by the sight of so many dogs that were obviously in need of proper care and nutrition. She turned to Lynn and asked her if there wasn't anyone that took care of the animals. Lynn shrugged and said,

"It doesn't look like it; they probably don't have a bylaw in place for keeping dogs on a leash or in the yard." Lynn had been on reserves before in British Columbia while executing search warrants and serving residents with subpoenas. So this was not the first time she had seen this type of desperate poverty. The thing that she could not understand was why it was happening in such a rich country as Canada? How could Canadians allow their own citizens to live like this?

Lynn was brought back by the sound of the drumming starting up again as the jingle dancers made their way into the arena for their competition. Besides the traditional men's dance this was her favourite. Their dresses were covered in rows of small bells sewn on by hand that all jingled and swayed with every move they made. It was beautiful to watch and hear. The traditional men's dance was her absolute favourite though. The raw testosterone that was obviously flowing through the men as they danced was exciting. Never had she seen such a display of masculine power and grace. No wonder the Pow Wows had been a place for "Strutting your stuff." as Owen had put it. This had been the forum for attracting the opposite sex and she could see how it would have worked!

The end of the evening was an open dance for everyone in the arena to participate in together. Lynn and one of the other women grabbed Owen and Jeff as they headed out to the floor.

"You are going to have to show us how this is done." they exclaimed as they fell into line with everyone else already on the floor. Trying to keep pace with Owen and Jeff, Lynn tripped along fighting her enforcement training that had pounded into her head the need for marching in step. Owen smiled sideways at her as she struggled to dance in step with him until she started looking around and realizing that the whole point of the dance was for everyone to dance to their own beat. An expression of the belief of all native people that everyone is free to do as they choose; this ideology ran counter to everything Lynn had been trained to believe with the RCMP. So she struggled along for most of the dance listening to the drummers and trying to not keep cadence with Owen. In amazement she looked around her at the roomful of people all dancing to their own beat, yet somehow still moving as one. As the night came to a close Owen and Jeff asked Lynn what she was doing for the rest of the evening.

"I don't know," she replied, "I hadn't really thought about it much." which was a full out lie, because all she had been thinking about was spending time with Owen.

"Well Jeff and I were going to try and get a group together to go out for a drink. Would you be interested in joining us?"

"Sure," she replied. "Sounds like a great idea."

"Okay, why don't you meet us back at the hotel in the lobby in about half an hour? We have to go back to our rooms to get our jackets and wallets. I have my own vehicle so I can give you a ride."

Delighted with the turn of events, Lynn took the bus back to the hotel with the rest of the group. When they arrived she headed back to her room on the fifth floor wondering if Owen was as intrigued by her as she was by him. Once Lynn was back in her hotel room she remembered her promise to call her husband back with her flight information. Crap, she had been enjoying herself so much that evening she had forgotten about him. Sighing Lynn reached for the hotel room phone. She tried to decide what she was going to tell him while the phone rang.

"Hello?" Olivia, her oldest daughter answered. Lynn was surprised to hear her voice so late in the evening.

"Hello honey, is your dad there?" sounding indignant Olivia responded.

"Mom he is not my dad! You know that so stop calling him that." Lynn sighed and rolled her eyes as her oldest daughter carried on.

"Okay, okay I get it. I won't forget again. Can you please go put Steve on the phone for me?" She could hear Olivia walk into the living room and hand the phone to her step father,

"It's mom" she said before stomping off to her bedroom.

"Hello?" Steve said as he put the phone to his ear. Lynn suppressed an urge to start an argument with him. What the heck was Olivia doing up so late at night? She decided to ignore it and just get this conversation over with as soon as possible with the least amount of arguing as possible.

"Hi, it's me. I have my flight information for you like you asked." Steve sounded like he had forgotten about their earlier conversation.

"Oh yeah, let me get a pen and paper first." she could hear him shuffling papers around while he looked for something to write on.

"Okay, go ahead." he grunted when he had found something to write on.

"I will be arriving on flight three hundred and fifty with Air Canada at eleven fifty five pm tomorrow night. Okay?"

"Yeah, thanks. Call me if your flight gets changed." Lynn could hear their two younger children playing in the background.

"Sure, no problem. Is that Eric and Marissa I hear playing in the living room?" Steve sounded surprised that she had noticed.

"Yeah, why?" he asked as she heard him sit back down in front of the television. Trying to stifle her frustration Lynn took a deep breath and explained to him,

"Because it is late and they should be in bed by now. Why are the still up?" Steve began to sound irritated with her and hissed a reply,

"It's not that late. Besides, they don't have school tomorrow. The teachers have the day off. One of those PA or PD days; whatever they call it." Lynn sighed as she gritted her teeth. This wasn't worth fighting over.

"Okay, just don't let them stay up much longer. Is there anything else before I go?" she could hear the fake smile in his voice as he growled,

"Yeah, don't screw around on me while you are out there." snorting Lynn replied,

"That's kind of like the pot calling the kettle black isn't?" without waiting for a reply Lynn hung up the phone. Why the heck was she still even putting up with this bullshit? She knew the answer even as she asked herself the question. She stayed for the kids' sake. She didn't want them to come from a broken home like she had. It was getting harder and harder to justify staying with Steve; even for the kids. All she wanted was peace and stability with someone that loved her and she loved in return. The thought of being alone was terrifying to her; terrifying enough to keep her married to Steve even as miserable as she was.

Fifteen minutes later she stepped off the elevator in the lobby wearing a pair of jeans and one of her favorite low cut shirts; as she waited for Owen and Jeff to reappear a couple of other individuals from their group wandered by. Lynn struck up a conversation with them and asked if they were interested in going out for drinks.

"The more the merrier, besides, it is our last night together as a group and it most likely we will never see each other again". It seemed fitting after sharing such an intense experience that day. Urma Reese one of the younger women agreed to go with them as well as Mike Holder, the tall blonde man that had sat beside her in the sweat lodge. Owen and Jeff appeared along with Renaud Montpellier, the group leader. Owen and Jeff volunteered to take Lynn with them to in Owen's vehicle and the rest agreed to catch a ride with Renaud. Out in the hotel parking lot Owen unlocked his Jeep Cherokee and apologized to Lynn for the mess in the back seat.

"I have been travelling for work for the past couple of weeks and I have not had time to clean it up." he explained. "Unfortunately there is no room in the back seat because my golf clubs are back there" he continued, "so you'll have to sit up front with Jeff and me. I am sure we can squeeze you in." he exclaimed as he laughed.

Jeff held open the passenger door as Lynn climbed in and squeezed between the gear shift and Jeff. Lynn tried to settle herself as best as she could without ending up in Jeff's lap. Not that he would mind Lynn mused. But she wasn't really interested in him. She was captivated by Owen and determined to get to know him in the time that they had left together. Owen looked at Jeff and said something to him in Blackfoot that Lynn couldn't understand.

"What did you just say?" she asked.

"Nothing," he laughed, "just that I need to go to a cash machine."

"Uh huh," she replied as she looked sideways first at Owen and then Jeff; wondering what he really said. It sounded more to me like keep your hands to yourself. Smiling, she looked out the front window and tried to get comfortable beside the gear shift.

"I hope we aren't going far," she commented. "This really isn't that comfortable."

"Don't worry," Owen replied, "we are just going up the street and then heading back to the bar."

They caught up with the rest of the group at the local country and western bar at the back of their hotel. It was a Thursday night and it was pretty dead. After everyone had one drink they decided to head back to the hotel; Renaud volunteered his room since it was the largest one. As everyone piled into his hotel room Renaud noticed that the sacred pipe and drum they used for the sweat lodge ceremony were lying on the coffee table in the sitting area. Renaud turned to Urma and Lynn and asked,

"Have either of you had anything to drink?" they both responded,

"No, nothing." so he asked,

"Could you please pick up the sacred objects and store them in that dresser?" They picked up the ceremonial objects and wrapped them up in their leather bag before placing them carefully in the top drawer of the dresser Renaud had pointed at.

"We will have to cleanse them later," he commented. "I should have put them away earlier. Oh well, nothing that can't be fixed later." Lynn and Urma looked at each other, confused. Did he mean that they had to be cleansed because they were women, or because they were not elders? Lynn decided not to ask.

The group of eight sat down on the couch and chairs in the room. Renaud was a Métis from Quebec and had been running the native awareness program for the federal government for the past couple of years. Jeff and Owen were both invited as friends of Renaud's to give him a hand since it was their reserve that had hosted the event this time around. Owen sat across from Lynn in a wing chair next to the hotel room door; Jeff had managed to claim the spot beside Lynn on the couch. Urma and Mike were next to the couch in the two dining room chairs in the room. Lynn was not very comfortable with Jeff sitting right beside her. He seemed to be getting more and more amorous as the night wore on. The more he drank the friendlier he got. Lynn kept trying to discourage him but it seemed that Owen would keep egging him on whenever he got discouraged. At one point Jeff announced to the room,

"I want to tie you up to my bed!" Leaning closer to Lynn he continued, "then I would strip you naked and," at that point Lynn cut him off,

"Stop, please I don't want to hear anymore and I am sure no one else in the room does either!" Owen was laughing so hard he nearly fell off his chair. Lynn was so annoyed with him for encouraging Jeff she said to him,

"I hope you fall off your chair and break something while you are at it!" looking extremely annoyed with the two of them she added "You know you could help me out here and tell him to stop!" This only seemed to make Owen laugh all that much harder. Renaud seemed to feel that there was a competition going on over who could sleep with Lynn first so he joined in the game by announcing,

"I am by far the best lover in the room and if you join me over there on the bed I can prove it to you!" At this point Lynn was starting to feel like a piece of meat that a pack of hyenas were squabbling over. In fact she commented to Mike sitting beside her,

"I think they are about to pull themselves out of their pants and slap them down on the table so we can measure to see who has the biggest one!" Mike burst out into laughter as he nodded his head and agreed with her,

"It certainly is starting to look like a brag fest to me!" it was about this time that Owen announced,

"I'm getting hungry, is anyone else interested in getting something to eat?"

Urma had already left for her room as well as Mike. Both saying they had flights to catch in the morning so they needed to get a couple of hours of sleep. Lynn had a flight first thing in the morning as well but she could not bring herself to leave. She really wanted to spend as much time with Owen as possible. Even though he was not trying very hard to spend any time talking to her apart from the group; in fact he was making the least amount of effort to get her attention. Lynn volunteered to try calling for pizza delivery but it was already past three in the morning so she had a difficult time finding anything that was open. Eventually she found a Humpty's across the street from the hotel that was willing to deliver some fries. So Owen paid for a round of fries for the group and the drank and talked until five in the morning until Lynn realized she only had an hour to pack and get ready for the shuttle bus to the Lethbridge airport. As she got up to leave Owen asked,

"Would you like to stay in touch? Here is my business card, call me or email me sometime."

"Of course."" she said as he handed her his business card. "I will." she said smiling and as he stood up he gave her a big bear hug and wished her a safe flight home. Lynn said goodbye to everyone else in the room and staggered back to her hotel room to pack and get ready for her flight home. As she stood waiting for the airport shuttle bus in the lobby Lynn yawned and smiled. She knew she would see Owen again and soon. She knew it in the depths of her soul. Although she was beginning to feel the effects of being up for twenty four hours straight and did not look forward to going home. The thought of going back home to her husband made her head hurt.

Travelling all day without any sleep was hellish. Lynn managed to get on the small plane that morning to fly back to Calgary. She had a two hour layover before her next flight to Toronto so she managed to sleep draped over one of the easy chairs in the airport gate area. She was so tired she barely managed to wake up when she heard the announcement for boarding her flight. Feeling stiff and mildly disoriented Lynn gathered up her purse and carryon and rushed for the gate. She was one of the last to board the plane and as soon as she sat down she pulled out her earplugs and sleeping mask and settled in to go back to sleep for the four hour flight. As she settled in beside the window she realized there were two small girls less than four years old sitting beside her in the other two seats. Their parents were Asian and did not seem to speak English, so she just smiled and curled up under her blanket with the blind drawn over the window. She was so tired she slept like the dead.

The next time she woke up the plane was landing in Toronto and the two little girls beside her were crying. Sitting up Lynn noticed there was food and toys strewn all over her. As she picked what looked like cereal out of her hair Lynn looked up at the girl's mother who was trying to apologize and clean up the mess they had made. Being a parent of three children herself, Lynn was not even bothered by the mess. She just brushed herself off and smiled at the girl's mother.

"Don't worry about it," she said, "I don't mind."

The airline stewardess came along and said, "Could you please sit down and put your seat belts on. We'll be landing shortly."

Lynn glanced at the girls beside her and settled in for the landing. The sat quietly through the landing and just smiled up at Lynn looking like a pair of little angels. Lynn couldn't help smiling back. Good Lord, I must have been really tired. Lynn stretched in her seat; the four hour sleep had done wonders for her. She had another lay over for a couple of hours before her last flight back north to Sudbury. But at least it was bearable. She just loaded up on Starbucks chai and devoured some kind of chicken sandwich roll while she sat and waited to board her last flight. It was almost midnight when Lynn finally took the airport shuttle bus home. Everyone was sound asleep when she let herself in and headed straight to the bedroom. Stephen was snoring lightly as she tip toed into the room and got undressed. She put on a pair of pajamas and slid into bed as quietly as possible. She didn't want to wake her husband. Not so much as to avoid interrupting his sleep but more in an effort to avoid having to talk to him. Sighing as she rolled over to face the wall Lynn closed her eyes and dreamt of seeing Owen again.

CHAPTER TWO

A Night to Remember

It would be weeks before Lynn decided to call Owen. She had been offered the opportunity to travel out to Coquitlam, BC to take the six week training course offered by the RCMP to become a firearms instructor. Lynn did not really like having to use firearms; it was an evil necessity as far as she was concerned. But she loved her job and this was a chance to improve her skills and her resume so she accepted. Besides, on her way back from BC she could probably make a stopover in Edmonton for a weekend. Lynn had a moral dilemma on her hands, she was still technically married and they were still living in the same house but both had agreed that they wanted a divorce. It had been a long time coming. Steve had left her once already for another woman and he had been cheating on her since with a string of different women. Their eight year marriage had already deteriorated to the point where they rarely spoke and they never slept together anymore. Half the time Lynn didn't know where her husband was, and she really didn't care anymore to tell the truth. They had three kids at home so she needed his help with the kids, especially when she travelled out of town for work. So she tolerated his staying with her even though she wished on a daily basis that she could be free of him and their marriage. Lynn had not slept with anyone outside of her marriage but she was so tempted by Owen that she had begun to consider divorcing Steve as quickly as possible if it meant she could be with him.

When she called Owen at his office she was surprised to be greeted by a receptionist who transferred her call. Looking at his business card she remembered he was the Director for Native Education. She was impressed. He sounded pleasantly surprised to hear her voice and they chatted for a few minutes about their trips back home after the workshop in Lethbridge. Lynn mentioned her lack of sleep and the long flight home. Owen laughed and told her he stayed in Lethbridge for the weekend and drove back on Sunday night to Edmonton. Lynn finally worked up the nerve to ask him if she were in Edmonton in about a month if he would be interested in seeing her again. Owen responded with enthusiasm,

"Yes, it would be great to see you again. I did not expect to see you so soon though."

"Oh, well I have an opportunity to train out in BC for the next month and I was planning on stopping in Edmonton on my way back home."

"That's great. I can meet you at the airport if you like. Do you have a place to stay while you are in town?"

"No I don't."

"I know a really nice hotel close to my office that I can book a room for you when you let me know the day you are arriving."

"Great, thanks very much."

"Okay, I have to go now but we will talk soon."

"Okay, good bye." As Lynn hung up she was feeling excited and mildly unsettled. Something did not feel right. Owen had been friendly, but there was a tone of professionalism in his voice that made her feel like she was talking to a stranger. It was a different side of Owen that she had not seen before.

Steve did not take the news of her travelling again with as much enthusiasm,

"Again and for six weeks?" Was his initial reply; "Do you have to go for that long? It is a lot of work looking after the kids on my own you know." She explained that it was for training to become a firearms instructor; an opportunity to advance and expand her resume. Steve agreed reluctantly to let her go but he made it clear that he was not happy about it.

"I suppose you will be sleeping with a bunch of different guys while you are out there too," he added. Lynn looked at him in disgust and snorted,

"No that would be your style, not mine." Their three kids were thirteen, six and five. They were not very happy with their mother when she told them she would be heading out to BC for a month for training.

"Ah mom do you have to leave again? You just got back home." It always made her sad to leave the kids for work. Even though it usually took a week or two before she really started to miss them.

"You know I will be home as soon as I can and I will call you guys every week. Okay? Mom has to travel for work. We have discussed this before." The kids reluctantly nodded their agreement before skipping off to play again. As sad as it was to say, getting away from Steve at any given opportunity was more appealing than staying at home with him; even if it meant leaving her children. Steve was only working sporadically, he was a framer in the construction industry and work was not very steady in Sudbury. So most of the time he was unemployed and at home anyways. They needed Lynn's income, and they needed her to get promoted as quickly as possible. Steve knew that so he always agreed to her working away from home. It was easier to let her be responsible for supporting the family and stay home to look after the kids anyways.

As Lynn flew out to Vancouver she thought about her trip to Lethbridge and Owen. He was not like any other man she had met before. She knew it would be weeks before she saw him but she couldn't help herself; she was looking forward to it already. It was pouring rain when Lynn's flight landed in Vancouver. It always seemed to be raining in Vancouver. Especially in the fall; it was early October already and the weather was not going to get any better. She had packed all of her rain gear and winter issue clothes. They would be spending every day on the outdoor firing range and she figured it would be raining almost every day; especially in Coquitlam since it was even closer to the mountains. Lynn had arranged for a ride with a couple of other officers that were travelling to BC for the same training so she started searching the airport for any sign of them. Giving up she dialled the cell phone number for the officer she knew from Thunder Bay, ON. Greg answered on the second ring,

"Officer White."

"Hey Greg, I will finish picking up my luggage and I will meet you at the car rental counter, okay?"

"Sure, sounds good." hanging up Lynn headed to the luggage carousal to pick up her bags.

Greg was a tall, lanky young man that fancied himself a ladies' man. Lynn liked him; he was a little hyper at times but usually a lot of fun to hang out with although the player attitude got on her nerves on occasion. She had been working in a male dominated field for almost four years now and she had found that the hardest part of the job was dealing with the good 'ole boy mentality. The guys considered her one of the boys but she still found it difficult at times trying to fit in. Men were easier to get along with than women in general. They said what was on their minds and if you pissed them off they let you know; you dealt with it and that was the end of it. Women were not that easy to get along with. You piss off a woman and you would end up hearing about it for the next couple of years, if they ever chose to speak to you again, that is. So even though it was awkward sometimes listening to the guys discuss the "rack" on that one or how they would love to jump that chick; she enjoyed herself hanging out with them most of the time. As Greg drove them out to Coquitlam he asked her if she knew the area.

"Well, yes kind of." she replied. "I grew up mostly in Burnaby and New Westminster but I have been out to Coquitlam and Port Coquitlam often to visit my father and his relatives. So I can probably find our hotel if we have a map."

The lower mainland felt different to her. It had been a couple of years since they had transferred from Vancouver to Sudbury and she had started to adjust to their life in Northern Ontario. The first thing she noticed was that no one was speaking French and there were no French language signs. She was living in a small community that was predominately French speaking so she had gotten used to hearing everyone around her speak French when she was in the grocery store or the only shopping mall in town. Lynn embraced the opportunity to expose herself and her kids to the language. They didn't have the same opportunity in BC to learn the language so she was determined to give her kids something she never had. So it seemed almost strange to her to hear only English and a handful of different Asian languages being spoken around her in the airport when she landed in Vancouver. She noticed when they checked into the hotel no one offered to speak French and none of the other officers were French speaking when they met up in the hotel restaurant that evening. Not that it mattered. She didn't speak enough French for it to make a difference. She just really noticed for the first time how little French was spoken out in BC. No wonder she had never really been able to get a grasp of the language.

The next six weeks went by quickly. Lynn was up early every morning and would head down to the restaurant in the hotel to have a quick breakfast with which ever officer was eating when she got there; although there was one Conservation Officer from British Columbia that caught Lynn's attention. He was a tall nice looking man in his mid to late forties with dark hair and bright blue eyes. He was in the midst of going through a bad divorce and he seemed to be preoccupied most of the time. Lynn sat down with him early one morning and ordered some orange juice with scrambled eggs and toast.

"Good morning Dan. How did you sleep? I was so exhausted from being on the shooting range all day in the rain yesterday I slept really well." Lynn said as she sat down. Glancing up from his pancakes and eggs Dan replied,

"Good morning, good thanks. I see you are up early today." smiling Lynn said,

"Yes, I guess it was the great sleep I had last night. Do you know what we are doing today?" shaking his head Dan replied between mouthfuls,

"No, I think we are starting on our presentations today. But I am not sure." grimacing at the thought of having to show everyone how to disassemble a shotgun and reassemble it Lynn said,

"Well, I hope it is not my turn today to do it. I am not very comfortable with disassembling a shotgun yet." smiling up at her briefly before turning back to his pancakes Dan responded,

"Don't worry about it. It's not that big of a deal." he finished his plate and pushed it towards the waitress as she brought Lynn's breakfast. Picking up his coffee he looked at Lynn and asked,

"So you are you married?" Lynn felt uncomfortable with the question, but decided to be honest with him,

"Yes, technically, but we have agreed to get a divorce."

"Oh, how is that working out for you?" Lynn put down her fork and looked out the window as she replied quietly,

"Not very good; it is very hard to live in the same house with someone you can't stand and just wish you could get out of your life." nodding his head Dan replied,

"I know what you mean. When my ex and I split we were fighting all the time. It just got to the point where we couldn't stand being in the same room with each other." Feeling like they might have something in common Lynn decided to ask,

"Do you like sushi? I can't find anyone else in the group that would like to go for sushi one night. I am getting tired of the steak and chicken wings." Dan looked interested as he replied,

"Sure, I like sushi. I would like to go one night this week if you are going to go. Do you know a good sushi restaurant nearby?" Lynn nodded her head and answered,

"Yes, there is a really good one just up the highway from here. We could even go for lunch if we wanted to, it is that close." standing up to pay his bill Dan glanced back while putting on his jacket and said.

"Okay, we can go for lunch today or tomorrow if you like." smiling up at him Lynn said,

"Sounds good, I will ask Greg if he would like to go with us. See you at the range."

"See you at the range." he replied as he walked out of the restaurant and passed a couple of other officers walking in for a quick cup of coffee before heading out to the shooting range for the day. Lynn found Greg out in the parking lot as he was getting ready to leave. He looked like he had just gotten out of bed and badly needed a cup of coffee.

"Oh, hey Lynn; are you heading out to the range now?"

"Hey Greg, I am. Can you give me a ride; I think just about everyone else has left." Greg answered,

"Sure, hop in. I am stopping at Timmy's along the way. I really need a cup of coffee." Lynn opened the passenger side door and got in as she replied,

"No problem. We still have lots of time." Greg grimaced at her and said,

"The way I feel this morning I don't think I care if we have enough time or not." Lynn turned and smiled at him and asked,

"Why are you so tired this morning? Didn't you get any sleep last night?" shaking his head, Greg mumbled,

"Not really, I went out for wings and beer with a couple of the guys last night. I am not sure what time we made it back. The bartender kicked us out so I guess it was past midnight." Lynn laughed and shook her head,

"Good grief Greg, most people don't go out on a bender on a Monday night!" Greg just shrugged and said,

"Ah, it's no big deal. We are just on the firing range today. I can do that with my eyes closed and a hangover." Lynn just shook her head in disbelief.

"Well, I know I couldn't do it. My hat's off to you." Greg grimaced in response as he drove through the Tim Horton's drive thru and asked,

"Do you want anything?" hesitating for a moment Lynn replied,

"Sure, can you get me a bottle of water?"

"No problem. One bottle of water as well please." Lynn started to dig in the pockets of her jacket for a loonie or quarters. Greg interrupted her and said,

"Don't worry about it. I got it." smiling Lynn said,

"Thanks Greg. I appreciate it. Hey, I forgot to ask you if you wanted to go for sushi for lunch today. I am going with Dan, the BC Conservation Officer from Penticton." looking slightly queasy at the idea of eating sushi Greg replied,

"Oh, no thanks; I don't think my stomach could handle it today. But I would like to go at least once before we leave." Nodding and smiling at the expression on Greg's face Lynn replied,

"No problem. I understand. I am sure Dan and I will find something to talk about." Lynn was not sure how comfortable she was having lunch alone with Dan. She was not interested in starting anything with him. She just wanted a ride to a sushi restaurant and he wanted to go. She would have preferred if Greg had gone with them. They had worked and trained together many times before and she enjoyed his company. Lunch time came and as Dan and Lynn jumped in his work truck Lynn said,

"The sushi place I was thinking of is just down the highway. We should be able to eat and be back in about an hour."

Dan nodded and said, "Perfect." Lynn turned to Dan and asked,

"How long have you been divorced?" shrugging he responded,

"Not long, we are still finalizing things. That woman is trying to take me for everything. She must be the most vindictive bitch on the planet!" Lynn was slightly taken aback by this comment; she was not really interested in hearing about his evil ex wife. Or any evil woman he may have encountered in his lifetime. In fact, in her experience any man that hated a woman that much was not really capable of loving or trusting anyone. Beginning to realize that this was going to be a very long lunch Lynn tried to change the subject.

"I'm sure you must be happy to get on with your life. Have you met anyone else?" Dan glanced at her and said,

"Yes, I'm seeing a woman back in Penticton. She seems like a nice person." relieved to have him on a more positive note she continued,

"Oh, that's great. How long have you been seeing each other?" Dan shook his head as he responded,

"Not very long, just a couple of months." Lynn nodded as she listened to Dan explain to her all of his new girlfriend's faults. This really is going to be a long lunch she thought as she looked out the passenger window and debated opening the door and jumping out at the next light. She decided against it; she was hungry and it was only for an hour. The sushi restaurant was busy but they were seated right away and both had their fill of sushi while Dan continued his litany of woes against women. Lynn was beginning to feel like a prisoner or his counsellor. This was certainly not worth suffering through just to have sushi. Oh please just hurry up and finish so we can get back to the firing range and some other people was all that kept going through her mind as she sat and smiled blankly at Dan. He got up and paid for his meal as she stood at the door and paid for her meal. She wanted to say,

"Hurry up! I can't stand much more of this." but she bit her tongue and waited for him as he counted out coins for a tip. Pulling a toonie out of her pocket Lynn dropped it on the counter beside the cash register and said,

"Here, let me get that." She turned and walked out of the restaurant towards the officer's work truck. The ride back was just as long and torturous. Dan never stopped talking about the evils of women and how he hated his ex wife. Lynn began to wonder if he realized she was a woman. For some reason the men she worked with often seemed to unload all their personal problems on her when they were alone. This wasn't the first time she had heard an officer cry the blues about the wrong done to him by some woman.

Lynn tried to avoid catching a ride with Dan for the next couple of weeks. She was polite and talked to him if he approached her. But she was not interested in repeating the disastrous lunch that she had suffered through previously. The last night of the training program before they were all scheduled to go home the group decided to go out for dinner together. Lynn was tired of being the only woman in the group but she agreed to go along. She didn't want to stay too late because she had an early flight out to Edmonton in the morning so Dan offered to give her a ride back to the hotel. She was not thrilled about his offer but she didn't want to pay for a cab so she accepted. On the way back to the hotel Dan smiled at her and said,

"We could spend the night together. No one else needs to know." taken aback but not entirely surprised Lynn tried to figure out how to turn him down as delicately as possible. She wasn't sure how bad is temper could get if he felt rejected. So she replied gently,

"That is flattering, really. But I am still technically married and I do not feel comfortable doing anything with anyone until I am divorced." Dan did not appear happy with her answer but he accepted it, even though he looked insulted when he said,

"Sure, I understand. Okay. Well here is the hotel. See you later." Lynn got out in front of the hotel lobby and watched as Dan drove back to the restaurant. That guy makes me really uncomfortable she thought as she walked into the hotel. There is no way I would ever have taken him up on his offer even if I was divorced.

Lynn was up early the next morning and caught a ride with Greg back to the Vancouver International Airport. Once they got there she shook his hand and said,

"Thanks Greg, I will see you back in Ontario. Have a great flight." bending down to pick up his luggage Greg smiled back at her and replied,

"Sure, you too. Bye" Lynn walked away as she looked for her line up to check her bags before boarding her flight to Edmonton. She caught her breath as she thought about seeing Owen in a couple of hours.

Standing in the airport smiling at Owen as he approached Lynn felt her heart skip a beat and something stir in her that she had not felt in years. He was as handsome as she remembered even though he looked really nervous and rushed.

"I just got here"" he panted as he came charging up to her. "I am sorry I am late. I got hung up in traffic."

"No worries," she replied, "I only landed about fifteen minutes ago and just finished getting my luggage."

"I see that!" he exclaimed as he surveyed the pile of suitcases on the luggage cart. "How much luggage did you bring with you?"

"Well I have been living out of a suitcase for the past six weeks so I think I have just about everything I own with me!"

"Okay well it should all fit in my Jeep. Let's get going. I have a hotel room booked for you in downtown Edmonton that I think you will like. It is still early and I have a few things to do for work yet so I was planning to drop you off at the hotel and then I can pick you up for dinner in a couple of hours; would that be okay with you?"

"Sure." she replied. Uncertain about how to feel about his plans; she had been hoping that he would spend all of his time with her while she was there. Although she knew that was not very realistic.

Owen helped Lynn check in and bring all of her luggage upstairs. She was surprised at how big the room was; it was a suite really. After she got settled in Owen excused himself and returned to work for a couple more hours. Explaining he had a presentation to complete for

Monday morning. So Lynn cleaned up quickly and called around until she found a store that had traditional sweet grass for sale. She had promised her Métis French tutor that she would try to pick some up for her in Edmonton. Locating one, she called a cab and headed out to Whyte Avenue to do some shopping. She was gone for about two hours and when she returned she changed into her clothes for dinner. The only nice outfit she had brought with her was a grey sweater set that had a flattering neckline and a pair of black dress pants that she always felt good in. It wasn't long before Owen called to let her know he was on his way to pick her up.

He waited downstairs for her in the lobby and suggested they walk to the restaurant just up the street because he remembered that she liked to walk. As they walked arm in arm Owen mentioned,

"My favourite Italian restaurant is one block up the street. I didn't make any reservations for us but I think we can still get a table." Lynn smiled and said,

"Well it is Saturday night, but if we can't get a table I am sure there are other restaurants nearby we can try." Shivering she pulled the collar of her jacket up, she had forgotten how cold and windy Edmonton could be. "It's a good thing I remembered to pack gloves." She commented. "I didn't need them in Coquitlam; it rained the whole six weeks that I was there." Owen chuckled.

"Edmonton always gets snow before just about everywhere else does."

"Oh I suspect there will be snow in Sudbury when I get home."

"Well here is the restaurant I was telling you about. I hope you like Italian food."

"Oh yes, I like most types of cuisine."

"Great, well let's go in and see if we can get a table." Owen opened the heavy wooden door for Lynn and stepped back to let her walk through first. He followed her as they walked in to the reception area and stood waiting for the hostess.

"Good evening, do you have a reservation?" inquired the young lady as she walked up from the kitchen area.

"No, I am afraid we don't."

"Oh, I am sorry, but we do not have any tables available until after eight this evening." Lynn and Owen looked at each other and Owen turned to the hostess,

"Thank you, but we are too hungry to wait for over an hour."

"Alright then, I am sorry. Have a nice evening." she replied as they turned and walked back out of the restaurant and into the cold night air.

"Well, where to now?" Lynn asked as they stood outside the restaurant doors shivering in the brisk wind.

"Hmm, I think there is a steak house just about a block from here that we could probably get into without a reservation. How does that sound to you?"

"Great, I am starved. I think I am on BC time now so that works just fine for me."

"Okay, we need to cross the street and head back the way we came." As Owen offered his arm to Lynn they quickly ran across the two lanes of traffic and started walking briskly up the street. "Are you sure you are not too cold?" Owen asked as Lynn started to shiver.

"No, I can manage if it is not much further."

"Just a couple of doors further and we should be there. Ah, here we are." Opening the glass doors Owen stepped back again to allow Lynn to enter first and as they walked into the restaurant Lynn could hear a band playing the blues.

"Well, that sounds pretty good," she exclaimed. "If the food is as good as the atmosphere this should be a great meal." Owen just smiled at her as her turned to the hostess and requested a table for two.

"Right this way" was her reply. With a sigh of relief they both followed her to a corner table next to the front window.

"This will be just fine, thank you very much." Owen stated as he handed both his and Lynn's jackets to the hostess. They sat down and smiled at each other over the menus as the hostess returned with water for them both. "So," Owen started a little awkwardly, "This is a very pleasant surprise. I was not sure if I would even hear from you after Lethbridge; let alone see you again." Lynn looked down at her menu and said quietly,

"I have a confession to make."

"Oh, what is it?" inquired Owen with a curious look on his face.

"I did not have any other reason for stopping over in Edmonton than to see you."

"Oh," Owen looked taken aback as he realized what she was saying. "You mean you are here just to see me?"

"Yes," nervously Lynn smiled at him and waited for Owen to respond. "Well, I think that is the most romantic thing anyone has ever done for me." relieved Lynn smiled and feeling a little more comfortable she continued.

"I knew before I left Lethbridge that I would see you again. I didn't know how or when, but I knew it wouldn't be very long before I saw you again."

"Really, why do you say that?" he asked as he leaned forward.

"Oh, it was just a feeling I had." looking down at her lap Lynn decided to ask Owen about their experience in the sweat lodge.

"Was that the first time you were in a sweat lodge?" smiling Owen replied,

"No, I have been in a few sweats over the years, although it has been awhile since the last one."

"Well that was the first time for me and it was an amazing experience. I never experienced anything like that before. Is it always so powerful?"

"Yes, usually it is a very powerful experience every time, for me anyways."

"Wow, I loved it and I would love the chance to do it again." Owen just laughed.

"You know, you can't rush these things, it will happen when it is supposed to. Everything happens when it is meant to." Lynn looked at him with a quizzical expression.

"You know my mentor said the same thing to me!"

"Mentor, I didn't know you had a mentor."

"Well, she is a spiritual mentor, of a sorts; she has been trying to help me work through some things in the past couple of months."

"Wow that is interesting."

"Yes, I suppose. She is a very interesting Métis spiritual teacher that I met first as my French tutor, but as time went on we began talking about other things. She has been encouraging me to explore some aspects of myself that I have tried to ignore for a very long time."

"What do you mean by that?" Lynn smiled at Owen and hesitated for a moment. Thinking; be careful, you don't want to come across as crazy. Even though the native tradition values dreams and intuition you still have to watch what you say.

"Oh, sometimes I have a flash of intuition, knowing something without knowing how or why."

"Ah, I understand, you are gifted."

Frowning Lynn thought about that for a moment and said "I suppose you could call it that, although sometimes it feels more like a curse than a gift. But I am trying to learn to live with it." Owen smiled and said,

"That would explain your comment about knowing you would see me again."

"Yes, I suppose it would."

Feeling uncomfortable about revealing too much of herself all at once Lynn decided to change the subject.

"So what do you feel like ordering?" Owen chuckled and looked down at his menu.

"I haven't really decided yet, but I usually order the prime rib when I eat here. So I guess I will just have that."

"Hmm it looks good but I think that is too much meat for me. I think I will order the steak and shrimp. I love seafood."

"Is that so?"

"Yes" Lynn replied, smiling at the memory of fresh seafood in Vancouver. "I grew up in the Lower Mainland, so we had a lot of fresh fish and seafood. I have never seen anywhere in Canada that has as good a selection as Vancouver's restaurants."

"I would have to agree with you there, I spent some time living in Victoria on the island and the seafood was amazing." Owen replied.

"Really, I didn't know you had lived out in BC."

"Oh yes, I lived on the island and the interior for a couple of years. I used to teach before I started working for the provincial government."

"Wow that is interesting. So where did you live in the interior?"

"Merritt, there is a reserve nearby where I worked as an elementary teacher for about a year."

"That is funny, my mother grew up in Merritt and my grandparents are buried there on the hill overlooking the town. It is a small world isn't?" Owen smiled and nodded. Lynn continued "I love the interior; it is so warm and beautiful. My favourite place is Nelson; it is like a secret hidden away in the mountains. What I wouldn't give to live there!" Owen looked interested as he asked,

"Nelson? I don't think I have been there."

"You would love it. The most gorgeous natural hot springs in BC are hidden away just north of it. You can sit in the hot springs pool and look out on Kootenay Lake and the mountains that form a ring all the way around it. I have never seen anything more beautiful or peaceful in my life." he nodded and said,

"I guess the next time I am out in the interior of BC I'll have to check it out."

"Oh you have no idea until you have actually seen it. If you ever get the chance check it out, you won't regret it." The waitress returned to take their orders and as they settled in they snacked on the complimentary fresh bread she had left with them.

The waitress returned with their drinks and as she walked away from the table Owen reached over and took Lynn's hand. Looking into her eyes he said softly,

"I'm very happy that you decided to come and see me." smiling, Lynn looked down as she tried not to blush. It took all of her self control to not blurt out how much she was attracted to him and if he asked, she would walk half way around the world just to see him.

As they finished dinner the waitress returned to ask if they would like to order dessert. Lynn was too full and Owen was not interested in ordering anything; so the waitress brought them the bill and thanked them for their business. Owen got up to pay for their meal and Lynn headed to the washroom before heading back out into the cold.

As they stepped back outside the restaurant Lynn could have sworn the temperature had dropped by another couple of degrees.

"Damn, I forgot how cold Edmonton can be." Lynn muttered, gritting her teeth. "I thought Sudbury was bad."

"So where to now?" Owen asked as he pulled the collar of his dress coat up around his neck "Would you like to go for a drink? I know a bar just down the street from here."

"Sure," Lynn answered, although she was starting to feel a little tired. She was on BC time so it was feeling later to her than it really was. Owen held out his hand and Lynn put her gloved hand in his. Smiling to herself she tried to get comfortable with the idea of holding Owen' hand; why not? It was harmless and it sure felt good. As they walked down the street towards the bar Lynn wondered if they would ever have a real chance together. Honestly, she was still trying to sort out the mess at home with her husband. She knew they were heading for a divorce and she didn't care anymore. It was only a matter of time. But technically she was still married; even if in her heart she was ready to move on. A feeling of guilt and confusion swept over her as she walked along with Owen. She was happy to see him again but she knew that she had to deal with her situation at home before anything could really happen between them. Owen looked at her sideways and commented,

"You seem awfully quiet all of a sudden. Is there anything wrong?" Lynn pulled herself away from her thoughts and said,

"No, I was just wondering if we could stay for just one drink and then head back to my hotel room. I am starting to feel the effects of the time difference."

"Sure, no problem. We can head back now if you are too tired."

"No I am okay for a while yet." Owen stopped in front of the bar doors and said, "After you."

Walking into the bar Lynn could hear the sounds of recorded music from the top twenty. It wasn't really busy in the bar, there were a few small groups hanging out at tables at the periphery. A couple of girls were dancing together on the dance floor, looking like they had had too much to drink. Owen gestured towards a booth at the back of the room and suggested they sit there. Lynn nodded and walked towards the booth. They stripped off their jackets before sitting down and piled them at one end of the booth. As they sat waiting for the waitress Owen's cell phone began vibrating and ringing. He glanced nervously at the phone and shut it off.

"Someone is looking for you." Lynn commented, thinking, a girlfriend possibly? Owen put his phone in his jacket pocket and said casually,

"Just an old drinking buddy looking for me."

"Oh" Lynn nodded and looked up as the waitress walked up to take their orders. "I think I will just have water please," Lynn said to the waitress, she nodded and turned to Owen,

"A rum and coke please." the waitress returned with their drinks and Owen paid for them, giving her a two dollar tip. "Would you like to dance?" he asked.

"Sure" she said, feeling a little uncomfortable. She was not really in the mood to dance but what the heck.

As they walked to the dance floor Lynn felt self conscious about her age. She must have been almost twenty years older than the two young girls dancing beside them. Turning her back to them she tried focussing on Owen and the music. It had a heavy dance beat and sounded like one of the newer songs on the radio. Owen smiled at her and started dancing, he moved pretty well for such a big man. Getting too warm Lynn decided to remove her sweater and hang it over the retaining wall surrounding the dance floor. Owen seemed surprised at the condition her arms were in after she removed her sweater. She had just spent the last six weeks working out and standing for hours at a time on a firing range holding her sidearm; so she was in pretty good shape. Lynn smiled bashfully and leaned in to Owen as she said,

"I feel like either they are too young to be here or I am too old. I'm not sure which." Owen smiled at her and said,

"You are in much better shape and much prettier than either of those two girls." Lynn smiled and said,

"Thanks," at the end of the song they both agreed to sit back down. Once sitting they finished their drinks and Owen asked Lynn if she would be interested in a game of pool.

"Okay, why not. Although I am not sure how good I will be." Owen laughed and said,

"Don't worry about it; I am not that good myself." Owen put a loonie in the pool table and set up the balls. He handed the cue to Lynn and said,

"Your break."

"Oh no thanks, I don't want to break them." she replied as she stepped back from the cue.

"Okay I can do it." Owen stepped up to the pool table and hit the balls with a loud crack. Impressed, Lynn took the cue from him and started looking for an opening. She was finding it very easy to line the balls up and hit them; easier than usual; it had to be the firearms training that had improved her aim. She sunk two low balls in a row and missed the third. She handed the cue back to Owen and grinned sheepishly at him.

"I guess my game has improved a little."

"I'd say," was his reply as he frowned and looked for an opening on one of the high balls. Missing his shot he handed back the cue to Lynn and watched as she circled the pool table. "I thought you didn't play this game much." she laughed and said,

"I don't but I seem to be doing better than usual. I think all those hours of target practice have improved my aim." leaning in Lynn took a shot at another low ball and sunk it. The ball rattled down to the basket at the end of the table. Considering her options she decided to throw the next shot. She had no real interest in winning the game.

"Oops, I think my luck has run out." she said handing the cue back to Owen and smiled at him.

"Hmm" he frowned at the table and lined up for another shot. Sinking it he circled the table looking for another opening.

"So just what were you doing in Coquitlam anyways?" he asked as he looked up from the cue.

"Mostly target practice, handling firearms and some public speaking; we were training to be firearm instructors."

"Right, I remember you mentioning that." sinking a second high ball Owen stood up and said,

"It looks like I am giving you a run for your money." Lynn just smiled as she watched him sink another high ball and then aim for the eight ball. After he had won the game she said,

"Congratulations, I think I would like to go back to the hotel now if that is okay with you." she was tired and had had enough of the game for the evening.

"Sure, not a problem." he replied as he put the pool cue away.

As they walked back to the hotel Lynn was trying to decide what she was going to say to Owen once they got back to her room. She was certain he expected to stay the night with her but she wasn't ready for that. She wanted him to stay with her and talk but she was not ready for anything more. Besides being married still, she was not interested in a one night stand. So when then walked up to her hotel room door still holding hands she turned to him and said,

"I would like you to stay, but I need you to understand that I am not ready to sleep with you. Are you okay with that?" surprised, Owen smiled at Lynn and said

"Okay, I understand. I would still like to stay." So she opened her door and as they walked in Owen took off his shoes and jacket and sat down on the couch in the sitting area. He watched Lynn as she got settled on the other end of the couch and fidgeted for a few moments before getting up again offering to bring Owen a drink of water. He smiled and said,

"No thanks I am fine. Why don't you sit down and relax?" Lynn went into the bedroom and pulled off the spare blanket from the closet shelf and brought it back to the couch with her. She cuddled up with the blanket and cushions on the couch close to Owen and smiled at him as she said,

"Tell me about your spiritual beliefs."

"What do you mean?"

"I mean, what do your legends say about the creation of the earth? Do you believe in the Great Turtle?"

"Yes, I guess I do. I am also Catholic so it is not always easy to balance both."

"Ah yes, I remember asking you about that after the sweat lodge. So you do believe in God?"

"Yes, I go to mass and pray." sighing, Lynn looked deeply into Owen' eyes and said,

"I believe in God, but more importantly I believe that there is more to life than what we see. It's what I sense in you that draws me to you more than anything else." Owen glanced downwards and smiled quietly.

"I feel the same way about you," he replied. She had the distinct impression that he wanted to kiss her at that moment, but didn't. Reaching across the coffee table Owen picked up the framed photo of Lynn's three children.

"Tell me about your children he said. I would really like to know more about you."

"Ah, my kids. I love them so much. I like having their photo with me when I am away for more than a couple of days." smiling Owen put the frame down and said,

"I can see that. How old are they?" pointing to their photo, Lynn said "Olivia is thirteen, Marissa is six and Eric is five."

"There is a big gap between the first two." "I know, Olivia's father died and I remarried a couple of years later."

"I see. So are you still married?" hesitating, Lynn answered "Yes, but we have agreed to get a divorce."

"Who is looking after your children now?"

"They are with their dad."

"Oh. How do they feel about you travelling for work?" Lynn laughed as she said "They hate it. I always get to hear about it before I leave and when I get back." changing the topic Lynn continued,

"How about your kids, do you see them often?"

"No, only once or twice a year."

"How old are they?"

"My oldest daughter is eighteen and my youngest daughter is fourteen."

"Do you have a picture of them with you?" Owen smiled as he replied "No, I don't carry pictures of them like you do." Lynn smiled at Owen and wondered what he was thinking as he became quiet and seemed to be lost in thought.

"So you are not married?" Lynn held her breath while she waited for him to answer

"No, not anymore." Owen answered sleepily,

"Are you tired?"

"Yes, it is after three in the morning now. Do you want to try and get some sleep?"

"Okay, but I am not sure that I will be able to sleep if I am lying down beside you." smiling, she said

"I know what you mean."

They both stood up and headed towards the bedroom. Neither one of them took off their clothes as they tried to get comfortable underneath the comforter. Owen reached out and wrapped his arms around Lynn's waist and pulled her close to his chest to spoon her. Lynn sighed as she closed her eyes and tried to get some rest but her heart was racing and she wasn't able to stop thinking about Owen being so close to her. Reaching behind her Lynn caressed Owen's face and unable to resist any longer she arched her back and turned her head to face Owen as she placed her lips on his for the first time. Their kiss was long and deep as Owen responded by pressing his body close to hers, moaning with passion. Lynn longed for Owen to touch her body, make love to her. But she knew she was not ready. It was still too soon. So she turned to face away from him and snuggled up as close as she could and closed her eyes. Lynn drifted in and out of sleep for the next couple of hours waking up whenever Owen moved. The slightest brush of his hand across her shoulder or her hair sent flames of passion burning throughout her body. Never before had she experienced so much passion for one man in her life.

Both were jolted awake by the sound of the phone ringing in the sitting area. They looked groggy and confused for a moment until they realized it was Lynn's wake up call. Owen staggered out of the bedroom and answered the phone,

"Hello." Lynn was already up and in the bathroom by the time he had hung up and headed back to the bedroom. She tried to clean up and pull herself together as she peered into the mirror, Lynn groaned.

"God I look awful. I guess that is what a couple of hours sleep will do for you. Ugh." she headed back to the bedroom to find some clean clothes and give Owen a chance to use the bathroom. He looked as tired as she did. Owen finished up in the bathroom and called to Lynn from the sitting area,

"Do you need help with your suitcases?

"Yes please, I can't seem to get one of them closed." Owen let out a snort of laughter as he walked back into the bedroom only to see Lynn perched on top of her largest suitcase trying desperately to pull the zipper closed between her knees. He smiled at her and said,

"What the heck do you have in there anyways?"

"Just my uniforms, duty belt, body armour and my work boots; what every girl takes with her on a trip." shaking his head Owen walked over and said,

"Here let me help." he picked up the overloaded suitcase with little effort and dropped it in the middle of the queen size bed. "I think you are going to have to repack it to get it to close." agreeing she started pulling everything out of her suitcase and piling it on the bed.

"What is this?" he asked, picking up the package of braided sweet grass.

"Oh that, I picked it up yesterday for my friend in Sudbury; she asked me to try and find some sweet grass for her."

"Is it sweet grass?"

"Yes." turning it over in his hands he said,

"Really, I didn't think it was possible to buy this stuff."

"What do you mean?" Lynn asked.

"Normally you are not allowed to sell ceremonial sweet grass. You have to have the elders' permission to do that."

"Oh, well the guy that sold it to me assured me that he had permission from the elders."

"Huh, can I see it?"

"Sure," Unwrapping the bundle Lynn showed Owen three braided strands of dried sweet grass.

"Well I am surprised, it is even wrapped properly. Does your friend know how to use it?"

"Apparently, she knew what she wanted and said she had a hard time finding any in Ontario. She said it is much more common in Alberta." Surveying the bundle in his hands Owen commented,

"Well it sure looks like the real thing. Did it cost much?"

"No, it cost me about ten bucks."

"Where did you say you got it?"

"A little store on Whyte Avenue, do you think it is alright? I haven't done anything wrong?"

"No, it looks fine and sounds like the guy is legitimate. Your friend will like her present." smiling and rewrapping the sweet grass she said,

"I hope so. " Owen helped Lynn pack up the rest of her suitcase and haul them out the hotel room into the lobby.

Lynn stopped at the front counter to pay her hotel bill and as Owen walked away to bring his car around to the front he patted Lynn on the backside and whispered,

"I'll be right back." Lynn nodded and felt herself blush, while thinking how wonderful that sounded to her. Pulling away from the hotel Owen asked Lynn if she wanted to stop for a coffee.

"Sure, is there a Starbucks nearby?"

"Yes there is we can stop there if you like."

"Oh that would be great. I need something to get me going. I am exhausted." Owen smiled and said,

"So am I."

They parked the car and walked hand in hand to the front door of Starbucks. Owen opened the door for Lynn and stepped back to allow her through first. Lynn smiled at him and said,

"Thank you."

Standing in line Owen looked down at Lynn and squeezed her hand as he asked her what she would like to order.

"Grande soy chai please; I love the stuff." he smiled and turned to order "One Grande coffee, black and one Grande soy chai please."

Walking back out of Starbucks Lynn nursed her chai as she tried to warm up and wake up. It was going to be a long flight home; one that she was dreading.

"Are you hungry?" Owen asked as they got back into his Jeep.

"A little, maybe we could get something to eat at the airport." nodding Owen backed up the Jeep and headed south towards the Edmonton International Airport.

"I really wish you could stay longer."

"I know, but I have to get home to my kids and work."

"I understand it just seems we never have much time together."

"I know what you mean. I feel the same way." forcing a smile Owen reached over and held Lynn's hand while they drove south down the highway.

"Well at least traffic is light on Sunday mornings. We will make good time getting to the airport."

"That's good; we will have plenty of time to get something to eat." Lynn replied, not that she was overly hungry. Being so tired made her feel queasy. She wasn't sure just how much breakfast she could eat before getting on the plane. But it was an excuse to spend a little more time with Owen so she didn't mind.

As they sat in the Rise n' Shine Restaurant Lynn nibbled at her breakfast burrito. It had seemed like a good idea when she had ordered it. Looking at all the greasy cheese she decided she should have gone with a piece of grapefruit or a glass of orange juice instead.

"Aren't you going to eat that?" Owen asked as he finished off his breakfast burrito.

"No, I don't think so; it is too much for me to eat." even though normally Lynn liked a healthy sized breakfast especially when she travelled. It seemed the combination of lack of sleep and the stress of returning home to her awful marriage was killing her appetite. Lynn sipped her tea as Owen drank his second cup of coffee.

"I have a question for you" Owen said as he put his coffee cup down.

"Okay, go ahead." Lynn waited for his question,

"Does it bother you that I am Native and you are not?" he hesitated waiting for her response,

"I think you are a very attractive, intelligent, articulate man" Owen interrupted her,

"You are just avoiding my question." Lynn smiled as she reached across the table for his hand,

"You didn't let me finish. I think you are a very attractive, intelligent, articulate man that I would be proud to be seen with anywhere that happens to be Native. It is part of who you are so I love that about you." Owen nodded and smiled as he squeezed her hand as she continued.

"How do you feel about me being a non-native? I am sure your family would have something to say about it." Owen laughed as her answered her,

"My family would be surprised if they met you but they would accept you." Lynn wasn't sure if she believed him but she decided not to press the issue.

"Well, it is getting close to your boarding time so I guess we should start heading down to your gate." Owen said as he pushed his plate back. Lynn's stomach sank even lower at the thought of getting on that plane and leaving Owen behind. Nodding, she got up and put her coat on as he headed for the cashier to pay for their breakfast. Sighing, Lynn picked up her purse and checked for her gloves. She walked to the front of the restaurant and met up with Owen. He smiled at her and held out his hand for hers as they made their way through the airport. He squeezed her hand as they stopped in front of the security entrance.

"Well this is as far as I can go." Lynn looked up into his eyes as he pulled her close to him and kissed her long and hard.

"My God you are beautiful" he whispered as he ran his hands through her long blonde hair and kissed her again. "I will be thinking of you."

"I will be thinking of you." she answered as she reached up to put her hand behind his neck to pull his face close to hers and kissed him again. Groaning, Owen straightened up and with a serious tone and said,

"You have to go now, before you miss your flight." Lynn frowned and stepped back, blowing him a kiss she walked up to the security gate and waited her turn to pass through the metal detector. Owen stood and watched as she submitted to a security search and then waved as she walked away. Lynn tried hard to smile as she waved, her heart breaking with the knowledge that it could be a very long time before she saw him again.

CHAPTER THREE

Run Baby Run

Lynn was right; it would be a couple of months before she even heard from Owen again. She wanted to pick up the phone and call him over a dozen times, but she resisted the urge. He will call me when he wants to talk. She kept reminding herself I already went all the way out to Edmonton to see him, so let him make the next move. Things at home had deteriorated. Steve had gotten more difficult to live with and they were starting to argue over everything. Things reached a peak that night when the phone rang and Lynn answered it.

"Hello?" a young woman's voice was on the other end of the line.

"Hello can I speak to Steve please?" surprised Lynn asked.

"Who is calling please?" the young woman sounded shocked that Lynn would ask.

"It's Sharon his girlfriend." dumbfounded Lynn put her hand over the phone and called into the living room.

"Steve your girlfriend is on the phone asking for you." Steve walked into the kitchen and took the phone from her.

"Hello?" Lynn watched him as he walked out of the kitchen into their master bedroom. She could see his face redden as he listened to Sharon on the other end of the phone and then replied,

"I am sorry Sharon but I can't see you or talk to you anymore. Please do not call here again." he hung up the phone and placed it back on its receiver without looking up. Lynn just stood in the middle of the kitchen still trying to process what had just happened.

"Was she who you were with last night?"

"Yeah, you said you didn't want me staying here so I stayed at her place."

"So why would she think she was your girlfriend Steve?" he shook his head as he started to walk away.

"I guess I might have let her think we were seeing each other." Lynn wasn't buying it.

"No, no I think it is more than that. A woman wouldn't call here knowing your wife might answer unless she had a history with you. You have to have been seeing her more than once." Steve shrugged as he replied.

"Yeah I might've seen her a couple of times before."

"Wow you don't even give a shit anymore do you? Sleep around and then tell them to call the house, my home. I want you to leave. I can't take this anymore." Steve had gotten so angry that he pushed her around the kitchen while screaming at her that she was a whore. He accused her of sleeping with a couple of the men that she worked with. He was not even rational. She was tired of trying to deal with the maniac and wanted him out of the house. So she had told him to find somewhere else to live and pronto. She despised a woman that had the nerve to call her house and ask her to put her husband on the phone. What the hell did she think she was doing? Was she that desperate that she couldn't wait for a married man to leave his family for her?

When Lynn was offered a chance to act as a supervisor for the four offices in Northern Ontario on a rotating basis with two other officers she jumped at the opportunity. The only problem was she would have to work out of the Thunder Bay office for a couple weeks at a time. After talking to her mother, Lynn agreed to take the job and told Steve that her mother would watch the kids. She was adamant that he find somewhere else to live. She did not want him living there when she got back home.

Lynn decided that she would email Owen and let him know how to find her. At least she wasn't calling him; although she disliked having to contact him again first. Owen emailed her back almost right away. He was delighted that she was taking on a supervisory position. He promised that he would call soon. He was just so busy with traveling and meetings he hadn't found the time to call. Lynn emailed him back asking him to provide her with his home phone number so she could call him some evening at home from Thunder Bay. The response she got back was disturbing to say the least. He ignored her request and promised to call her soon. Now Lynn did not think of herself as an overly paranoid person but when a man refuses to give her his home phone number or tell her where he lives a red flag goes up.

Lynn thought about his response for days, confused and very concerned. What was she supposed to think? Was he hiding something, more specifically someone? Was she being a fool thinking that they actually had something special developing between them? She had tried to be honest with Owen about her crumbling marriage and the fact that she was in the midst of trying to get a separation. Had he been scared off by her situation, or had he gotten tired of waiting for her to put out? Worse was the thought that he was living with another woman and just playing her. She tried to put it out of her mind as she spent the next couple of days making her travel arrangements and getting ready to leave for Thunder Bay. By the end of the week Lynn was ready to fly up to Thunder Bay. She would be gone for at least three weeks before she would fly back to Sudbury and work out of that office for a couple of weeks. She would be on this schedule for a month or two, possibly longer depending on how her managers decided to split the work load.

That Sunday afternoon Lynn took an airport shuttle bus out to the Sudbury airport; loaded down with suitcases and boxes of office equipment. Checking in for her flight on Bearpaw Airlines Lynn grimaced at the thought of flying on such a small aircraft. She really didn't like eight seat planes very much. They always felt like flying culverts to her. There was something unnerving about being able to see your pilot while he was flying the plane. It was late afternoon when she finally crossed the tarmac with her carryon bag and boarded the tiny aircraft. The co pilot greeted them and went through the safety talk with them before attempting to do a check for seatbelts. Attempting is the operative word here; the fellow was so tall and had such broad shoulders he could only fit about half way down the plane before he had to make a three point turn to head back to the front of the plane. Lynn stifled a laugh as she watched him struggle to return to the cockpit with what remained of his dignity. There was only one row of seats on each side of the plane in the tiny aircraft and the noise level was high enough to drone out a normal conversation. So the only thing left for Lynn to do was curl up against her window and take a nap.

As Lynn leaned her head against the window and watched the sun set she started to drift off. Half asleep she closed her eyes and immediately found herself sitting in a hospital room holding Owen's hand as he lay in bed. His hair was still jet black with only a hint of gray. She sat looking down at him as he smiled up at her and she said,

"All those years were worth it."

At that moment she walked past the open door of the hospital room and she looked up at herself. Lynn's eyes snapped open. What had just happened? Confused Lynn bolted upright and shook her head. Had she been dreaming or awake? Lynn thought back to the last conscious thought she had had just before closing her eyes. She had decided that she was going to email Owen from Thunder Bay and tell him to leave her alone. She did not want to be involved with him if he was living with another woman and lying to her. Her life was crazy enough as it was. It was for the best, she needed to sort out her personal life first before she could start anything with him. So why would she dream about being with Owen in the future? It didn't really feel like a dream. It felt more like a premonition or waking dream. Was this something that would happen in the future? And what did she mean by,

"All those years were worth it?" Trying to shake off the feeling of confusion and frustration Lynn closed her eyes again and pulled her jacket over her to no avail. She was not going to be able to sleep now. There were too many thoughts running around in her head.

Sitting up Lynn looked around and realized they were getting ready to make their descent into Thunder Bay. She had never been there before and was wondering how the next couple of weeks were going to work out. The first order of business was going to be emailing Owen. The quicker she dealt with this the better. After an uneventful landing Lynn disembarked and went looking for her luggage. One of the staff from the Thunder Bay office was supposed to be picking her up. She started looking around the small airport for Greg White. As she stood out front with her suitcases Greg pulled up in a work truck and jumped out.

"Hey Lynn, how was your flight?" he asked as he started picking up the bag nearest him.

"It's been a while since I've seen you. Coquitlam was the last time wasn't?" he said casually while dropping her suitcases in the back of the pickup. They climbed into the crew cab and headed off. Lynn couldn't see much because it is already pitch black out so as she tried to get her bearings she asked,

"What street are we on?"

"Main street." he answered. "We just have to turn left up here and your apartment is only a couple of more blocks away. You are going to be pretty close to the office. I will pick you up in the morning and then you can bring one of the other work trucks home tomorrow night. There is a grocery store nearby and a gym as well if you are interested."

"Yes, that sounds good." she replied still peering out the passenger's side window. It was late when she finally got settled in her basement apartment and fell into the double bed for a couple of hours of much needed sleep.

It seemed like the alarm clock started buzzing not more than ten minutes after she had put her head down on the pillow. Dragging herself out of bed Lynn stumbled into the bathroom and started looking for her toothbrush. She dropped it and cursed while she watched it roll behind the toilet. Too tired to care, she left it and wandered back out of the bathroom after splashing water on her face. There was no food in the apartment so she was going to have to get Greg to stop somewhere for her to grab some breakfast and a cup of tea on their way into the office. Grumbling to herself about the state of her life Lynn put on her uniform, loaded her firearm and holstered it as Greg started buzzing her from the lobby.

"Hold on, I'm coming!" she yelled into the intercom as she glanced around quickly making sure she hadn't forgotten anything before heading out the door.

With a cup of green tea and a breakfast sandwich in hand Lynn followed Greg into the Thunder Bay office. He was in an exceptionally chatty mood that morning. Lynn had barely managed to get a word in edgewise for the past forty five minutes; which was unusual for her. He showed her to her new office and said,

"It is pretty bare, but you have the basics. You have your laptop with you right?"

"Yes, right here in my carry on."

"Good, you should be able to dock it and hook up to our network without much trouble. If you do have any problems just call the helpdesk and they will walk you through reconfiguring your computer."

"Great thanks, I will give you a call if I need anything else."

"Okay, I will be in my office down the hall if you need me."

Balancing her tea and laptop bag Lynn edged her way through the office door and sat down. Putting her tea on the desk Lynn looked around and decided to deal with her laptop first. That usually was the most time consuming part of setting up anyways. Nothing is as easy as it seems. Smiling she thought, how true on so many levels. Sure enough her email wouldn't work and she ended up on the phone with the helpdesk staff for the next two hours while they walked her through reconfiguring her settings.

Hanging up the phone Lynn sighed and looked out the window in front of her desk. The view wasn't much, just the parking lot and an old abandoned dock. It was almost noon already. She had taken all morning just trying to get herself set up and she hadn't been able to do any work yet. Thoughts of Owen floated across her mind as she closed her eyes and remembered their last kiss. The mere thought of him made her body ache. No, this is not worth it. He is hiding something and it is getting too complicated. It would be best if I just ended things now. So taking a deep breath Lynn opened up her email and wrote Owen a long letter explaining that she felt he was hiding something from her and she was still in the middle of her separation so it would be best if they just left things alone for now. She sat and wiped away her tears for a few moments before pressing the send button. It felt like she had just ripped her own heart out with the simple click of a button. Sitting back and shaking off her grief Lynn went to work answering all of the emails that had piled up in her in box for about half an hour before Greg knocked on her office door and asked,

"Are you interested in going out for lunch?" she replied,

"Sure." and grabbed her jacket as she followed Greg out of the office and into the parking lot.

"You seem awfully quiet today Lynn, that is unusual for you." trying to muster up a smile Lynn laughed weakly and said,

"I know, I have a lot of stuff on my mind lately. I have been having trouble at home with my husband."

"Oh, sorry I asked" Greg replied as they pulled into the parking lot of the restaurant. "By the way did you get the email from Brian? He is planning to be in the office tomorrow and he wants to have a staff meeting."

"Yes, I saw it. I think we will be holding a quick meeting before the staff meeting just to go over things for the supervisory position. When are you scheduled to act in the position again?"

"In about six weeks after your rotation and Ray's." nodding Lynn asked,

"Is there anything that you wanted to let me know about before the staff meeting?"

"No, there is only one hot file in the area right now and I have left all of the information for you in the file drawer of your desk."

"Great, I will look it over this afternoon." as they walked into the restaurant and seated themselves Lynn asked "Is anyone else from the office joining us?" picking up his menu, Greg replied,

"No, they are all either away on training or they eat in the office." wanting to get back to the office as quickly as possible, Lynn said,

"Okay, let's order then."

The rest of the day was just a dull blur as Lynn went through the motions of doing her job and trying to care. All she could think about was how much her heart ached and how she wished things could be different. Her life had not turned out anything like she thought it would. She had ended up married to a man that was a fraud. He had been so loving and fun to be with for the first year and then he had turned into a moody, callous, and manipulative man that expected her to support him while he cheated on her with a string of different women. When she met Owen she thought she had finally met someone that could answer her heart and love her with all of his soul. Someone that she felt connected to on a level that left her breathless at times. But it seemed at that moment that she had been wrong. Maybe this was it, her personal life was destined to be a disaster and there was nothing she could do about it. Sighing Lynn packed up for the evening and headed back to her lonely apartment.

The silence was the worst; she was so used to her children and the dog making enough racket to raise the dead that she found it very difficult to stay home alone at night and not feel lonely.

Lynn cried herself to sleep that night, feeling more alone than she had in years. She knew there was no way she and Owen would be able to be together anytime soon, but the thought of him being out there thinking about her had always filled her with so much joy. It made her loveless marriage almost bearable most days. Slipping into the refuge of deep sleep Lynn dreamt of the night she and Owen spent together; the memory of their passion blazing through her dreams.

The next morning as Lynn sat in her office talking to Brian, her manager, about the expectations of her acting position her phone rang. Surprised she answered it while apologizing to her manager.

"Fishery Officer Thompson speaking"

"Lynn, its Owen can we talk?" shocked at the sound of his voice on the other end of the line she was at a loss for words.

"Uh, okay, I am in a meeting right now. Can I call you back in say half an hour?"

"Sure as long as you are not trying to blow me off."

"No, I'm not. I will call you back as soon as I am done. Okay."

"Okay, I will be waiting." apologizing again for the interruption Brian just smiled and said

"Don't worry about it, I have a personal life too and it's difficult when you are away from home." nodding, Lynn agreed with him and changed the subject.

"So Greg had mentioned a hot file in the area, I went through the information he left me but I was wondering if you had any more details for me?" they finished up their meeting and Lynn shut her office door as her manager left the office. She called Owen's office and was greeted by his receptionist. She transferred her right away and when Owen answered he sounded stressed.

"Give me just a minute okay?" she could hear the sound of him closing his office door and sitting back down again. "There, I was just closing my door."

"Uh huh."

"I got your email this morning and I was very disturbed by it."

"Okay, why were you disturbed?"

"I don't understand why you are upset with me."

"Owen, you refuse to give me your home address or your home phone number. You must be hiding something from me, most likely another woman that you are living with or even married to." Owen sounded almost relieved when he said,

"No, there is no one else, I just don't have a home phone and I was embarrassed to tell you." Lynn burst out into laughter,

"Are you kidding me? Why would you be embarrassed to tell me that? Lots of people only keep a cell phone. You could have just told me."

"I am sorry, it was wrong of me not to tell you. I just wasn't sure what you would think if I did."

"Oh Owen, you have to communicate with me if we are ever going to make anything work between us."

"You are right." a wave of relief swept over Lynn as she realized that Owen was trying to impress her and not hide a woman from her. That she could deal with. Owen continued the conversation by adding,

"As for your separation I thought you were working on getting things finalized."

"Yes, I am trying but it is difficult and he does not seem to want to do anything about getting divorced right now. It is very frustrating."

"I'll say. It bothers me that you are still married." sighing, Lynn agreed,

"I know it bothers me too; I am trying to figure out what to do about it though. It is just one big ugly mess."

"I realize that but I need you to finalize your divorce as soon as possible if we are going to continue seeing each other."

"Okay I get that. But it takes time. You can't give me a little more time to deal with it?" Lynn could hear Owen sigh with frustration,

"Yes I guess I can wait a few more months." shocked Lynn replied with a sinking feeling,

"A few more months? I will need at least six more months before I can get it finalized. Between my ex-husband refusing to cooperate and the lawyers dragging out everything it is an uphill battle. I already sped up the divorce by suing on the grounds of adultery rather than waiting for a legal separation for one year."

Lynn felt some relief as he agreed reluctantly, "Well I guess I can wait six more months for you. We have already waited this long."

"Thank you, I appreciate your patience."

"There is one other reason why I called you."

"Oh, what is that?"

I wanted to ask you to meet me out in Winnipeg in two weeks. I am flying out there as a guest speaker for a Round Table session with the Privy Council on Native Education. Do you think you can get permission to come out and attend?" hesitating Lynn thought about it for a moment,

"I don't know. I have been the lead officer for all Native training and communications, so it's possible. Can you email me with the details and I will talk to my manager today."

"Okay, I will do that right away. It would be great to see you again. All I do is think about you and how much I want you." Blushing Lynn felt a wave of desire rush through her body. She wanted him too. It was all she thought about every moment she had to herself.

"I feel the same way Owen; I just want us to be ready for this."

"I am ready, all I do is think about being with you Lynn."

"Okay, I will email you when I get an answer from my manager."

"Alright, I will be waiting to hear from you. Good bye."

"Bye." closing her eyes for just a moment Lynn felt her body rush with a wave of heat as she thought about Owen touching her and kissing her again. She ached for his touch. Damn, this was getting so confusing. She knew she would probably get permission to attend the Round Table in Winnipeg; she just wasn't sure if seeing Owen was a good idea. She wished she had someone that she could talk to about her feelings. After lunch Lynn approached her manager and presented him with the details for the Round Table that Owen had forwarded to her. Her manager was very supportive and gave her the green light immediately.

"Sounds like an excellent opportunity to me. If it is only for three days go ahead and book your flight. I will sign off on your travel authority."

"Great thanks," walking back to her office Lynn felt excited and nervous. She could go, but what did she want to happen when she saw Owen in Winnipeg? Lynn sent him a quick email letting him know she had gotten permission to go and that she would forward him her flight information once she had it. Smiling, Lynn couldn't help relishing the thought of finally making love to Owen. It was all she been longing for.

Lynn spent the next two weeks trying to immerse herself in her work to keep as busy as possible so she wouldn't miss her kids or think about Owen. It didn't work very well. All she did in the evenings while alone in her apartment was long to call Owen and talk to him. She tried reaching him a few times but he never answered his cell phone. So she contented herself with calling home and talking to her kids in an effort to stave off the loneliness she felt. Lynn visited the local gym a couple of times a week and worked out for over an hour, just to fill the time.

Landing in Winnipeg Lynn felt a rush of emotion. Finally, she could hardly wait to see Owen again. Leaving the plane and heading down to the main level Lynn looked around expectantly for him. He was nowhere in sight. Puzzled Lynn checked the flight information that he had sent her earlier that week. He should have landed over an hour ago. Where was he? Digging out her cell phone she called Owen. He answered with an enthusiastic,

"Hello, where are you?"

"I am in the airport where are you?"

"I am upstairs in the lounge with my new friend why don't you come on up and meet us?"

Mildly annoyed Lynn said "Okay," and hung up. What was going on? What happened to I can hardly wait to see you? Pulling her two suitcases along behind her Lynn headed for the nearest escalator.

Once she got to the second level she had no trouble finding in the airport lounge. Owen was sitting in the front window with a young man she had never seen before. As she approached Owen jumped up and rushed out to give her a big hug and exclaimed,

"I am so happy to see you! Come here and meet my new friend Mark Greene, he flew into Winnipeg with me. We have been sitting here and having a couple of drinks waiting for your flight to arrive." It was obvious Owen had been drinking; he looked like he was feeling pretty good. Lynn felt she had never seen this side of him before; he was wearing a bright red track suit, runners and a heavy gold chain around his neck. He reminded her of a rap star; a look that really wasn't working for him. Lynn perched herself on a bar stool between Mark and Owen, still feeling a little confused. What exactly were they doing? She had been dying to see Owen and she thought he felt the same way. So why were they wasting valuable time with some stranger when they could be alone; especially when they had waited so long to see each other? Lynn gave the waitress her order for a glass of water and smiled weakly as Owen told Mark the story of how they had met early that summer in Lethbridge.

"Isn't she the most beautiful woman you have ever seen?" he demanded of Mark. Mark agreed,

"Yes, she most certainly is." while Lynn wondered if he felt he had the option of saying no.

Owen grabbed her hand and kissed her.

"I am so happy to see you." he said while smiling at her. I told Mark all about you on the flight from Edmonton." all Lynn could think was poor Mark and what a pair of drunks! Lynn was rapidly getting bored with the conversation and anxious to head out to their hotel.

"It is getting late Owen; do you think we could head out soon? I am sure Mark has someone expecting him." Mark seemed to consider her comment for a moment and glanced at his watch.

"You know you are right. I do have family expecting me to show up pretty soon. I guess I should get going."

"You can catch a cab with us!" Owen exclaimed. "It will be cheaper that way!" Mark agreed and as they settled the bill Lynn gathered up her suitcases and jacket. Owen followed her out of the lounge, commenting on the fact that she was hauling two suitcases for just three days.

"I know, I know, I bring everything with me when I travel. I hate not having something I didn't think of when I packed so I pack everything possible." Owen just laughed and pointed to the one bag on his shoulder.

"This is all I brought. It has everything I need and if I don't have it I either buy it or go without." Lynn just shrugged,

"What can I say?" as they rode the escalator down to the front doors.

Once they got outside Owen spotted a limousine sitting along the curb in front of the doors,

"Would you like to take limousine instead?" Owen asked Lynn.

"Sure, I haven't ridden in one of those things for a long time, why not." laughing Owen left Lynn on the curb and walked up to the limo driver.

"How much?" the limousine driver replied,

"Forty bucks for an hour" turning to Mark, Owen said

"Do you want to split the limousine? It will be almost the same cost as a cab."

Mark shrugged and said, "Why not, you only live once."

Lynn handed her bags to the driver and they climbed into the back seat of the stretch limousine. Owen put his arm around Lynn and they leaned back while sitting and chatting with Mark. After a short drive the limousine driver dropped Mark off in front of his relative's house and continued downtown to the Marriott Hotel. As they drove through the downtown core Owen noticed the large number of natives hanging out on the street.

"Wow, there sure are a lot of my brothers here." he commented while laughing nervously. Leaning forward Lynn looked out the window and realized that there were a lot of native people hanging out on the streets.

"Hmm, I never noticed before."

"Winnipeg has the highest population of natives in Canada." Owen replied, "That is one of the reasons why the conference on Native education is being held here." nodding she replied "Oh, that makes sense."

Owen paid the driver and Lynn headed into the lobby with her suitcases looking for the reception desk.

"Did you make a reservation?" Owen asked.

"Yes, I did, how about you?" Lynn responded.

"No. I assumed we would be sharing the same room."

"Oh, okay, that works." she said while squeezing his hand. Owen turned to the hotel staff at the front desk and announced loudly,

"My girlfriend and I would like a room please. I believe you have a reservation under Lynn Thompson."

"Yes sir, we do. We have the king corner room suite reserved. Will that be acceptable?"

"Perfect," turning to Lynn he said,

"You reserved a king suite?" smiling Lynn said,

"Yes, I figured we would be more comfortable." he laughed and shook his head.

"I should have guessed." Once they had checked in and found their room they both changed into formal evening wear and took the elevator down to the reception that was being held for the Members of Parliament and the Grand Chief of the Assembly of First Nations.

Owen held Lynn's hand and smiled at her as they walked past security into the reception. The room was full of dignitaries and wait staff. Lynn was wearing a full length black skirt with a sheer gold shirt. She had swept her hair up and put on her Austrian crystal earrings. Owen looked as handsome as ever in his black pinstriped suit and black tie. As they walked into the room Owen was greeted by his manager, the Executive Director of his department. He introduced Lynn to his manager and then said to her,

"Mary Glenn this is Lynn Thompson. Lynn this is my manager Mary Glenn. Isn't Lynn the most beautiful woman in the room?" Lynn blushed and looked down as she tried not to feel silly after such a compliment. His manager only smiled and said,

"Why yes, she is." Lynn was grateful for her gracious response. It was getting to be dinner time and both Lynn and Owen were getting hungry. The reception was only serving cocktails and finger foods. Lynn went looking for something for them to eat and brought back a small plate for them to share as they sat and listened to the speeches of the dignitaries. Everyone began mingling after the speeches and Lynn was introduced to a number of different officials. The one that caught her attention was the Member of Parliament who was the Minister of Education and Youth Services. He was a former NHL hockey player and most of the men in the room were tripping over themselves trying to talk to him and shake his hand. Owen was no exception. He started to sweat and leaned over to Lynn and motioned towards him while he was on the other side of the room.

"See that man standing over there?"

"Yes." "He is a former NHL hockey legend. I would love to meet him."

"So why don't we go over and introduce ourselves then?" Lynn asked.

"Oh, no, we couldn't do that." he whispered back.

"Oh my goodness Owen, he's just a guy. He doesn't even play hockey anymore."

Being a woman with very little interest in hockey Lynn was not really that impressed by the guy or his former hockey career. So Lynn waited for a moment when he was not being mobbed by men pumping his hand and asking for autographs and walked over to introduce herself and Owen as he followed along behind her.

"Hello, I am Lynn Thompson and this is Owen Proudfeather."

"Allen, pleased to meet you." breaking into a profuse sweat Owen held out his hand and shook the Minister's hand.

"It is a real pleasure and honour to meet you." smiling, Lynn watched as they started discussing hockey and his career.

Lynn soon lost interest and started talking to the two men standing beside her waiting to shake the Minister's hand. They all seemed awestruck by the fellow, something that was completely lost on Lynn. The Minister noticed that she was not reacting to his reputation nor did she seem to recognize him. He seemed to find this amusing and after talking with Owen he stood chatting with her for quite awhile as the men kept coming and going pumping his hand and uttering phrases like,

"You are a legend. I am still a fan." he seemed to take it all in stride and enjoy the conversation. Owen's manager joined them at one point and seemed to find the men's reaction to the former hockey star just as amusing as Lynn did. She made polite conversation with Lynn and Owen for a bit and then wandered off to talk to another group of people on the other side of the room. While she had been standing with them her daughter had walked up and she had introduced her to both Lynn and Owen.

"Owen I believe you have already met my daughter Linda. Lynn Thompson, this is Linda Whiteside. She works out of Ottawa with the Native Women's Association."

Linda was a beautiful Métis woman in her early thirties. She had beautiful long, dark hair and the most gorgeous complexion Lynn had ever seen. Lynn was surprised that Owen seemed to show no interest in her. And she commented on this after they had left.

"What a beautiful young woman, surely you must have been interested in her?" shrugging Owen just answered,

"I never noticed." after about an hour Lynn whispered to Owen,

"I am starving." he smiled down at her and said,

"So am I. This thing is coming to an end, why don't we go and try and find a restaurant nearby?" agreeing, they headed back to their hotel room and changed into jeans and sweaters before heading out.

Lynn was too hungry to worry about the last couple of hours. She just wanted to find a quiet restaurant and have a nice, romantic meal with Owen. There was no point in getting all stressed out about his behaviour at the airport. Besides he had just spent the last couple of hours treating her like royalty. Hand in hand they walked down the main street of downtown Winnipeg looking for a restaurant they both could agree on. They were not having much luck. There didn't seem to be many restaurants on the main street. So they ended up walking over five blocks before they started seeing anything that even looked like a restaurant. It was getting late and the temperature was dropping. The wind in Winnipeg is legendary for its bone chilling effect and Lynn and Owen were finding out first hand why. They spotted a little Italian restaurant that looked good so they both agreed to check it out. Honestly, Lynn was so cold and hungry she didn't really care anymore. She just wanted to find someplace and get inside out of the cold. Stepping into the restaurant Lynn sighed with a breath of relief, warmth finally. They were seated almost right away by a friendly hostess that directed their attention to a black board with all of the night's specials.

"Looks great, I am so hungry I think I will start with the lasagne." Owen replied and Lynn agreed.

"Make that two please." While they waited for their food Owen ordered another drink and Lynn decided to have a hot blueberry tea to warm her up.

"What is in one of those?" Owen asked her. "Tea, amaretto, Grande Marnier and a cinnamon stick."

"Wow, that must pack a punch." he chuckled.

"Well it certainly warms you up." Lynn agreed. She settled in and relaxed as their meal arrived as they enjoyed the pleasant atmosphere and good food. It was late; they stayed until the restaurant closed and headed back to the hotel.

"I have a very early morning breakfast meeting tomorrow and I really need to get some sleep." Owen explained to Lynn as they walked back into the hotel.

"Okay, no problem. I understand. We have the next couple of days to spend together so there is no hurry."

"Good, I am glad you understand."

They walked back to their hotel room still holding hands and smiling at one another. After letting themselves into the room they settled down on the king size bed and turned on the television. Owen lay back in the bed and flipped through the channels.

"There is nothing worth watching and I am too tired to watch TV." he said. He handed the remote to Lynn and asked,

"Do you want to watch anything?"

"No," she replied, "I am not interested in watching TV."

"Okay. Let's get some sleep then." feeling disappointed she said,

"Sure." she got up headed into the bathroom and changed into her negligee and brushed her teeth. She opened the bathroom door and walked back into the room with the complimentary house coat wrapped around her. She dropped her housecoat on the sofa chair at the foot of the bed and slide under the blankets. Owen lay in bed watching her and smiled.

"You are beautiful." he said and kissed her good night. Lynn said,

"Thank you." and kissed him back. Then Owen rolled over with his back to Lynn and promptly fell asleep. She lay in bed listening to his heavy breathing as he slipped into a deep sleep and began to snore.

Shaking her head Lynn put her ear plugs in and rolled over to go to sleep. As she drifted off Lynn wondered to herself. What did I do wrong? Lynn had never been alone before in a hotel room with a man that didn't seem interested in having sex; at least at some level. Even if nothing did happen there was at least the interest or attempt. Owen had shown neither. In fact he had acted like they were an old married couple that had been together for about thirty years and he had lost all interest. This was very confusing behaviour coming from a man that she had never actually had sex with yet and had seemed so eager to see her. Either way it felt like a blow to Lynn's self esteem. Maybe Owen did not find her very attractive after all. It was her marriage all over again. Steve never touched her or looked at her either. Maybe she really was just too big and fat for any man to want her. Feeling lonely and unlovable Lynn curled up on her side and drifted off to sleep with tears welling in her eyes.

Owen had set the alarm clock for six thirty am; Lynn was jolted out of her sleep by the sound of it buzzing and groaned as she pulled the covers over her head. Owen staggered out of bed and once dressed in his suit he said goodbye to Lynn and promised to meet up with her for lunch. She tried to curl up and go back to sleep. She managed for about an hour or so and then started feeling hungry so she got up and got dressed. Remembering a breakfast buffet was being served on the tenth floor Lynn headed out of the hotel room towards the elevator. Reaching the tenth floor Lynn stepped off and walked over to the restaurant entrance and stood in line. As she stood there waiting her turn to be seated Owen rushed past her looking hurried and preoccupied.

"Owen," she called out as he was about to walk past her.

"Oh, Lynn good morning." he grabbed her hand and kissed her briefly before saying, "I have to attend the first session this morning; I will see you at lunch." with that he was gone and she was left standing alone in the restaurant. Lynn was used to travelling alone. She had been doing it for the past couple of years with her job. But still somehow she was disappointed. She had been hoping they would spend more time together. Lynn spent the rest of the morning reading the newspaper and then meditating for about an hour before deciding to go for a walk through downtown. She had been hoping to sit in on some of the discussions, but she was not on the guest list and security refused to provide her with a pass.

While on her walk Lynn picked up some candles in a little gift shop across the street from their hotel. She decided that she would try and create a very romantic atmosphere that evening to try and get Owen in the mood. She had brought along her favourite rose coloured satin negligee and some unscented massage oil. Around five o'clock Lynn showered, changed and filled the room with lit candles. She put the massage oil in a hot water bath and waited for Owen to return to their room. It was about five thirty when Lynn heard Owen unlock the door and walk in. She was laying in the middle of the king size bed waiting for him, surrounded by the burning candles in the darkness. As Owen rounded the corner he stopped in his tracks and smiled.

"Wow, this is amazing," he exclaimed. "I didn't expect this!" Lynn smiled and sat up in the bed, patting the covers beside her.

"Come join me." she said.

"Okay," taking off his shoes Owen stretched out on the bed beside Lynn. "You look amazing," he said as he ran his hand along her arm and down her side. "This is so beautiful on you. I can't believe how many candles are in the room. It looks like a church!" smiling Lynn said,

"Would you like me to give you a massage? You must be tired after being in meetings all day."

"No that's okay, I don't feel like one."

"Oh, okay. Well why don't you change into something more comfortable."

"No, I would rather go out for a drink. I could really use one after the day I just had." sitting up Lynn said.

"Okay, I guess we can do this later."

"Sure, it was really nice of you but I would rather go out right now." feeling disappointed and rejected Lynn got up and got dressed while Owen relaxed on the bed. Lynn blew out the candles in the room and put her coat and boots on.

"Okay, I am ready to go." she said. Sitting up Owen got his coat and put his shoes back on. Heading down the hallway Owen took Lynn's hand and looked at her sideways.

"You are not pouting are you?" he asked. Lynn shook her head and didn't say anything. She was struggling with her overwhelming feeling of rejection. The last couple years of her marriage had been awful. Her husband never looked at her or touched her and if she tried to get him interested in sex he usually rejected her; especially during both her pregnancies. So Lynn was sensitive to rejection and this was hammering her self esteem. If Owen is already rejecting me what would our relationship be like if we were together for a long time? I don't think I can handle this type of a relationship. They walked out of the hotel in silence and crossed the street looking for a bar. It was obvious to Lynn that Owen was determined to get something to drink. He was on a mission. He barely spoke to her as they walked along retracing their steps from the night before. They found a quiet little bar down the street from the hotel and sat in silence while Owen had a couple of rum and cokes and Lynn had a cup of tea.

"Don't you want anything to drink?" Owen asked her.

"No, I am not in the mood." she replied.

As they walked back to the hotel Owen seemed more relaxed. He held Lynn's hand and smiled at her, sensing she was still upset he tried to get her to smile. Frustrated with her lack of response he gave up. Opening the hotel room door he looked at her and said,

"Why don't we put the music channel on?" he flipped on the television and found the music channel, Mariah Carey's song *Vision of Love* played as he pulled her close to him and said,

"I guess this is our song now." as he kissed her, smiling Lynn said,

"I guess so." and kissed him back. She pushed her feelings of rejection aside and looked into his brown eyes and said.

"You know I only wanted to make you happy." Owen smiled back at her and said,

"I know. I just wasn't ready."

"Okay." sinking down onto the king sized bed together Owen started to undress Lynn as she kissed his face and neck. They made love that night for the first time. Passion blazed through Lynn's body with an intensity she had never experienced in her life before. The slightest touch or kiss from him made her body ache for more and burn with a bright flame of desire. She felt the intensity of her desire rise and flow throughout her body as it filled her senses. Moaning with desire Owen pulled Lynn up onto his broad chest. He kissed her slowly, deeply as his hands caressed her body. Lynn rolled onto the bed and Owen mounted her as he kissed her neck and breasts. "You are so beautiful" he whispered in ear as he slide his hand across her hip and down her thigh. Lynn moaned deeply as Owen entered her. He thrust deeply into her body as she arched her back. "Owen" she moaned as she felt a great wave of love and intense passion sweep over her body. Lynn grasped his shoulders and arched her back again as she climaxed with such intensity she could feel her toes aching with passion. That night Lynn slept in Owen's arms; the same way that they had slept their first night together.

The next morning Owen was up early again for more meetings and Lynn was getting restless. She had not agreed to attend the conference just so she could wait around all day for Owen to reappear. She had been planning to attend the meetings, she knew she would not be asked to participate, but she would have liked to have at least listened. Lynn had brought along everything for a workout in the hotel gym. She decided to go for a walk first and found herself standing outside a beautiful Anglican church situated right behind the hotel. A service had just started so she slipped in the wooden double doors as quietly as she could and sat down in the back pews. Lynn loved the ritual of church services. The catholic services were the most beautiful, although she didn't get much out of the actual sermons. She preferred United or Baptist sermons. She had not attended an Anglican service in a very long time so she was content to just listen and go along with the kneeling and prayers. There was something so comforting about the ritual of kneeling and praying.

Heading back to the hotel after the service Lynn mulled over her feelings. She could not sort them all out, there were too many. Her feelings for Owen were so strong, yet his behaviour at times made her feel frustrated and uneasy, as if he were taking her for granted. She did not like feeling that way and was having trouble understanding why he behaved the way he did; especially his need to drink. It seemed to be more important to him to drink than just about anything else. She had barely survived growing up with her abusive, alcoholic mother and had stumbled into her disastrous marriage to Steve and his drinking. She could not get into another relationship with another alcoholic. Lynn was becoming very confused. Was she making another mistake?

Lynn went back to her hotel room and changed into her tee shirt and shorts. She took the elevator down to the third floor and started running on the treadmill. She had not gone for a run in days so she had a lot of pent up energy. It was about an hour later when panting with exhaustion she headed back to her room to find some water. She felt better after her run and decided to have a quick shower and meditate while she waited for Owen to return from the last of his meetings. He had promised her that he would only be gone until about three that afternoon. Feeling like a kept woman Lynn settled down in the hotel room with her ear plugs in and started meditating. She loved to mediate. It always made her feel so much calmer and grounded.

When Owen got back it was after four and Lynn was starting to wonder where he was. Opening the door he apologized for being late and sat on the bed looking exhausted.

"I am worn right out." he sighed and lay back in the bed flipping through the television channels. Lynn was feeling neglected and bored, so she tried to cuddle up to Owen while he watched TV. Looking mildly annoyed with her he shifted his weight and sat up. Not knowing how to interpret his behaviour Lynn sat up and left him alone. After about half an hour Lynn asked Owen if he wanted to go out for something to eat.

"No, I am too tired to eat." he replied. Lynn was starting to get very hungry so she decided to order room service. Sitting at the small table in the corner of the hotel room Lynn ate her dinner while watching the television show Owen had on.

After she ate Lynn put her tray with all of her dishes out in the hallway and coming back into the room she asked Owen,

"Would you like to go out for a walk?"

"No," he answered, "I am too tired to do anything right now. I just want to sit here and relax while I unwind." confused, and feeling rejected by his behaviour Lynn made herself comfortable on the bed while making sure she did not bother Owen. She was not ready to be rejected again. Around nine thirty Owen announced,

"I am tired; I think I am ready to go to bed." Lynn agreed, even though she was bored and would have liked to do something, anything for a couple of more hours before going to sleep. But she got ready for bed quietly. Owen rolled over as he said,

"Good night." and promptly fell asleep with his back to her. Lynn was getting used to this behaviour and rolled over to sleep on her side of the bed, choking back tears of disappointment. This certainly had been a strange weekend. Not what she had expected at all.

The next morning the two got up around nine and started packing for their flights home. Lynn put on a pair of jeans and a sweater and packed her bags. She sat and watched Owen ironing his suit while he wore a towel around his waist from his shower. Neither of them said much as Lynn sat feeling disappointed and confused. She didn't say anything to Owen because she didn't know what to say. Noticing that Owen didn't have his bag fully packed Lynn finished packing it for him. Owen glanced up after she had finished his packing for him and smiling briefly he thanked her,

"I appreciate your help, thanks." Lynn just smiled and sat down on the bed.

"I've had enough," Owen said as he continued to iron his suit.

"What do you mean?" Lynn asked.

"Nothing." he responded and went back to his ironing. Lynn's flight was not until late that afternoon so she decided to stay at the hotel and relax before heading back to the airport. So once Owen was dressed he gave her a quick hug and said.

"Bye, I will call you later in the week."

"Okay, have a good flight home." smiling weakly, Lynn watched him leave and sat back down with a sigh. What had happened? This weekend had not turned out to be anything like she expected. Shaking her head, Lynn decided to go for breakfast and then take a quick walk around the block before leaving for the airport. Checking out of the hotel Lynn asked the front desk clerk for the bill,

"The bill has already been paid Madame," was his reply. "The gentleman paid it this morning."

"Oh, okay, that is a pleasant surprise." Lynn was puzzled. Why would he pay for the hotel room and not mention it to her? Strange, but most of the weekend had been strange. Handing him her room key, Lynn said "Thanks very much. Do you think you could call me a cab for the airport?"

"There should be one sitting outside that door Madame." was the clerk's response. Pulling her suitcases behind her Lynn let herself out of the revolving doors and found a taxi cab.

Her flight home was uneventful. She mostly sat in silence while she mulled over the events of the past couple of days. Landing in Toronto she headed through the airport terminal straight for the Starbucks counter. She loved her soy chai and when she was feeling down or stressed nothing made her happier than sipping on a grande chai while she contemplated her life.

CHAPTER FOUR

Gone Baby Gone

Lynn dragged herself in to work the next day. She was exhausted from the long trip back to Thunder Bay the night before. Delays in Toronto held her flight up for a couple of hours, so it was well past midnight before she finally arrived back at her lonely apartment.

She dropped down into her high back office chair and put her boots up on the desk. Taking another sip of her green tea she noticed the message indicator was blinking on her phone.

"I guess I have been gone for at least one whole day so I suppose I shouldn't be surprised." she muttered under her breath. Sighing, she dug in the desk drawer for the yellow sticky notepad that had the pass code for the voice messages. Lynn jotted down all the phone numbers she had to call back until she got to the last message. It was from Owen. Her heart skipped a beat as she listened to his voice. That was quick! But why hadn't he called her on her cell phone or at the apartment phone number? He had both numbers. Focussing on the message Lynn couldn't believe what she heard,

"Hi Lynn, this is Owen. I just wanted to tell you I don't think we should see each other anymore. Okay. Goodbye." shocked Lynn sat back and thought what the heck was going on? She knew something didn't feel right when he left but this caught her off guard. Sitting in her office staring out of the window, Lynn felt as if the floor had been pulled out from under her feet and she was going into a free fall. Chocking back her tears Lynn got up and locked her office door and closed her blinds. She sat quietly as tears streamed down her face and onto her hands supporting her head. Never in her life had she felt so much grief over losing someone after knowing them for only a couple of months.

Sitting up she dried her tears and decided that she deserved an explanation. He was not going to get off this easy. Owen could explain to her over the phone what the problem was. Pulling out his business card she dialled his number and waited while his receptionist transferred her call.

"Good morning, Owen Proudfeather speaking."

"Owen, this is Lynn." she was greeted by silence. Continuing she added,

"I got your voice message and I am very confused. What is wrong?" hesitating Owen replied in a wooden tone,

"I don't think we should see each other anymore Lynn." it was if he had pierced her chest with a sharp blade; the pain was that intense. Clutching at her heart Lynn drew a ragged breath and gritted her teeth against the pain.

"Owen, you and I are connected. Can't you feel it? Don't you know what you are doing to me?" sadly, but with resolve he answered,

"I know, I can feel it. But we can't see each other anymore." Lynn took her hand off her chest and braced herself against the desk.

"Tell me why." was all she could manage to say between the waves of searing pain wracking her body. Quietly he replied,

"I spoke to my mother about us. You know I respect her opinion highly and she does not approve of my seeing a married woman." drawing another painful breath Lynn pleaded with him,

"Please Owen, don't do this. You know I am trying to end my marriage. It takes time to finalize a divorce. You said you were willing to give me six more months."

"I know what I said. I just can't wait." he replied sternly. "What we are doing is wrong. There is nothing more to say. Goodbye Lynn and take care." with that he hung up as Lynn sat holding the phone willing her heart to continue beating as each breath become more painful than the last. Blind with grief Lynn stood up and groped for the phone. She replaced the receiver and grabbed her jacket. Picking up her keys she walked out of the office without a word to anyone and drove to the nearest Starbucks to get a soy chai.

As she sat in her truck drinking her chai Lynn contemplated her options. Staying in Thunder Bay was out of the question. She was getting lonelier by the day and she could not bear another two weeks in that apartment before she was scheduled to fly home. Setting her resolve Lynn drove back to the office and called back all the people that had left her messages. Once that was done she called her manager,

"I have a family emergency. My mother is not well and I need to go home." sounding concerned her manager replied,

"Of course, make the arrangements to fly back to Sudbury as quickly as you can. I will sign off on everything."

"Okay, thank you. I will try and book a flight back in the next twenty four hours." sighing with relief Lynn hung up and started packing up her laptop and sorting out her files. Greg came by about an hour later and knocked on her door.

"Hey Lynn, Brian called and said you have to head back home right away. Is everything okay?"

"Well not really," she replied, which in a manner of speaking was the truth, "My mother is ill and I need to get home to take care of her and the kids."

"Hey, I understand completely, family first" Greg said as he helped her pack up her office.

Lynn packed up everything in the apartment that night and caught the first flight out in the morning. She was so distraught she didn't even sleep that night. She just lay in bed and wept until there were no more tears to cry. Then she curled up into a ball and pulled her covers up over her head. She rolled out of bed over an hour before her alarm went off and was ready long before her cab arrived to take her to the airport.

Arriving back home late in the afternoon she was greeted with surprise and delight.

"You're back home early!" her mother exclaimed, "Glad you decided to come back, things have been crazy around here." The kids bounced around her as they squealed,

"Mommy's home, mommy's home. Hurray!" Forcing a smile Lynn bent down and hugged her kids. Burying her face in Marissa's hair she murmured,

"It's good to be back." standing up, she stroked Eric's head and put her arm around Olivia's shoulders. "I hope you guys have been good for Nana." her mother snorted as she replied,

"Are you kidding? They have been little monsters. Nothing has changed around here." smiling at her mother, she hugged her as she said,

"I can certainly see that. Okay guys give me a hand hauling my luggage into the house." and with that the three children charged out of the house in a race to be the first to bring back a suitcase. Laughing quietly, Lynn paused for a moment and glanced around her. It is humble but it is ours. We have each other and that counts for something. For a moment the ache in her heart was eased as she realized she was loved and she was not alone. Her relationship with her mother even made her feel loved and supported. It had been hard growing up with an abusive alcoholic for a mother. But she had been sober for over fifteen years and had made a huge effort to make amends for what she had put them through. Lynn was willing to forgive and forget.

Lynn slept that night; happy to be back in her own bed. Even though she was alone it didn't matter. Being alone was better than being trapped in a loveless marriage with someone you despised. Besides, she preferred to be alone with her grief. As she lay in her bed drifting off to sleep she reached out across the miles between them to feel for Owen, as she had done many times before. Except this time he was not there; it was if he had put up a wall and she could not feel him. Saddened by this she slipped into a deep sleep where she dreamt of his loving touch and the feel of his arms around her. Longing wracked her body even as she slept.

Months passed and Lynn marched through her days in a haze of pain and grief. She prayed every day for some way to remove the part of her that was connected to Owen. Every day she repeated the same mantra "I don't need another alcoholic in my life." Finally the day came when Lynn woke up and she did not immediately feel the agony of her loss. In fact her first thought was not of Owen, but how beautiful the sun rise looked that morning. Smiling and humming under her breath Lynn greeted everyone in the office as she made her way to her desk.

"Good morning Judy, good morning Carrie." both just looked up startled and replied,

"Why good morning Lynn you're in a good mood today."

"I sure am," she responded as she breezed past and into her office. Dropping into her chair and digging her gun holster out of her hip, Lynn started checking her email. Nothing grabbed her interest just routine requests for until she got half way through. She froze as she read it entirely and then re read it in disbelief. Slowly, the pit of her stomach sank into her feet as she absorbed the implications of the email. She was being sent to Calgary for training, again. Bloody hell! This was the last thing she needed right now. She was just getting over Owen and settling into her single life. Going back to Alberta would just put her on the crazy train, she could not handle being anywhere near him right now. Even though he would still be more than two hours away from her it was too close. Shit. What was she going to do? Trying to pull herself together, Lynn leaned back in her office chair and thought about trying to get out of the trip. She could make up another excuse; but that wasn't a smart career move.

Deciding to talk to someone about her dilemma Lynn walked down the office corridor to Carrie's office. She was one of the biologists that Lynn worked with. Lynn liked Carrie Madison she had a dark, twisted sense of humour that she could relate to.

"Hi Carrie, do you have a couple of minutes? I really need to talk."

"Sure Lynn, sit down. What's up?" sitting in the spare chair in Carrie's office Lynn started to explain,

"I have this problem, I met this amazing guy out in Lethbridge last summer and we have kept in touch and we've seen each other a couple of times since."

"Okay," Carrie replied as she encouraged Lynn to continue.

"But the last time we saw each other in Winnipeg he ended our relationship right after."

"Oh ouch, I see," she replied, "that sucks." "I know, I have been trying to get over him and move on with my life but it has been really difficult."

"Uh huh I can understand that." continuing Lynn added,

"I have been doing better up until today,"

"Oh what happened today?"

"I got an email today from Rob saying all officers have to fly out to Calgary next month for mandatory training. I don't want to go. I am tired of being away from my kids and I don't want to be in the same province as Owen. That would be too hard to take." sitting back in her chair Carrie pushed her dark, wide rimmed glasses up her nose and asked,

"What can you do? If you have to go do you really have a choice?" her voice heavy with resignation Lynn responded,

"No, I don't think I do have a choice. If I want to keep my job then I have to go. Damn, this is so frustrating. Sometimes I feel like this bloody outfit owns me." standing up with a heavy sigh Lynn said, "Thanks for listening Carrie."

"Sure, no problem, anytime." as Lynn walked back to her office.

Sitting down at her desk Lynn looked like a condemned woman as she wrote her reply to the email from the training coordinator; I will make my travel arrangements, please forward me a travel authority number to my flights, regards. Pushing herself away from the desk Lynn looked out her window and wished she could start her day all over again. She had gone from being cheerfully optimistic to being a tortured soul once again in a matter of minutes.

Lynn tried to keep herself busy with work for the next month in an effort to keep her mind off the impending trip. She spent long hours driving all over Northern Ontario working with the Ministry of Natural Resources Conservation Officers. She even flirted with the idea of dating again. Although she couldn't bring herself to actually go on a date, her scars were still too fresh.

Hauling her suitcase off the luggage carousel Lynn looked up at the dinosaur display. Still the same, I wonder if the bronze statue of the wild horses is still here. As she walked through the Calgary airport she looked up at her favourite statue and smiled. Some things never change. In a small way the thought was comforting. Lynn walked out the front doors of the airport terminal and looked around for her single girlfriend Maggie Jeffery. She had emailed her a couple of weeks ago and arranged to stay with her while she was in town. They had been friends for years. They met when both were originally hired by the department and sent to Cornwall, Ontario for training. It had been over five years now but they always managed to stay in touch and visit at least once a year. Even though Maggie was more than ten years younger than Lynn with no children they always got along very well and enjoyed each other's company. Lynn was looking forward to seeing Maggie they had a lot of catching up to do and Lynn always enjoyed teasing Maggie about meeting men. This was the only good part about her trip to Calgary. As she stood out front waiting for Maggie to arrive she looked around at the dirty snow and brown grass. She never really liked Calgary that much. It always seemed dry and dusty, even in the winter. The grass was always brown and the trees were few and far between. It's only redeeming quality was the Rocky Mountains on the horizon; promising something better if you could only reach them. But getting to them was the trick. It seemed like Calgary held onto her, pulling her down and preventing her from reaching the mountains. Making her feel trapped within the city limits. When she had lived there years ago in what seemed like another life time she had felt anxiety over the thought of never being able to get out of the city again. Trapped in its dirty, windy confines forever only to gaze longingly at the mountains she had been borne to. Never to go home and feel the cool mist of a waterfall or hear a mountain stream again. Closing her eyes momentarily she remembered the clear water rushing and tumbling over the grey stones. Laughing and babbling past her feet as it made its way towards the sea. Opening her eyes, Lynn shuddered as she looked around her. It was only a dream; we can not base our lives on dreams. Get a hold of yourself. Just then Maggie pulled up to the entrance of the airport and honked at Lynn. She put her truck in park and jumped out.

"Hey Lynn it's great to see you!" she exclaimed as she walked around to the front of the vehicle and gave Lynn a hug. "Is this your only bag? You usually never travel with less than two. What happened to you?" she chided as she helped Lynn load her suitcase into the back of her truck.

"Oh very funny Maggie, I decided to travel light. I got tired of hauling all those bags around and it is great to see you too!" Lynn jumped into the passenger side of the truck and Maggie got back in. Her long brown hair was pulled up in a ponytail. Lynn noticed she looked as slender and athletic as the last time she had seen her.

"You look great Maggie! Guys must be tripping over themselves to ask you out." Maggie just smiled shyly and shook her head.

"Oh Lynn you know I am not good with dating. That is more your thing." Lynn just laughed and shook her head. Maggie changed the subject,

"So do you want to head back to my place right away or are you hungry? We could go out for some noodles if you want."

"You know that sounds fantastic, I am starving and I have not had any kind of Asian food in months." "Okay then, I know a great little noodle house near my place." smiling Lynn said,

"Perfect, we can catch up while we eat."

Lynn and Maggie walked into a small, crowded little restaurant. The young woman that seated them handed them a menu that was written in Korean, after surveying the menu Lynn put it back down on the table covered with a greasy table cloth and said,

"I don't think I can read this Maggie."

"Oh, don't worry," she responded, "I already know what we can order, I will order for both of us." agreeing to that Lynn shrugged and said,

"Okay, that works for me." the waitress didn't speak any English but it didn't seem to matter to Maggie. She happily ordered a bowl of noodles and a bowl of rice for each of them and turned back to Lynn to inquire,

"Would you like green tea?" nodding Lynn said,

"Sure, sounds good." leaning back in their rickety old metal chairs, Lynn commented,

"This place is pretty old looking; it looks like mostly locals eat here." Maggie glanced around the restaurant and replied,

"Yes, most of the people that eat here live in the neighbourhood. No else seems to know about it. I like it because the food is good and cheap."

Just as Maggie finished what she was saying the waitress appeared with a pot of green tea and their bowels of noodles. She placed plastic chopsticks down in front of each of them and a couple of china spoons. She smiled and walked away after they thanked her. Lynn loved the noodles, it had been months since she had been to a good

Asian restaurant and she enjoyed getting out for different food once in awhile.

"So what is new in your life?" Maggie asked as she slurped down a noodle.

"Well, let's see. You know that Steve left us and moved back to BC to work."

"Yes, I remember you telling me that last month." "Well, that has turned out to be a good move for all of us. It is much calmer at home and we all seem happier." Maggie smiled gently,

"Good, I am glad to hear it. It is unfortunate that you guys couldn't work things out, but at least it seems for the best." Lynn smiled back and continued,

"Since then I have been working away from home and travelling quite often. My mom watches the kids for me most of the time."

"That's nice that your mother can help you out like that."

"Yes, I am grateful for the help, but she can be difficult at times. She does not get along with Olivia, my oldest daughter. They fight often and I end up having to try and referee arguments over the phone while I am away. It can be really stressful." Maggie looked up from her rice bowl and agreed,

"No kidding, I would find that stressful too."

"Oh, well it works for now so I just do the best that I can."

Smiling, Maggie asked, "Anything else interesting going on in your life? No new man? You usually have something interesting to tell me."

"Well I did meet this amazing guy this summer while I was in Lethbridge on that Native awareness workshop that I went to." nodding Maggie said,

"Oh yes I remember you telling me about that. So tell me more." looking slightly embarrassed Lynn continued,

"His name is Owen and he is full status Blackfoot. He is gorgeous. He is well over six foot five and he is a big man. There is just something about him that I can't explain. It is like we are connected, I don't know what happened. I think it might have been the sweat lodge that we did together. Somehow we are tuned into one another. I can feel when he thinks about me and I think he can feel when I think about him." looking surprised Maggie sat up and said,

"Go on, I am very interested now." smiling with a faraway look in her eyes Lynn tried to describe to Maggie her relationship with Owen.

"We seem to have this strange relationship, on again, off again. I dump him, he dumps me. We don't talk for months and then he calls me out of the blue and I go see him again. I don't know. He seems to drink a lot. He comes across as so professional and well educated but in a personal relationship he seems to act like he is eighteen. The man is almost fifty for God's sake; you would think he would have figured out how to be in a relationship by now, wouldn't you?" Maggie just laughed,

"Oh Lynn you sure know how to pick them!" Looking down at her bowl and trying to not show the pain she still felt Lynn agreed with her,

"Yes, you are right I sure know how to pick them."

"So are you still seeing him?" Maggie asked,

"No, I don't think so. He ended things between us a couple of months ago. I haven't heard from him or tried to contact him since. Although being here in Alberta makes it much harder for me. Knowing he is only a couple of hours drive away is very tempting. I didn't want to come out here for that reason. I am trying to work on letting him go. I don't need to get involved with another alcoholic. I have had my fill with Steve." Maggie reached across the table and squeezed Lynn's hand,

"Don't worry, I am around for the next couple of days for the training session as well so we can hang out together in the evenings and keep your mind off him." squeezing Maggie's hand back Lynn looked relieved,

"Thanks Maggie, you're the best."

Lynn and Maggie headed back to Maggie's apartment. Lynn curled up on the couch as she watched Maggie make them a cup of herbal tea. "Do you want any help with that?" Lynn asked from the couch.

"No, you relax. I am done anyways." Maggie said as she walked into the living room and handed Lynn a cup of herbal tea. "Thanks," Lynn said as she took the tea cup and wrapped both her hands around it warming her hands. She looked thoughtful as she added,

"You know I think I finally figured out why I am so stuck on Owen. He reminds me of my father in so many ways." Maggie looked interested as she sat down in the recliner across from Lynn on the couch.

"Oh, how?"

"Well, he is intelligent and professional like my father was but I think it is more than that. I think it is because he is cold and emotionally detached like my father that I am having so much trouble letting him go. I spent most of my childhood longing for my father to come back to us, to me. All I wanted was for him to come back home and tell me how much he loved me and missed me. He never did. Even when I spent a couple of weeks with him during my summer vacation after my parents were divorced he never once hugged me or told me he loved me."

Maggie sat and listened, nodding her encouragement when Lynn glanced up from her cup. "Well that would explain why you are feeling so attracted to someone that is emotionally unavailable. That sounds like the way Owen is behaving with you." Lynn sat quietly as she mulled over her revelation. Could it be possible? Was she really just attracted to Owen just because he reminded her of her unresolved issues with her father? She had tried to get some closure with him just before he died of colon cancer four years earlier. It was becoming obvious to her that she still had more work to do.

"You know something Maggie. I think I have some serious thinking to do. I think I may have to work on some issues I thought

I had dealt with already." sighing with resignation Lynn put her tea cup down.

"That's enough talk about me for one night. I have been selfish. How are you doing? We haven't even talked about your love life yet!" Maggie blushed as she looked uncomfortable and answered,

"Oh well, there is someone I have been seeing. It has only been a couple of weeks but I really like him."

Finally, sometime around midnight they called it quits and Lynn crashed on the couch. She slept very well considering that she was sleeping on a couch in someone else's living room. Maggie woke Lynn up early the next morning and they got ready to head off to their training session together. The next two days were pretty uneventful. Lynn spent every day sitting in training all day; she socialized with some of the other officers that she hadn't seen in awhile. Her department was pretty small and everyone normally managed to keep tabs on everybody else. By the end of the second day they were tired of sitting around all day and eating. So that afternoon Maggie and Lynn decided to go for a hike in a nearby park. That evening Lynn packed up her belongings and thanked Maggie for her hospitality.

"I am sorry that you have to leave tonight, I have to head north for work and I want to leave this evening so I can get an early start in the morning." Maggie said as she helped Lynn pack.

"No worries, I have a hotel room reserved for tonight close to the airport and I will take a shuttle bus there after I check out. I really enjoyed our visit. You know if you ever get back out to Ontario you have to come and stay with the kids and I." hugging Lynn, Maggie said,

"Of course, you know it."

Smiling Lynn picked up her jacket while placing her purse on her suitcase. "My cab should be showing up any minute, do you want to come downstairs with me while I wait for the cab?" grabbing her jacket, Maggie said,

"Sure sounds like a good idea." as they walked down the three flights of stairs Maggie said,

"Don't worry about Owen, I am sure you will get over him soon and find someone that is even better."

"I am sure you are right, I just need a little more time." the cab was waiting for Lynn outside the front doors of the apartment building so Lynn gave Maggie a quick hug and headed out the doors and down the front steps to the curb. Opening the passenger door Lynn greeted the taxi driver and tossed her suitcase onto the back seat. She waved at Maggie as the cab pulled away from the cab and smiled again. Maggie waved back and turned to go back up the stairs. Lynn gave the address of the hotel to the cab driver and sat back in her seat. Watching the apartment fall behind her she couldn't help thinking I hope you are right Maggie. I really do.

Lynn checked in and lugged her suitcase into her room. Flopping down on the queen size bed she looked around the room and wondered what to do next. It was still early and she hadn't eaten supper so she ordered a stir fry from room service and waited for it to arrive. She started to pace and began to feel anxious. I wonder what Owen is doing right now? I wonder if he is thinking about me. Damn it, I promised myself that I wouldn't do this anymore. Feeling like a woman possessed she dug through her day timer until she found Owen's cell phone number. She had thrown his business card away but she still had his phone number written down with all of her other contact numbers. She sat on the bed and contemplated calling him until there was a knock on her door.

"Room service." getting up she walked over to the door and let the waitress into the room. "Good evening, was there anything else I can bring you?" inquired the young woman while Lynn feigned a smiled at her and signed the restaurant bill.

"No thanks. I don't want anything else. Have a nice evening." closing the door behind her the waitress smiled and responded,

"Thank you, you too." Lynn turned the television on and started flipping through the channels while she sat on the bed and ate her meal. She hated eating alone. It made her feel so isolated and lonely. Finishing her food she carried her tray to the door and placed outside on the hallway floor. She still hadn't had her chamomile tea so she dropped a spoonful of honey into the tea cup and poured herself a cup of tea. As she drank it she stared blankly at the television. Not really noticing the screen. All she could think about was Owen. It was only about a two hour drive from here. She could make it if she left soon and be there for the morning. Her flight wasn't until late tomorrow afternoon so she would have enough time to drive back again in the morning. Feeling slightly crazed Lynn reached for the phone and decided to call him. Maybe he would be willing to talk now that a couple of months had passed. As she dialed his cell phone number her heart raced. What if he answered? What if he didn't answer? The phone rang for a minute or so and then switched to his voice mail,

"Oki, you have reached Owen Proudfeather I am not available please leave a message. Have a nice day." taking a deep breath Lynn decided to leave a message,

"Owen, it is Lynn I am in Calgary for the next day or so. Please call me. I am staying at the Airporter Inn and I have my cell phone with me. I am sure you know the number. Bye." Lynn hung up the phone feeling disappointed. She would have really loved to talk to him. Even the sound of his voice still made her heart soar.

Feeling like she was committed to her course of action, Lynn paced the floor in the hotel room. I am sure he won't call me back. I think I would rather just drive up to Edmonton and see if I can find him. I really don't think I can handle sitting here much longer. She picked up the yellow pages and started looking through it for rental cars. Then it occurred to her that many of the hotels close to the airport either had a rental car outlet close by or sometimes they were right in the hotel. She picked up the phone and called the front desk,

"Hi, do you have a rental car service in the hotel?" the woman on the other end of the line responded,

"No, I am sorry we don't but there is a rental car outlet just across the street from us. It is close enough for you to walk to it." smiling Lynn replied,

"Perfect, thank you very much." dropping the phone back on the bed Lynn grabbed her jacket and purse and headed out the door. She figured the rental car outlet wouldn't be open much later than six so she would have to hurry. Lynn walked briskly down to the front lobby and out the revolving glass doors. She hadn't planned on renting a car but she hadn't spent much money staying in Calgary so she figured she could afford it.

Spotting the rental car outlet Lynn broke into a sprint and dashed across the dead end street to the front doors. Letting herself in Lynn walked up to the front counter and smiled at the young man standing behind the counter.

"Hi, would you happen to have any economy cars available for one day?" checking the computer the young man looked up and said,

"Yes, we have one left. It is a Honda Civic, will that do?" smiling with relief Lynn said,

"Great, I'll take it." she dug in her purse and pulled out her Ontario Driver's license and her credit card. Picking up her identification the young man said,

"Thank you, it will be just a minute while I print everything up and I will have someone bring the car around front." elated, Lynn walked out of the building and hopped into the Honda. She drove it back to the front of her hotel and parked it in the parking lot. Getting out she smiled as she headed back to her hotel room to take a quick nap for a couple of hours before checking out of her room. There was no point in leaving anything there. She would not have time to come back for it tomorrow before her flight left.

As Lynn headed north of Calgary towards Edmonton she hummed along to the radio. Things were looking up already. She should have done this sooner! She was certain that once she found Owen and talked to him he would see reason and everything would be alright again. They could work out their differences. Even his drinking didn't seem to be that big of an issue. How could he be so successful if he was an alcoholic? She was probably exaggerating his drinking because she was overly sensitive due to her mother's serious addiction that lasted until she was well into her forties. The two hours flew by as she drove just over the speed limit. The weather was clear and it was a beautiful evening. Lynn watched the moon grow fat and waxy on the horizon, wondering if Owen was looking up at the moon while she was. She only got lost once when she got into town. She knew that Owen worked in the provincial building just up the street from the hotel that she had stayed in when she visited him in Edmonton last fall. She had lived in Edmonton about fifteen years ago and she still remembered her way around for the most part.

It was early morning when she found the building and circled it weighing her options. She could check into another hotel for a couple of hours or just hang out in the car and the front lobby of the building until Owen arrived. It was already past six in the morning so she decided to park the car in the parking lot across the street, lock all the car doors and take a cat nap. She woke up around eight o'clock and decided to try and walk over to the building and see if the front doors were unlocked yet. Feeling a little tired and in need of some breakfast Lynn walked up to the double glass doors and pulled. They were unlocked, so she opened the door and walked in. She noticed there were a couple of sectional chairs and a sofa arranged in a semi circle in front of an artificial waterfall. So she walked over and sat down. It was the perfect vantage point. She could see the front doors and the elevators in case Owen came in from a back door and by passed her.

She only had to wait about a half an hour before Owen came through the front doors walking at a brisk pace with his head down. He walked right past Lynn without noticing her and headed for the elevators. Lynn called out to him from her sofa chair,

"Owen," but he didn't seem to hear her so she stood up and followed him to the elevators. She had to walk very quickly to catch up to him; she wanted to get his attention before he got onto an elevator. As she rounded the corner she saw him step onto an elevator at the end of the corridor, breaking into a trot she managed to slip onto the elevator as the doors slide shut. Standing in the front of the elevator Lynn looked across at Owen and smiled,

"Good morning," she said, feeling nervous and amused by the expression on his face she waited for his response.

"Good morning Lynn; I am surprised to see you here." looking mildly annoyed with her he pushed the button for the first floor and said,

"What can I do for you?" Lynn took a deep breath and said,

"I would really like to talk." Owen glanced nervously at the other man standing in the elevator with them and said,

"Okay, let's get off here." as the elevator stopped at the first floor, he then headed straight for the cafeteria doors and without looking back said to her,

"I only have about fifteen minutes to spare before I have to be in a meeting. You are going to have to make this quick." walking along behind Owen, Lynn started to wonder if she had made a mistake. It was too late now. She had come all this way and she was going to see this through. There was no turning back now. Following Owen to a small table with two plastic chairs they sat down facing each other. Lynn tried to calm down and gather her thoughts for a moment before she began,

"I tried calling you last night, I left you a message." Owen nodded as he replied quietly,

"I know. I got it this morning."

"Okay, were you going to call me back?" shaking his head Owen replied,

"No, I don't think so." Lynn took a deep breath; this was harder than she thought it would be.

"I really want to talk about this Owen; I don't think you really want to end what we have between us. I think there is something else going on and you don't want to talk about it so you are using your mother as an excuse. I knew that we shouldn't have slept together it was too soon." Owen looked at her in silence for a few moments and then glanced down at the table,

"There is something else that is bothering me. I never told you that I was in trouble with the police once." reaching up to touch his lower lip Owen said,

"I have been in relationships in the past and I have gotten hurt. The last real relationship I was in I ended up with this scar." Lynn nodded her head and leaned forward as she tried to understand what he was trying to say. Owen continued,

"The night I got this scar I was in a fight with my ex wife and she threw a bottle at me. The cops ended up coming to the house and they put me in jail over night." Lynn sat back. This was not what she was expecting to hear. She was not thrilled with the idea of Owen having a police record.

"Okay, were you charged? " Owen shook his head and answered,

"No, I wasn't charged. But it bothers me that you are in law enforcement and I have a history with the police." Lynn couldn't help smiling as she said,

"Owen, you weren't even charged. I doubt that you have a record of any kind. I think I can deal with you being in a domestic dispute. Everyone that has been in a bad marriage has been in a fight. I have been in an argument with my ex husband that ended up in the police showing up at our house. It is not that the end of the world. Staying in a relationship that continues to be that violent is worse. At least you got out of it."

Owen looked like he was starting to relax as he leaned forward and said,

"Okay, I feel better now that I told you. But I still am having trouble with your being married. Are you divorced yet?"

"Oh, Owen I told you I am working on it, a divorce can take years. I am nowhere near getting my divorce yet. Why is that such a big deal to you? I am not living with my ex and I have filed for a divorce. What more can I do?" Owen thought about what she said for a moment then he said,

"I have been thinking about that for the past couple of months. You are right I should not be so judgemental. You are not sneaking around behind your husband's back to be with me. I should try and give you a chance to work things out. I did agree to give you six months." smiling Lynn reached across the table and touched Owen' hand,

"Thank you. That means the world to me." looking at his watch Owen stood up and said,

"I am sorry I have to go, I am already late for a meeting. I can call you later if you like." Lynn was elated. This had turned out better than she could have hoped for.

"Okay, I will be home tonight. I have a flight back home this afternoon. I will be looking forward to hearing from you." with that Owen was off. As Lynn stood in the cafeteria watching him leave she wondered if he would call her or if he would have another change of heart. It didn't matter, she had gotten to see him and talk to him. If nothing else she had managed that much.

Lynn drove back to Calgary while eating her breakfast sandwich and sipping a green tea. She couldn't help feeling pleased with herself. Maybe, just maybe Owen would call her tonight and she would get to hear his voice again. He had no idea how much she loved the sound of his voice. It was all she had of him most of the time. Lynn made her flight with an hour to spare after dropping off her rental car and taking a cab to the airport. Owen had no idea what lengths she would go to just to see him. She wondered if it would scare him if he did. Her flight back to Toronto was right on schedule and her flight back to Sudbury was also on time. Lynn figured the gods must have been smiling on her that day. Everything went right. Once Lynn got home she settled down into bed right away, it was late and she was tired. The kids had already been asleep when she arrived so she tried to stay as quiet as possible so as not to wake them up. She brought both her phones into her bedroom with her just in case Owen called her cell instead of her home phone number. Just as she was about to drift off to sleep her phone rang.

"Hello" she mumbled into the phone.

"Hi, it's Owen," as if he needed to identify himself she thought, I would know that voice anywhere.

"Hi, how are you?"

"Good, I want you to know I was really surprised to see you at my office today. How did you find me by the way?" laughing Lynn answered,

"Owen, it is my job to find people that do not want to be found. You were easy. I know where you work so I just figured if I waited there long enough you would show up." Owen laughed and replied,

"I should not be surprised by anything you do. You are not like anyone I have ever met before." Lynn sat up in bed and said,

"You got that right," she continued, "So are you sorry that you talked to me? Are we still okay?" Lynn could hear the affection in his voice as he said,

"No, I am not sorry that I talked to you today, I am glad you forced me to see you. I missed talking to you." Lynn was wide awake; her heart soared as she heard the emotion in his voice. They talked for almost an hour as Owen told her how much he missed her and thought about her all the time; even after he had broken things off with her. As she hung up the phone and snuggled back under the covers she thought about what they had just talked about. Owen seemed so interested in her; she knew she was very interested in him. In fact she was becoming very emotionally attached to him. Was she starting to fall in love with him? Neither one of them had said that word to each other. She wasn't sure yet and she didn't want to scare Owen off. Besides, she wanted to take her time and be careful about getting involved to deeply with him. There were still a lot of things she did not know about Owen. His drinking was worrying her. He seemed to need it to function on a personal level. Even tonight she noticed that he had a couple of drinks before her called her. He always seemed to be able to express his feelings so much better once he had a couple of drinks. Or was it just the booze talking? That thought made her nervous. As she drifted off to sleep Lynn could hear the distant sound of the train whistle. She loved that sound. It was comforting even though it stirred something up in her. The sound made her long to go, travel anywhere, it didn't matter where, just go. She dreamt that night of travelling back to Owen in Alberta and staying with him; never having to be apart or saying good bye ever again.

CHAPTER FIVE

One More Time

It wasn't long before Lynn received another email request for her to book a flight to Edmonton for training. This time it was for enforcing some new federal legislation that had just been passed. It was early spring and Lynn had spent the last couple of months dreaming about seeing Owen again. So she was delighted with the training request. Even though it was short notice she made her travel arrangements and emailed Owen to let him know that she would be in the following week.

While she sat in the Sudbury airport waiting to board the plane for what seemed like the hundredth time she noticed a good looking man in his early thirties smiling at her. Lynn smiled back and as he sat down next to her he made a casual comment about the spring weather they were having. Lynn nodded her agreement and noticed the Canadian flag tattooed on his left hand, just above his thumb. She motioned towards his tattoo and commented,

"Nice tattoo, why the Canadian flag?" he glanced down at his thumb as if he had forgotten it was there and replied,

"Thanks, I am in the military and we all got a Canadian flag tattoo before going to Afghanistan on my last tour of duty." surprised, Lynn sat back and answered,

"Oh, how long were you there?" frowning he replied,

"Six months, a long hot, dry six months. I just got back from two weeks in the Dominican Republic before flying to Sudbury to visit my family."

"Wow, that is impressive. I have nothing but respect for anyone that chooses to serve in the military. What do you do?" the soldier looked down at his hands as he rubbed at the tattoo and answered,

"I am a tank driver. I've done it for ten years."

"I am an enforcement officer myself. But it is nothing like being a soldier." interested, he leaned forward and asked,

"Enforcement officer? Are you with the RCMP?" shaking her head Lynn responded,

"No, Fisheries and Oceans. I am a Fishery Officer." smiling he replied,

"Ah, I don't really know what that is." laughing, Lynn responded,

"Don't worry about it; most people don't know what that is!" they were interrupted by the boarding announcement for their plane. Standing up Lynn nodded and said,

"Nice talking to you, enjoy your flight." the soldier smiled and replied,

"Same here." Lynn smiled and picked up her bags as she headed for the line up to board the plane. Once they had landed in Toronto Lynn decided to try and get something to eat. She took the escalator upstairs for the lower level where they had disembarked and started looking for a cafeteria. Walking down to the end of the terminal, past all of the shops offering books, soap and chocolates for sale she noticed a cafeteria with salads and stir fry for sale. As she stood in line to place her order she looked up and noticed the soldier she had been talking to earlier sitting alone at a corner table eating his lunch and watching her. She smiled vaguely and turned back to place her order. As she walked over to the sitting area Lynn was approached by a reporter for a local television station. She was armed with a microphone and had a camera man in tow. Stopping in front of Lynn she said,

"Excuse me Madame, but would you be interested in doing a brief interview regarding the cost of food in the airport?" Lynn had just paid over ten dollars for a salad and a bottle of water so she was more than happy to do the interview.

"Sure, I can do that." she replied.

"Great, just give us a minute to set up and then I will ask you a couple of questions." the reporter turned to the camera man and set up the equipment. Turning back to Lynn she said,

"Okay, we are ready." the camera man turned on his video camera and signalled that he was taping. Looking at the camera the reporter started with her introduction,

"We are standing in the Toronto International Airport and I am speaking to this young woman regarding the cost of food in the airport." turning back to Lynn she continued, "So would you say the cost of food in the airport is higher than food offered in restaurants outside of the airport?" Lynn nodded and replied,

"Yes, I just paid over ten dollars for a salad and a bottle of water. I would say the cost is a couple of dollars higher than in other restaurants."

"Okay, thanks very much." was the reporter's reply as she signalled to the camera man to turn off the video camera, "You can catch your interview on the six o'clock news tomorrow night." she said to Lynn before heading off to find another person to interview. Lynn turned back to the sitting area to find a table to eat her salad when she noticed the solider from the Sudbury airport still watching her. Feeling awkward about sitting nearby and not acknowledging him Lynn walked over and asked,

"Do you mind if I sit with you?" smiling briefly he replied,

"No, I don't mind. Have a seat. I saw you give that interview a few minutes ago." laughing while she opened her salad Lynn said,

"Yes, well I just paid way too much for this salad so I was happy to do the interview." shaking his head the soldier said,

"You are braver than I am. She asked me earlier to do an interview but I refused." they finished their meals and Lynn excused herself as she picked up her bags and headed for the women's washroom before going getting in line to board their next flight to Edmonton. When they arrived in Edmonton, the soldier walked up to Lynn while she was standing at the luggage carousel and said,

"My name is Rick Easton by the way," smiling Lynn shook his outstretched hand and replied,

"Lynn Thompson, nice to meet you."

"Hi Lynn. Would you be interested in going out for dinner with me later this evening?" while handing her a piece of paper with his phone number. Lynn took his phone number and said,

"Sure, why not." smiling Rick said,

"Great, give me a call once you get to your hotel. I can pick you up."

"Okay, thanks very much Rick, I will call you in a couple of hours." picking up his suitcase off the luggage carousel he smiled at Lynn as he waved and walked out of the airport. Lynn was not overly interested in going for dinner with Rick. He had to be nearly ten years younger than her and the conversation had not been very stimulating. She had the impression that he was a tank driver for the army for a reason. He did seem like a nice guy and she wouldn't mind some company for dinner so she decided to call him once she got to her hotel room.

"Hi Rick, I am at my hotel and if the offer for dinner still stands I am interested."

"Hi Lynn, sure but I have to deal with a couple of things here first so it will be another hour before I can head out to pick you up. Is that okay?" Lynn nodded and tried to sound enthusiastic,

"Okay, no problem."

"Great, what is the address of your hotel? " Lynn replied,

"I am staying at the Highlander on the south side, I am not sure of the street address. Do you know where it is?""

"Yes, I know it. I will give you a call when I get there. See you in about an hour."

"Okay, see you then." hanging up the phone Lynn decided she had enough time for a quick shower, she was feeling grimy from spending the whole day in airports. An hour later Lynn sat on her hotel bed wondering if Rick was on his way; getting bored she turned on the television and flipped through the channels.

"Nothing on as usual." she commented while turning it back off. Checking her watch she noticed that it had been almost two hours since she called Rick. She was getting hungry so she decided to call him to see if he was on his way.

"Hi Rick, its Lynn. Are you still planning on picking me up for dinner?" sounding distracted he replied,

"Yes, I just took a little longer than I thought to fix up my window. My roommates broke one while I was away and I wanted to deal with it right away."

"Oh, okay, well if you don't have time I understand. Some other time."

"No, no, I am done so I will be heading out right away"

"Okay, I will be waiting down in the lobby. Bye"

"Bye"." hanging up the phone Lynn picked up her jacket and purse, slipped her heels on and walked down stairs to wait for Rick to show up. He appeared about fifteen minutes later and suggested that they check out a pub just down the street.

"I miss pub food; we couldn't get it in Afghanistan. Do you mind?" Lynn smiled and said,

"No not at all. I like pub food." so they drove a couple of blocks down the street from her hotel and parked in front of a local pub.

"You will like the food here; it is one of my favourites." Rick said as they got out of his car and walked up to the front doors. He opened the door and walked through, letting Lynn hold the door open for herself. Hmm, not very impressive; she thought as she walked along behind him. They sat down in a booth and ordered burgers and fries. While they waited for their food to arrive Lynn was having a difficult time getting Rick to focus while she tried talking to him. He was so busy staring at all of the waitresses as they walked by. There were a couple of nice looking young woman working in their section and Rick was having trouble focussing on anything else. She knew he had just spent six months in Afghanistan but she figured the two week vacation he had in the Dominican Republic would have provided him an opportunity to get laid. Fed up with his behaviour Lynn said,

"Well it is late and I have an early day tomorrow. Would you mind driving me back to my hotel?" looking surprised Rick said,

"Sure just let me pay the bill." he stood up and went looking for their waitress and Lynn put on her jacket and picked up her purse. She was ready to go when he got back. They drove back to the hotel and Lynn smiled at Rick as he pulled into the parking lot across the street from the hotel.

"Thanks for the great meal. Here is my business card. If you are ever in Sudbury look me up." she reached over and gave him a quick hug and went to open her car door.

"Sure, you're welcome," he replied looking puzzled. "You are not going to invite me up?" Lynn smiled gently and said,

"No, I don't think so. I am too tired and I am not really interested in a one night stand." with that she got out of the car, waved vaguely in his direction and crossed the street to her hotel. As she headed up to her room Lynn shook her head. She couldn't get the image of him screwing some prostitute in the Dominican out of her head.

"Just what I need; to catch AIDS off some guy I just met in the airport." she muttered as she unlocked her hotel room door. Closing the door behind her Lynn headed for the phone to see if she could track Owen down. She had sent him an email to let him know she was going to be in town but he hadn't responded. It had been short notice so she wasn't surprised. She just hoped he would be in town for the three days she was going to be there.

"Hello," he sounded like he had been drinking.

"Hi Owen, did you get my email?"

"I did, are you in Edmonton now?" smiling she responded,

"I am. I am staying at the Highlander at the south end of town."

"Oh, how long will you be here?"

"For three days. I have training for two days and I finish up on the morning of the third. I fly back home that evening. Are you interested in getting together?"

"Sure, why don't you take a cab over and I will meet you at the Rose and Thorn pub on Jasper Avenue." frowning Lynn replied,

"Okay, you can't pick me up?""

"No, my jeep died and I bought a new car. But it won't be delivered until next week." sighing, Lynn agreed,

"Okay, I should be there within an hour. See you soon."

"Sounds good, I look forward to seeing you." hanging up Lynn picked up her jacket and purse and headed back down to the lobby to look for a cab. One was sitting out front so she hopped in the back seat and said to the driver,

"The Rose and Thorn Pub on Jasper Avenue please." leaning back in the seat Lynn looked out the window as they drove through town. How much is this cab ride going to cost me she wondered as she watched the meter climb. That man, he has no idea how much I do just so I can see him. Hell, I wonder sometimes if this is worth it. The cab pulled up in front of the pub and Lynn got out handing the driver a twenty.

"Keep the change." she said as she closed the cab door and walked towards the pub. Opening the front doors she walked in looking around to see if Owen was there already. He was sitting at the bar by himself nursing what looked like a rum and coke.

"Hi," he said as she noticed her approaching him. Giving her a big hug and a kiss he said, "It is so nice to see you. Did you have any trouble finding the place?" Lynn kissed him back and shook her head,

"No, the cab driver knew where it was." she sat down at the bar beside Owen and smiled up at the bartender. Owen put his arm around her shoulders and said to the bartender,

"I would like you to meet my girlfriend. She flew out all the way from Sudbury, Ontario just to visit me." the young lady behind the bar smiled at Lynn and said,

"Wow, Ontario. That is a long ways away. Nice to meet you Lynn; my name is Kelly. Would you like something to drink?" Lynn thought about it for a moment and said,

"Sure, a Caesar please."

"One Caesar coming up." Lynn turned back to Owen and smiled at him as she put her hand in his.

"I have been thinking of you a lot." she said, "I was delighted when I found out I was being sent to Edmonton for training. It has been too long since the last time I saw you." Owen just smiled at her and said,

"I know I was very happy when I got your email." he turned back to the bartender and said,

"My good friend, could I have another rum and coke please?" the bartender just shook her head and laughed,

"You know my name. It's Kelly and yes you can have another rum and coke." Lynn took a good look at Owen and realized that he had been drinking for awhile. He was pretty drunk and he looked like he had no intentions of slowing down.

"My mother called me today." Owen said as the bartender served him his drink.

"Oh?" Lynn replied,

"She wants me to come and see her. She is not feeling well."

"Oh, I am sorry to hear that. What is wrong?" Lynn asked genuinely concerned.

"What isn't wrong with her?" Owen exclaimed, "She is eighty years old!" Not sure how to respond to that Lynn picked up her Caesar and said,

"So how long have you been here?"

"Oh, I don't know. A couple of hours I guess. I come often after work. I like relaxing here before I go home."

"Oh, well I have training in the morning so I have to get up early tomorrow. " waving his hand vaguely at her Owen said,

"No problem, we can leave as soon as we finish our drinks."

"Okay, that works." Lynn looked up and noticed a karaoke screen had been turned on. "They have karaoke here?" she asked.

"Yes, do you like to sing?" Owen replied. Smiling Lynn shook her head,

"Well not really, I sing at home when I am alone but I am not sure how much anyone else wants to hear me." smiling at her Owen reached over and grabbed the karaoke selection book. He pushed it across the bar to Lynn and said,

"Pick a song. I would love to hear you sing. I sing you know. It was me you heard singing in the sweat lodge." Lynn smiled and said,

"I know. I thought you were amazing."

"Okay then, it is settled you will sing a song for me!" Lynn felt uncomfortable as she thought about singing in front of him; in front of anyone for that matter. She flipped through the book looking for a song that was familiar to her. Finding a song she liked Lynn made her choice and said,

"Okay, brace yourself; I am not sure how good this will sound. I am going to sing *I'm gonna make you mine* by Lou Christie." feeling very nervous and uncertain how good she was going to sound Lynn waited for the cue on the lyrics. She started singing as the words came up.

"It's gonna take money, a whole lotta money, it's gonna take time, a whole lotta time. But I'm gonna make you mine." turning to Owen she smiled at him as she kept singing. A couple of the other patrons in the bar joined in with her as she sang. Owen sat and smiled while watching her. Never taking his eyes off of her while she sang. Finishing the song, Lynn sat down relieved and smiled nervously at Owen.

"I like that," he said, "you can sing!" looking embarrassed Lynn blushed and said,

"Well, I sing well enough to get by. But I don't think I should quit my day job just yet." Owen just laughed and ordered them both another drink. Lynn checked her watch and noticed that it was almost midnight.

"Don't you think we should get going soon?" she asked Owen as their round of drinks showed up.

"What time is it?" he asked as he paid the bartender for the drinks.

"It is almost midnight; we both have to be up early for work tomorrow." nodding in agreement, Owen replied,

"Okay, let's finish this drink and then we can go back to my place. It is just around the corner." Lynn was not really interested in having another drink when she had to be up early the next morning. She didn't handle booze very well. Usually two drinks were her limit and even then she was pretty hung over the next day. So she just sipped slowly at the drink and by the time Owen had finished his she was not even half way done.

"Aren't you going to finish that?" he asked pointing at her drink.

"No, I don't think so. I have had enough for now." shrugging Owen said,

"Okay, well I guess if you are ready we can get going." Lynn nodded in agreement and got up to put her coat back on. They both started to walk out the door when Lynn remembered that she had brought her overnight bag with her and stashed it behind the bar.

"Good thing I didn't forget this," she said as she retrieved it from behind the bar.

"I would be really unhappy tomorrow morning." smiling at her Owen held open the doors and then took her bag from her as they started walking through the parking lot.

"Here, I will carry that for you." he said as he held out his hand.

"Okay, thanks very much." Lynn said as she handed him her bag. It was late out but Lynn could not see any stars in the sky. The city lights washed them out, making it impossible to see anything. Sighing Lynn took Owen's free hand and squeezed it. He turned and smiled at her as he said,

"My apartment is just up this street about a block. It is a really short walk."

"Good, I am getting tired and the wind is still pretty cold at night." Owen laughed and said,

"For someone that spends a lot of her time outside and in the bush you seem to get cold pretty easy!" Lynn looked up at him and said,

"Hey, watch it. I may not have my gun with me but I can still take you out!" they both started to laugh as they continued walking back to the apartment and Owen continued teasing her,

"Well you are the prettiest woman I have ever met that carries a gun! Are you sure you really do carry one and you are not just making it up?" Lynn hit his arm playfully and said,

"Whatever tough guy. Is this your apartment building?" as they walked up to a four storey apartment building; Owen nodded as he let go of her hand and began digging in his pockets for his keys.

"They are in her somewhere." he mumbled, "Ah, here they are." opening the front doors he held them open for Lynn as she stooped down and picked up her overnight bag and walked into the lobby,

"Thank you," she said as she passed Owen. He nodded in acknowledgment and said,

"This way, I am downstairs in the basement." Lynn followed him down the hallway as he gestured at the doors,

"A guy from China lives there and another guy from Africa lives next door to me," he said as he laughed, "it is like the United Nations around here!" Lynn smiled and nodded as they stopped in front of his apartment door. He dug out his keys once more and fumbled with them until he got the door open. Waving his hand in a grand gesture he said,

"Welcome to my humble abode. I hope you like it." Lynn smiled and walked in the door. She stopped to put down her bag and take off her shoes. Looking around Lynn replied,

"It looks great to me. I love the art work in the living room. Are those by local artists?" smiling at her Owen replied,

"Yes, one painting is from a local native artist here in Edmonton and these two paintings are by two different native artists in southern Alberta. They are all originals." Lynn stepped closer to get a better look at the paintings and then turned to Owen and said,

"Wow, beautiful. I didn't know you like art." Owen just smiled at her and sat down on his sectional couch.

"Would you like me to put some music on?" he said as he leaned forward to pick up the remote for his stereo.

"Sure, why not." Lynn replied as she sat down on the couch. Turning on the stereo Owen put the remote down and turned towards Lynn and said,

"You look so beautiful tonight. I am very happy that came to see me. I have been thinking about you since the last time I saw you." Lynn just smiled and moved closer to him.

"I know, I have been thinking about you too." leaning towards Owen she kissed him slowly and passionately as she wrapped her arms around his neck. Owen leaned in to her and engulfed her in his large embrace. He held her so tightly she could hardly breathe. It didn't matter though. She loved every moment he touched her. Moaning and pulling away slightly Owen said,

"Why don't we go to bed?" Lynn agreed and started to get up to head towards the bedroom. Owen stopped her and said,

"No, I don't have a bed we can sleep on the futon. You will have to set it up though." confused, Lynn crossed the room and stopped in front of the futon and said,

"You mean you want me to unfold it so we can sleep on it?" looking impatient Owen replied,

"Yes, you have to pull the front down and towards you and then make sure the supports are unfolded in the back. I am not sure how exactly, I don't use it much. I just sleep on my couch most of the time." shaking her head Lynn grabbed the front of the futon and pulled. Nothing much happened and she was getting frustrated. What kind of guy slept on his couch or on a futon for that matter? Feeling as if the moment had passed Lynn just wanted to get the thing set up so she could get some sleep.

"Okay, I can't find any kind of release mechanism to make it unfold. Do you know where it is?" she asked as she dropped down on the floor to see if it was underneath the front support bar.

"No, I don't know where it is." Owen said as he started to lean to the side. Lynn was sure he was going to pass out any moment and leave her to struggle with the darn thing on her own.

"Oh, I found it!" she announced sitting up and pulling on the futon again. It flattened out and was starting to look more like a bed until Lynn put her weight on it. The back side of the futon collapsed under her weight and she slide to the floor. Landing on the other side of the room Lynn stood back up again and said,

"There must be a support bar in the back to keep it from doing that!" Owen responded with a snort with laughter as he said,

"I think you need some help! You are not very good at this are you?" he staggered over and dropped to the floor as he reached underneath the futon looking for the supporting legs. Lying on the floor he groped around underneath the futon aimlessly while trying to keep his eyes open. Lynn looked at Owen and said,

"I give up, let's just try and get the back support legs to stay down. That should keep this thing level." grunting his agreement, Owen rolled onto his back and passed out while Lynn struggled with the back legs. She managed to get them to sit against the floor but she could not get them to lock into place. Giving up she found a couple of blankets in Owen's hall closet and picked up the cushions off his couch. After she had made a close approximation of a bed Lynn nudged Owen who was already starting to snore and said to him,

"The bed is made if you want to get up on it." groaning and mumbling something Lynn couldn't understand Owen hauled himself up onto the bed and rolled over to go back to sleep. Lynn took off most of her clothes and pulling out a tee shirt from her bag she slide in beside Owen on the futon. It wasn't anywhere near long enough for either of them. Both of their feet hung off the end of the bed and Lynn was having trouble getting enough room to sleep. Owen woke up as she was struggling to pull some of the blankets out from under him and rolled over to wrap his arm around her.

"I really think you are beautiful." he whispered as he started to kiss Lynn. Kissing him back she smiled and said,

"I know, but you are really drunk right now. We should just get some sleep." opening his eyes Owen looked at her and said,

"No, no I really want to make love to you. " Lynn smiled as she looked into his eyes and said,

"I would really like that Owen, but you have had too much to drink. There is always tomorrow."

"No, no" he insisted as he rolled up onto his elbow and started kissing her. Pulling at her tee shirt he managed to get it over Lynn's head and he started to fondle her breast.

"I love your breast, they are beautiful," he whispered as he kissed her. Owen rolled over and mounted Lynn.

"I really want to make love to you." he said as he penetrated her and started to thrust himself deeper and deeper. Lynn loved how he felt inside of her. Groaning she arched her back as she reached up and stroked his face and chest. A few moments later Owen rolled over and begged her to get on top of him.

"Please, I would love it if you sat on top of me." smiling Lynn said,

"Sure, I would love that too. " she straddled Owen wrapping her legs around his and started to make love to him. Owen moaned and reached up to fondle her breasts and play with her hair.

"I would love to make a baby with you." he whispered. Surprised, Lynn smiled down at him as she leaned forward and kissed him.

"So would I sweet heart." Lynn would have loved to have a child with Owen; she was that deeply in love with him already. But it would never happen. She had had a hysterectomy over four years ago and having any more children was impossible. Owen began to lose his focus and as Lynn kissed him he fell asleep.

"Oh well, there is always tomorrow." she said as she slide down off of Owen and cuddled up next to him. Lynn tried to settle down to sleep as Owen began snoring louder and louder. Sighing with exhaustion and frustration Lynn got up and rummaged through her overnight bag. Pulling out a pair of moulded ear plugs she muttered,

"It is a good thing I always travel with these." Lynn put her ear plugs into her ears and slipped back under the blanket to try and get some sleep. Owen tossed and turned throughout the night and at one point Lynn woke up to find Owen sleeping with his head at her feet. His feet were stuck in her face and as she tried to figure out how to push them out of the way, he rolled over on top of her. The sudden shift in his weight dislodged the back supports and the back half of the futon dropped to the floor. Owen slide head first into the floor with a thud; Lynn held her breath expecting him to wake up or start flaying about on top of her. Instead he only groaned before starting to snore again. Lynn decided to lower the other end of the futon and turned around to sleep with her head beside Owen's head. As she settled in beside him he muttered something incomprehensible and kissed her on her shoulder. Lynn smiled, for some reason the kiss meant more to her than anything he could have said at that moment. Lynn repositioned her earplugs to maximize their noise blocking effect and closed her eyes.

Lynn was woken up a couple of hours later by Owen as he started to fondle her and rolled over on top of her again. He started to make love to her without a word. He pounded Lynn into the futon with all of his three hundred pounds and when he finished he rolled off and got up to go to the bathroom. Lynn could hear him running the water for the shower and retching. She tried to close her eyes and get a few more minutes sleep when Owen's cell phone started ringing so Lynn staggered up from the futon to try and find it. Picking up his cell phone from the kitchen table Lynn shut it off and handed it to Owen as he came out of the bathroom. Without saying a word he took his cell phone and put it in his jacket pocket.

"What happened last night? I feel awful." looking down at the futon he said, "What happened to the futon?" Lynn shrugged and said,

"It collapsed during the night. So I didn't bother fixing it. You slept right through the whole thing." Owen grunted,

"Huh, I must have. I don't remember it falling." picking up her clothes and making her way to the bathroom Lynn said,

"I won't be long; I just need a quick shower." Owen waved vaguely in her direction and said,

"Sure, no problem." while she was standing under the shower head enjoying the feeling of the warm water on her back she wondered what to make of what just happened. Sex with Owen had been okay to begin with but now it seemed to be getting worse. She figured they had hit an all time low. She had not had such an awful lover since she had slept with that eighteen year old guy from her college days. That had lasted less than five minutes and he had not even bothered to undress. He had jumped her right in the middle of the living room on the floor. Without a word he had pulled down her pants to her knees and then he pulled down his pants to his knees. The carpet burn she got on her butt hurt for days. Even though she really cared for Owen his apparent lack of sexual finesse was starting to become a problem. Sighing Lynn turned off the shower and towel dried her hair while looking into the mirror. Ugh, I look awful. I feel like shit too. I didn't even drink very much; it must be the lack of sleep. Lynn dressed in the clothes she had brought with her and did her makeup as quickly as she could. She tried to minimize the dark circles under her eyes but it was no use. Giving up she packed her makeup and carried her bag out into the hallway.

"I think I am just about ready to go," she called into the living room. "I just need to blow dry my hair for a couple of minutes."

"The hair dryer is in the closet," Owen responded from his bedroom. Lynn fished the hair dryer out of the closet and dried her hair in the bathroom. Finishing up she put the hair dryer back and checked to make sure she had everything packed in her bag. She stood by the door holding her jacket and wearing her dress shoes as Owen walked out of his bedroom dressed in a dark brown suit.

"You look nice," he said as he smiled at her briefly. Lynn smiled at him and glanced down as she said,

"Thanks, I love this blue jacket. It is the perfect colour for my eyes. You look nice yourself." smiling back at her Owen put on his dress shoes and picked up his overcoat.

"Okay, it looks like we are ready. Let's go." Lynn pulled the handle up on her bag and pulled it along behind her on its two wheels.

"I didn't know that thing had wheels on it." Owen exclaimed as they walked out of his apartment, "I didn't have to carry it all the way here last night." Lynn shrugged and said,

"Sorry, didn't think of it, besides the wheels don't work very well in gravel parking lots and on bumpy sidewalks." nodding, Owen agreed,

"You're right. It was too rough to pull it all the way here from the bar. As they walked outside Owen called a taxi on his cell phone. Glancing down at her he said,

"It should be here in ten to fifteen minutes." Lynn sighed and wrapped her arms around his waist. "I am sorry that we can't spend the day together. I would really love to do that."

Frowning down at her Owen stepped back and said, "I have to go to work, you know that. Here is the cab." Lynn turned around and walked over to the passenger door of the taxi as Owen picked up her overnight bag. He handed it to her as she got into the cab and then walked around to the other passenger door. Sitting down in the cab he leaned forward and said,

"Good morning my good friend, can you please take us to Jasper Avenue."

"Certainly sir." replied the cab driver. Lynn reached over and squeezed Owen's hand. He looked at her and smiled.

"I will get him to drop me off at my office first then he can take you to the south side, okay?" Lynn nodded and said,

"Sure, that makes sense." arriving in front of Owen's office building the cab pulled up to the curb and Owen handed Lynn a twenty dollar bill.

"Here, this is for the cab fare." Lynn protested but he pushed the money into her hand and gave her a quick kiss before jumping out of the cab.

"Take it, I have to go. Good bye," he said as he closed the door and smiled before the taxi pulled away from the curb. Lynn gave the cab driver the address of her hotel and sat back. She was damn tired and really not looking forward to spending all day in a conference room learning about some new piece of legislation.

Lynn staggered into the front lobby of the hotel about fifteen minutes before her training session was scheduled to begin. She headed back to her hotel room and dropped off her bag. When she got to the conference room she headed straight to the table with the coffee and muffins. She hated coffee, it was too bitter for her taste but she needed something to keep her awake. The other officers in the room were getting settled down in their seats. Rob, one of the officers that she had worked with for the past couple of years watched her as she crossed the room and sat down.

"You look very tired this morning Lynn, what were you up to last night?" Lynn just smiled and said,

"Oh, nothing much; I just met up with an old friend." laughing, Rob said,

"I'll say, he must be one heck of a friend. You look like you have had about an hour's sleep!" Lynn had a sheepish grin on her face when she replied,

"Yes, he is alright." Rob asked,

"So are we going to meet this friend of yours?" Lynn just smiled mysteriously and said,

"Oh, I don't think so. I don't want to scare him off." they were interrupted by the officer that was doing the presentation as he walked into the room and introduced himself. The rest of the day was a blur for Lynn. She was so tired she had to fight to stay awake during the presentation. She drank cup after cup of coffee and then switched to orange juice when she couldn't stand the taste of coffee any longer.

That evening after the presentation was finished for the day Lynn headed back to her hotel room for a nap. She just couldn't stay awake any longer. She woke up around eight o'clock and decided to call room service for some dinner. She wolfed down her chicken cordon bleu and dessert before deciding to call Owen. She figured he must have taken a nap after he got home from work too. Lynn dialled his cell phone and listened to it ring. It switched over to his voice mail; disappointed Lynn left a brief message for him to call her back. Turning the television on Lynn flipped aimlessly through the channels trying to find something to watch. She jumped when her room phone rang. Picking it up she was surprised to hear Rick's voice on the other end.

"Hi Lynn, its Rick. How are you?"

"Hi Rick, good. Yourself?"

"I am good; I have been trying to get everything organized here after being away for almost six months so that has kept me pretty busy." Lynn was only half listening to Rick talk. Her mind was busy whirling with possible reasons why Owen hadn't called her yet.

"Uh huh, well at least it sounds like you got almost everything taken care of." she responded in a distracted tone. Sensing her lack of interest Rick asked,

"Is this a good time? I am not interrupting anything am I?" shaking her head Lynn said,

"Oh, no. Sorry I am just tired. It has been a busy couple of days."

"Oh, okay, well then I guess you would not be interested in going out for drinks tonight or something to eat?" Lynn sighed, why couldn't the right guy be asking her this question. It always seemed to be the wrong guy.

"No thanks, I think I am going to call it an early night and try and get some rest for tomorrow. I have training all day again."

"Sure, I understand. Well, if you change your mind give me a call."

"Okay, thanks. I will. Good bye." hanging up the phone Lynn decided to try and call Owen again. There was still no answer. Getting annoyed she decided to call a cab and try to see if she could find him at his apartment. As the cab pulled up in front of his apartment building Lynn paid the taxi driver and got out of the cab. She walked over to the front doors and pushed the buzzer for his apartment. It rang a couple of times and then went to his voice mail on his cell phone. Lynn was getting frustrated with the way the evening was going and she was starting to get suspicious of Owen. What could he be doing? She walked along the building trying to guess which apartment window was his, but she could not see into any of them so it was difficult to figure out which one was his. She decided the third one from the front door on the right had to be it but there were no lights on in the apartment so she could not see anything. She tried calling his cell phone again but it went directly to his voice mail. Feeling angry and frustrated Lynn left Owen a long message,

"Owen this is Lynn, if you did not want to see me again you should have told me that instead of hiding from me. I am only here for one more day and I thought we were going to try and spend some time together. I am really disappointed in you." she hung up and called another taxi. Climbing into the taxi she asked the driver to take her to the bar that she and Owen had met in the night before. Just in case he might be hanging out there. She couldn't imagine him going drinking again after last night but it was worth a try. The cab waited while she walked into the bar and checked for Owen.

She walked up to the bartender and asked if she had seen him that night. Shaking her head she replied,

"No, I haven't seen him tonight. He usually only comes in a couple of nights a week." Lynn thanked her and left. She got back into the cab and asked him to drive her back to her hotel. She paid the cab fare and got out of the taxi. As she turned to walk back into the lobby she heard a familiar voice,

"Hey Lynn, I am surprised to see you out here." startled Lynn spun around to see Rob and the rest of the group from her training session standing just outside the lobby doors. Smiling and waving vaguely in there general direction Lynn said,

"Oh hi, what are you guys up to?" Rob and the rest chuckled as they looked at each other and he said,

"We are going out for a couple of beers; do you want to join us?" Lynn shook her head and said,

"No thanks, I know where you like to go for beer, I am not into watching strippers." the men just laughed and walked away as Lynn headed back into the hotel lobby. She was in no mood to hang out with a bunch of men at that moment. In fact she was not in the mood to see any man. Owen was pissing her off and she was getting really frustrated. His behaviour was inexcusable. He did this to her every time. He always managed to disappear after the spent some time together. She figured she would be used to it by now but for some reason his behaviour caught her off guard every time. Maybe because deep down she had hoped he would change. Shaking her head and muttering under her breath Lynn took the elevator back to her hotel room. She was getting fed up with this game of cat and mouse. She had better things to do with her time and if Owen wasn't interested in her then she was determined to move on, no matter what.

Lynn got ready for bed and as she lay there alone in her hotel room staring up at the ceiling she wondered what she was doing with her life. She loved her job and she was good at it. She had a career with the federal government and she was determined to stick with it. But her personal life was not going as well. It seemed that every man she got involved with was either a loser or a jerk. She was working so hard to get Steve out of her life and now she was getting emotionally involved with a guy that couldn't seem to sustain two days in a row. How the heck was she supposed to build a relationship with a guy like that? Maybe she was being unrealistic about things with Owen and should call it quits now; before she got hurt any worse than she had been already. *You tried that already, remember? It didn't work very well.* Lynn thought. There was something that kept her tied to him even when they didn't see each other for months and had two provinces between them. That night Lynn drifted off to sleep exhausted and full of conviction to end things with Owen the next day.

Lynn got up early the next morning feeling refreshed and determined to deal with Owen even if she had to hunt him down to do it. She knew that he would be finishing work around four and then probably head back to his apartment. She had to finish up with her training session for a couple of hours that morning and then get ready to fly back home late in the day. She had deliberately booked herself a late flight out of Edmonton to ensure she had the most time possible to spend with Owen before returning to Sudbury. As Lynn walked into the conference room the other officers were sitting around the board room table nursing what looked like some serious hangovers.

"Why good morning gentlemen, you all look a little tired this morning. Had a bit too much fun last night?" she smiled at them as she walked to the back of the room to find an assortment of tea bags and hot water waiting for her along with the coffee and muffins.

"Well this is nice, someone remembered us poor tea drinkers!" she exclaimed while digging through the basket.

"Yes," replied the instructor "I reminded them yesterday that we need tea here as well." he grimaced at the sound of his own voice and then continued at almost a whisper, "I know you asked for tea yesterday, a day late is better than never I suppose. Do you mind keeping it down. I seem to have a splitting headache this morning."

Lynn laughed and said,

"Sure, no problem. That must have been one heck of a strip show." the rest of the men in the room just nodded and some made an attempt to laugh; which only resulted in more groans and requests for aspirin or Tylenol. She dug in her purse and found a bottle of pills.

"Here, I just happen to have a bottle of Tylenol. Help yourselves." she tossed them into the centre of the table and seated herself at one end while watching the others nurse their hangovers. Feeling mildly amused at their suffering Lynn couldn't help thinking maybe there is a God after all.

"Well I guess we should get started." the instructor began. "I have printed off all of your certificates for your training session and you can pick them up on your way out. We just have a couple of things to go over quickly and then a few housekeeping items before you can all go and check out if you haven't done so already. I am assuming everyone has a flight out sometime this afternoon so I won't keep you past ten thirty." Lynn sat back and tried to listen to what he was saying but for the most part she was already making plans for tracking down Owen and ending things with him. She was determined to get closure before leaving Edmonton. The session ended and everyone was preparing to leave. Lynn stood up and shook hands with the others and picked up her certificate.

"Thanks very much. I will see you back in Ontario Rob." she said before leaving to check out of her room and stow her luggage with the hotel service. She figured she had a couple of hours to spare before Owen would be heading home. She tried his cell phone one more time but he didn't answer; even though she wasn't really expecting him to answer during the day. He was normally busy in meetings or conference calls. She decided to spend the next couple of hours checking out the mall nearby to do a little shopping. Around three thirty she called a cab and hopped in the passenger side,

"Jasper Avenue, I don't remember the street name but I will show you where to turn." Lynn said as she did up her seat belt. For some reason she was feeling nervous at the thought of seeing Owen. As they pulled up in front of his apartment building she got out of the cab and paid the driver. Turning to look up the street she decided to wait in front of the building until someone came along to let her in. It didn't take very long until a young couple unlocked the front doors and held them open for her as she walked through behind them.

"Thanks." she said as they held the door open.

"No problem." they replied as they walked away.

Lynn tried calling Owen' s cell phone again but it was turned off or the battery was dead so she sat down on the steps in the lobby and waited for him to appear; about half an hour later Lynn noticed Owen walking up the street towards his apartment building. Lynn remained seated as she watched him walk up to the front doors and look for his key. He looked up as he turned the key and noticed her watching him from inside the lobby. Smiling he opened the door and walked through.

"Hello, I am surprised to see you here." he said as he walked up to Lynn and smiled down at her sitting on the stairway.

"Hello Owen, nice to see you too. Why are you surprised? I told you I was here for a couple of days."

"I meant I was surprised to see you inside the lobby. How did you get in?" Lynn smiled up at him and said,

"It's really not that hard. I do this for a living remember." shaking his head Owen laughed and said,

"I forgot; I should not be surprised by anything you do anymore." Lynn couldn't help thinking I probably could have waited for you in your apartment if I really wanted to. I just didn't want to go that far and upset you.

"You're right, you shouldn't be surprised." she answered as she followed him down the stairs to his basement suite. As Owen let them into his apartment she stood quietly and watched him. He seemed to be mildly uncomfortable with her; like they hadn't already spent the night together more than once. His behaviour confused her; was he uncomfortable because she was waiting for him or was it something else?

"Come in, sit down." Owen said as he walked into his bedroom to put away his brief case and take off his dress shoes. Lynn sat down on the sectional couch in the living room and waited for Owen to join her. He sat down on at the other end of the couch and smiled weakly at her.

"So, it is nice to see you again." he said in what seemed like an almost formal tone. Lynn was becoming more confused by the minute.

"Thank you," she said, "I wanted to see you before I left. I purposely booked a late flight out today so I could see you. I tried reaching you on your cell last night but you never answered. Were you trying to avoid me?" Owen shook his head and looked amused.

"No, I was just really tired from the night before and I came home from work and passed out on the couch. I guess I didn't hear my cell ring." feeling uncomfortable, as if she were in a job interview, Lynn shifted her weight and leaned forward,

"So you weren't avoiding me?" looking mildly annoyed with her Owen responded,

"No, I already told you I was just really tired and fell asleep." Lynn was confused, she felt angry that Owen did not try to call her last night but she was relieved that she was able to see him and talk to him before she left.

"Owen I don't know if you realize how much of an impact you have on me. I was going crazy last night trying to figure out what was going on. You weren't returning my calls and I couldn't find you. All I wanted to do was see you. I couldn't understand why you didn't feel the same way. "Owen looked down at the floor as he replied quietly,

"No, I didn't realize." Lynn continued,

"It's as if you reach inside of me and grab some part of my soul. I can't even begin to describe to you how much I feel for you. I care more for you than any other man in my life. I feel more for you than I ever did for my husband. " Owen smiled shyly and glanced downwards as he replied,

"That is one of the most flattering things anyone has ever said to me. Thank you." surprised by his response Lynn replied,

"You're welcome, I meant it." Owen stood up and walked back into his bedroom. He came out with an overnight bag and said,

"I am sorry, but I am planning on catching the bus to Lethbridge to go see my mother. If you like we can take a cab together and you can drop me off at the bus station on your way back to your hotel." Lynn wasn't sure how to interpret what had just happened between them so she decided to just go along with Owen for the moment. Still she couldn't help wondering, did he have any feelings for her?

"Okay, that works. Oh, by the way. I left you a couple of messages on your cell phone last night. Please don't listen to the last one. I was pretty upset when I left it." Owen picked up his cell phone and started listening to his messages. Lynn could tell when he got to the last one. He cast her an annoyed glance as he listened to it and then deleted it.

Shrugging Lynn said, "Sorry, I was upset." Owen just shook his head for a moment and then said,

"Okay, we have to get going. The bus is leaving in less than an hour." feeling childish Lynn followed him out the door as he locked it. When they got outside he called for a taxi. They stood outside for a few minutes quietly holding hands as Owen looked down at her with an expression of mild annoyance and affection. As they cab pulled up he opened the passenger door for Lynn. She got in and slide across the seat to allow him to get in beside her. Lynn squeezed his hand as he gave the cab driver the bus station address. Leaning back he put his arm around her shoulders for a moment and smiled at her.

"I will try and give you a call next week when I get back into the office." he said as they pulled up in front of the bus station. He gave Lynn a quick kiss and then jumped out of the cab. Without glancing back he walked away briskly towards the front doors of the bus station. Lynn watched him walk away and then leaned forward as she said,

"The Highliner Hotel on the south side please." Lynn hated flying late in the day when she was travelling back east. It meant for a very long day. She would lose two hours in the time difference between the provinces and by the time she got home that night it would be well past midnight. All of that didn't matter. She would do anything just to spend a couple more hours with Owen. She was just not so sure that he felt the same way about her.

CHAPTER SIX

The Night The Lights Went Out

Summer was fast approaching and Lynn was making arrangements to send her two youngest children out to Vancouver to spend a month with their father and his parents. The kids were excited and nervous about flying unaccompanied and Lynn was worried about them flying alone. But she needed a break from the kids and they needed to see their father. She knew that his parents would be sure that they were well taken care of and if Steve needed any help with the kids they would be right there.

Lynn and Owen had been keeping in touch every other week either by email or by phone. He mostly called her at the end of the day at the office just before she headed home. She didn't really like that he called her at her office. She would have liked him to call her at home where she would feel more comfortable talking about her personal feelings. But he insisted on calling her there, so she accepted it. Besides, it was better than nothing. At the beginning of June Lynn mentioned to Owen that she was sending the kids out to Vancouver to be with their dad and she would be alone for about a month.

"Would you be interested in coming out here to visit with me, or I could come out to see you? I could stay with you at your apartment and we could spend some time together getting to know each other better."

Owen sounded interested in the idea but was not certain he could manage it, "I have to work for all of the month of July. The only time we could really spend together would be the evenings and the weekends if you came out here." he replied.

"That would be alright," Lynn said, "I can catch up on some reading, go for walks and work on my meditation and yoga. I could have dinner ready for you every night when you come home. We could go for walks or a bike ride on the weekend. I would love it. I think I have enough vacation time and overtime banked that I could come out for at least three weeks." sighing, Owen answered,

"Oh, I don't know Lynn I would have to think about it. I travel a lot with my work and I am not home for days at a time. I think you would be bored. Let me think about it okay? I will see how much vacation time I will have coming to me." Lynn felt disappointed. She really would like to see him, but it sounded like he was not overly enthusiastic about the idea.

"Okay, think about it and let me know in the next week or so. If I am going to take that much vacation time I need to get approval for it." Owen agreed to call her back by the end of the week with his decision and hung up. Sitting in her office Lynn looked out her window. This long distance relationship thing was a lot of work. She wasn't even sure if relationship was the right word to describe what they had between them. Owen called her back about a week later and told her that he was not able to spend that much time with her in July. He had been mulling over a job offer and he was seriously considering taking it. That would mean he would have to move over the summer and start a new job by August. So he didn't think he would be able to spend any real amount of time with her in July. Disappointed, Lynn asked,

"What is the new job?" trying to sound supportive.

Owen explained, "It would be a principal position with one of the elementary schools back on my reserve; but that means leaving the provincial government and moving back to Lethbridge. I am still not entirely sure I want the position. What do you think?" Lynn was surprised to hear him ask her opinion,

"Well, to be honest I think you are unhappy in your current job and if this would make you happier than you should seriously consider it. Although, I will add that I have been on your reserve and there is a lot of violence and dysfunction going on. How do you feel about going back to that?"Owen was silent for a moment as he considered what she had said,

"You are right, I am unhappy in my job. I am stressed out most of the time and I do not feel that my manager and I get along very well. I would be happy going back to the school system and working with my own community. I know that there are a lot of problems back there but I am willing to deal with that. Besides, I have my own home on the reserve and it would be nice to live in it again." Lynn was interested in his comment about having his own home back on the reserve.

"I didn't know you had a home there. You never mentioned it before."

"I guess it never came up before." he replied. Lynn thought about that for a moment and then said,

"Owen you should do what you think is right. You are the one that has to live with your decisions. Don't stay in a job that you find stressful and unfulfilling just because you think you have to. The job as a school principal would certainly be one that gave back to your community and I would think that would be very satisfying. I would be proud of you if that is what you decided to do. Besides,

I love Lethbridge and wouldn't mind living there someday myself. I envy you." laughing Owen replied,

"Who knows, maybe one day you will move to Lethbridge and would could be together." Lynn smiled at this and said,

"You never know." she was happy for Owen, he seemed to be a very successful man and that made her proud of him. Yet she couldn't help feeling empty inside as she hung up the phone. She was going to spend the summer alone; without her kids and without Owen. The idea was disturbing to her. She was not used to being home alone for such a long period of time. Her kids had never gone anywhere without her. She was not sure how she was going to handle them leaving for the summer. More than anything else she hated being alone. It was going to be a long, lonely summer.

Lynn drove Eric and Marissa down to Toronto and they stayed in a hotel overnight before she put them on a flight to Vancouver the next morning. As Lynn waited for the plane to leave the runway she felt a flood of tears wash over her. This was going to be harder than she thought.

The days flew by quickly and Lynn kept herself as busy as possible. She had a small hobby farm that she and her ex husband had started together before he left. So when she wasn't working she was at home looking after the chickens, pigs and goats. She loved working in the barn. It made her feel grounded. She would spend hours cleaning out the stalls and hauling feed for the animals. One of the nanny goats was expecting and Lynn was looking forward to having the newborn kid running around on the farm. It also meant she would have goat's milk. She made goat's milk soap whenever she had a supply of milk. She just froze it in large milk jugs until she was ready to make the soap.

It had been an exceptionally hot and muggy day and Lynn was wondering how she was going to get any sleep that night. She didn't have air conditioning in her old farm house but usually she managed with the ceiling fans and opened the windows at night. She was not so sure that would be enough that night. All of Ontario had been experiencing a real heat wave and she was hoping that it would let up soon. When she got up the next morning to get ready for work it was already getting hot and muggy.

"Wow, it is going to be a scorcher today." she muttered as she got into her work truck. She turned the radio on as she pulled out of the driveway and drove towards the highway.

"Record high temperatures expected today. We should see temperatures in the mid to high forties in Southern Ontario and close to the same in Northern Ontario with the humidity." said the voice on the radio. It certainly was going to be hot. Lynn just hoped the air conditioning in her truck could keep up. As she drove into the office Lynn wondered how her kids were doing in BC. She had talked to them a couple of nights ago and they seemed to be having fun swimming almost every day and spending lots of time with their grandparents.

Walking into the office Lynn smiled at Judy St. Amour, the administrative assistant and said, "Hot enough? The radio was said we are getting record high temperatures today! Thank goodness for air conditioning!" Judy just laughed and said with her thick French accent,

"No kidding, can you imagine what it would be like in here without it!" Lynn walked into her office and turned on her computer. Sitting down she lowered the blinds on her window. She didn't need any more sunlight in her office. Not ten minutes after her computer was booted up it went dead, along with every other computer in the entire office. Sticking her head out of her office Lynn called out to Judy,

"Is the power out?"

Judy answered, "It looks that way. Everything is off." Lynn walked out of her office and stood in the front lobby. Everyone else from the office came out to join them as they stood their wondering how long the power outage would last.

"Does anyone have a battery operated radio?" Judy asked. Carrie came back from her office carrying a small portable radio.

"I always keep one just in case. You never know when you might need one." She laughed as she added,

"For the end of the world!" Lynn and Judy just shook their heads. They were used to Carrie's sense of humour. Carrie tried to turn the radio on,

"I think it needs new batteries." Judy dug a couple of AA batteries out of her supply drawer and Carrie put them in the radio. She turned the dial trying to find a station.

"It doesn't look like we are the only area without power." she said.

"Well, why don't we just hang out here for awhile and see if the power comes back up on its own. Normally a power outage only lasts for an hour or so anyways." Lynn said as she made herself comfortable on one of the counters as she tried to loosen her body armor. "Besides, it is almost time for coffee. Does anyone want to go for a Starbucks and Timmy's run in about an hour?"

"Sure, I will go with you if the power is still out. Maybe we can find out how far the power outage extends. I am sure it is only for a couple of blocks." Carrie volunteered. About an hour later Lynn and Carrie left the office and drove across town; as they drove they could not find anything open or with power.

"This is getting to be surreal." Lynn muttered as they kept driving.

"I know it looks like no one has power. I have never seen anything like it." Carrie answered as she stared out the passenger side window. "Maybe it really is the beginning of the end." Lynn glanced sideways at Carrie as they both burst out in nervous laughter.

"Well, I guess we should head back to the office and let everyone know." Lynn said as she pulled into a parking lot and turned the truck around.

"Okay, that sounds like a plan to me." They drove back to the office in silence; both straining to see any indication of power in any of the buildings they passed. When they pulled back into the parking lot for their office they noticed all of the businesses were closing.

"I guess everyone has decided to go home and wait this out." Carrie said as she got out of the truck. "Maybe we should do the same." nodding her agreement Lynn followed her back into the office. Everyone was sitting up front waiting for them to return with coffee.

"Sorry, no coffee; it looks like the power is out all over town." Lynn announced as they walked back in the side door of the office. She was met with groans and sighs of resignation. "All of the businesses in the rest of the building are closing up. Maybe we should do the same."

"I called Brian down in the Parry Sound office and he said give it another hour and if the power does not come back up then we can go home." Wayne Bradley, the senior biologist said as he walked out of his office. "They don't have any power down in the Coast Guard Base either."

"Wow, this is a pretty big outage. I wonder how far it extends." Lynn answered as she walked back to her office to pick up her gear for the truck. "I guess I could go for a drive and do some field work. But if everyone else is going home I won't be able to call in with my location. So I guess that is out of the question." Wayne nodded his agreement.

"That is not a good idea. You would not be able to get any back up if something went wrong."

"Okay, I guess we sit and wait. I sure hope the air conditioning comes on soon. It is getting pretty hot in here, especially if you happen to be wearing work boots, dark pants, body armour and a duty belt; like me." Lynn said as she tried to get comfortable. "I wish I had something lighter to change into." the next hour seemed to crawl by as everyone waited expectantly for the power to come back on. At the end of the hour Wayne called their supervisor at the Parry Sound Coast Guard Base.

"Okay, we have permission to go home. If the power is back up tomorrow morning it is business as usual. If not don't bother coming in to the office."

"Really, how long can the power be out for? Have they heard anything down in Parry Sound?" Lynn asked.

"Apparently it is most of Ontario and maybe into the US as well."

"What, are you kidding?" Lynn asked incredulous. "That can't be possible. How could such a big area lose power all at once?" everyone else in the room nodded their agreement.

"Tabernac, all of Ontario?" Judy asked shaking her head, "Are you sure? That sounds pretty hard to believe."

"Hey, I am only repeating what Brian told me. I don't know any more than that."

"Okay, well I guess it is time to go home. I have to go and check on my animals. I am not sure how I am going to get them water. Both of my water pumps are electric. Do you think I could take one of the bottles of water for the water cooler home with me?" Lynn asked,

"Sure, do you want help loading it?" Wayne said. Lynn appreciated the offer; he was younger than her and in very good physical shape. She knew he could handle the large water bottles much easier than she could.

"Yes please. Those things are heavy." Lynn and Wayne hauled one of the large bottles for the water cooler out and put it in the back of her work truck.

"Thanks, I am going to go home and check up on my livestock. They must be dying from this heat." Driving home Lynn wondered just how bad it would be when she got back to her farm. She had given all of her livestock water before leaving that morning but it was so hot she knew they were going to be really thirsty. Lynn turned the radio on as she drove hoping to hear something about the power outage. There was nothing but silence. It was eerie not being able to get anything on the radio. When she got home Lynn worked for hours hauling water into the barn and feeding the animals before going inside to empty out her fridge. She cooked everything she could on the barbeque in the back yard and put the rest of it back in the fridge hoping it would last for at least another day before she would have to throw it out.

The next morning she woke up to another hot, muggy day. The power was still out and she was out of water. Remembering there were still two more large bottles of water for the office water cooler Lynn decided to drive into town and bring them back to the farm. Her own personal vehicle was nearly on empty when she checked the gas gauge so she decided to drive back with her work truck. She didn't have any real cash on her even if she could find an open gas station. She knew the cash machines weren't working because she had already stopped at one on the way home the night before.

"I guess I will have to stop depending on my debit card so much," she muttered. "I think I will try and keep some cash on me and some gas in the car just in case in the future." It had never occurred to her until that moment how dependent she was on having access to her money all the time. Lynn drove back into town mesmerized by the strangely quiet streets. Nothing was open. Not a single gas station or convenience store. It made her uncomfortable seeing everything so quiet. Once she opened the office door she rolled the water bottles out to the back of the truck and managed to hoist them up one at a time into the bed of the pickup.

"Damn, these things are heavy." she grunted as she pushed and heaved. The water bottles rolled to the back of the truck and she tied them down the best she could before locking everything back up and heading back to her farm. She spent the rest of the morning hauling the water into the barn and feeding her livestock before collapsing under a tree in as much shade as she could find. Looking down at her dog lying next to her in the shade she said,

"I sure hope this heat wave lets up tomorrow. I don't know where I am going to get more water." her cell phone rang at that moment, startling her. She dug around in her short's pocket and answered.

"Hello?"

"Hi Lynn, this is Beth Mackenzie. Bob Wilson and I are scheduled to arrive tomorrow morning in Sudbury. Will you be around to meet us?" Lynn just laughed and replied,

"Didn't anyone tell you? There is no power in Sudbury. Our office is closed. I am at home trying to make sure I don't lose my livestock."

Beth sounded surprised as she said, "you still don't have any power? We thought Northern Ontario had gotten power back now."

"No, not here. Sudbury is still without power. Where are you calling from?"

"We are in Thunder Bay. We have power up here."

"Great, I hope we get it back here soon. Do you know how far the power outage goes?"

"Well from what we have been hearing it was most of Ontario including Toronto and into New York. Apparently we are all on the same power grid. I think Toronto and New York have power now. They are still working on getting power to the rest of Northern Ontario."

"Wow, that is huge." Lynn said as she stood up and dusted her shorts off. "Sorry I won't be able to commit to picking you guys up. I think it would be better if you by passed us on your tour. I don't know how much longer the power outage is going to last and I have to make sure I have water for my livestock."

"Okay, no problem. If things change later this evening give me a call. We can probably still make it down there."

"Sure, I will do that." hanging up Lynn shook her head and muttered "I am too busy with this mess to worry about driving you guys around all day tomorrow." Lynn went to bed that night praying for rain or a break in the heat at the very least.

Lynn woke to find another hot, muggy day. But at least there were clouds on the horizon. She looked up at the sky; squinting into the sun trying to decide if the clouds looked like they might offer some relief later that afternoon. It didn't matter. By lunch time the power started fluctuating. It flickered off and on a couple of times before it settled down and stayed on. Lynn was so happy she could have danced in the street. The first thing she did was fill everything she could find with water. Just in case. After eating what was left in her fridge she headed out in her own car to see if she could withdraw some cash from an ATM machine. She stopped at a gas station on the way home and filled her car with gas. It seemed like everyone else was thinking the same thing she was, the line ups at the pumps were long and everyone looked nervous. She also noticed the line up for the drive through at Tim Horton's was out to the road. Apparently everyone missed their coffee.

Lynn was happy to have everything return to normal the next day. She got up and took care of the livestock before driving to the office. Everyone was there and they all seemed relieved to have life return to normal.

"I watched the news last night and it was saying that the power outage was a black out for most of Ontario and the Northern part of New York. Apparently the heat wave created a demand for too much power when everyone turned on their air conditioners. The power grid couldn't handle it." Judy said as Lynn walked in to the office.

"Wow, I guess there will be some changes to the power grid now. I am sure we will be seeing an increase in the amount of power that Ontario will be producing. I never realized New York State bought our power before this. It goes to show you how easy it is to disrupt everything, doesn't it? I know I will do things a little differently from now on." Judy nodded while she brushed her long brown hair back,

"No kidding, we were almost out of gas when the power outage hit. It is a good thing we didn't need to go anywhere."

Lynn laughed, "I know, I was in the same situation. I don't think I will let my car get that low on gas anymore just in case."

"Good idea, the first thing we did was fill up both cars. Oh, by the way I increased the temperature of the air conditioning. They asked that everyone raise it by two degrees to try and alleviate the heavy demand on power."

"Okay, sounds like the least we can do." Lynn walked back to her office and sat down at her desk. What had just happened? It all seemed surreal, right out of a movie. Booting up her computer she reached for the phone. I wonder if Owen is in his office yet. He will get a kick out of hearing about this. As the phone rang Lynn stood up and closed her office door. Smiling with contentment Lynn leaned back in her chair; enjoying the guilty pleasure of air conditioning.

"Owen Proudfeather"

Smiling, Lynn replied, "Hi Owen have you seen the news lately?"

"Lynn, yes I did see the news last night. Do you have power now?" laughing Lynn replied,

"Yes, we have power now. It has been out for the past couple of days. I am so happy to have the power back on. I even missed air conditioning."

"Wow, your power was out for a couple of days? How did you manage?""

"Oh, I hauled water for the livestock and barbequed everything. The office closed down. Everything was closed down in town for two days."

"Well that sounds like quite an adventure to me. You sound like you are no worse for the experience though."

"I am okay. Nothing really serious happened. I just got a good scare; I decided to keep some cash on me and more gas in my car.

"That sounds like a prudent course of action. How are the kids?" Lynn smiled as she answered.

"My two youngest are still out in BC and my oldest daughter is at a sleep over. She stayed there during the power outage."

"Oh, was that planned or did it just work out that way?" Lynn laughed as she replied,

"It just worked out that way. It is a good thing too. I was having trouble getting enough water for the livestock and myself. I am glad I did not have to worry about her as well. She spent the whole time playing with her friends and swimming." "I am sure we will remember this as the great blackout of 2005." Lynn paused and then asked,

"Do you realize that it is almost a year since we met? It will be exactly a year next week."

Owen sounded surprised when he answered, "It has been a year already?" Pausing to think about it for a moment he continued, "You are right. The workshop was in the first week of August. Time sure does fly by quickly. Well I have to get going now but I will try and call you next week. Take care."

"Bye, you too." She added, "Happy Anniversary, Owen." Hanging up Lynn wondered why Owen was still so stiff with her on the phone. It seemed like she was talking to a different person at times.

The month of August flew by quickly and the two kids were back before she knew it. Life always got crazy the two weeks before school started. Lynn always took those two weeks off so she could do all of the back to school shopping for the kids and get them organized for the first day of school. Her birthday was also coming up really fast. The end of September and she was dreading it. She hated celebrating her birthday alone. Secretly she hoped Owen would call her or send her an email at least; something to make her feel like he remembered.

Saturday afternoon Lynn's phone rang. She was on her way out to the barn as she picked up the phone.

"Hello?"

"Hello is this Steve's wife?"

"Yes who's calling?"

"My name is Amanda. I was seeing Steve for a couple of weeks before he dumped me. I thought you be interested in knowing that we were sleeping together." Lynn felt surprised and mildly annoyed with the woman.

"Really? Why would you think that?"

"Oh I just thought you might like to know that after he gave me some of your goat's milk soap he came over to my house and screwed me on the couch." Lynn shook her head as she tried not to laugh.

"Oh honey if you are stupid enough to have sex with a man you barely know then I can't help you."

"I knew him for at least a couple of days before we had sex and I have three children that were in the other room when he screwed me. What am I supposed to tell them? He told me that he was going to stay with me and take care of us."

"Jesus Christ you are crazy, lady! I don't give a damn about you or what you did with Steve. Don't ever call me again. I have nothing to say to you." Lynn hung up the phone and walked out the back door to the barn. Jesus there were some seriously messed up women in this world. Steve wasn't even living with her and he was still causing chaos in her life.

The end of September came and went. Her birthday was lonely. The only person that remembered was her mother. She had a bouquet of balloons sent to the office. The ladies in the office had a cake at the end week for Lynn and two of the other staff in the office with birthdays in October. Lynn's kids tried hard to make her birthday special by making her breakfast in bed on the weekend. It was a disaster but she loved that they tried so hard to cut up the oranges and put them on the burned eggs. The effort was all that mattered.

The next couple of months were difficult for Lynn and the kids. Lynn had started her Law degree by distant education. She studied every spare minute she wasn't working or looking after the kids. One Saturday afternoon she was sitting in her living room studying while the kids were out in the backyard playing with the dog. She had been reading her latest assignment while sitting in the early October sunshine when suddenly she wasn't seeing her text book in her lap anymore. Instead she seemed to be seeing through someone else's eyes. She could only see what was directly in front of the person she was joined to and they seemed to be standing on an arched bridge in an indoor garden. The garden looked familiar to Lynn; she just couldn't remember where she had seen it before. She could hear a woman's voice calling to them.

"Owen, are you ready to join us? We are about to begin." her field of view changed as he turned towards the speaker and then their connection stopped. As if a cord had snapped or been cut. Lynn sat upright in her recliner and caught her breath. What the hell had just happened? Had she just seen what Owen was seeing? Holy Crap! Was their connection so strong that she could see what he saw when he concentrated on her? Shaking her head Lynn closed her eyes and tried to relax. The indoor garden looked like the one in the hotel in Lethbridge where she had first met Owen. It had been over a month since they had talked or emailed. Owen seemed to have disappeared. Like he did so often; Lynn would go for months without hearing anything from him. She thought about him all the time. She often wondered if he thought of her as much as she thought of him. Maybe he was thinking about her. It was possible. They seemed to have some kind of connection. Shrugging, Lynn got up and stretched. It was time to make dinner. If and when she talked to Owen again she would have to ask him about what had just happened. She wondered if he would have felt their connection.

Thanksgiving had always been a family event and it was hard for them all to be without any other family to celebrate the holidays with. Lynn loved cooking a big meal for Thanksgiving. So she made a turkey dinner for her and the three children. Sitting at the table Lynn said a small prayer quietly. Please make us a whole family a again.

It was late almost one in the morning when Lynn's cell phone began to ring beside her bed. She was pulled out of a deep and dreamless sleep by the sound. Feeling mildly annoyed and groggy with sleep she groped around on her nightstand for her cell phone.

"Hello?" she mumbled into her cell,

"Hi it's Owen! Did I wake you?"

"Owen? What time is it?" sitting up in bed Lynn tried to focus,

"Oh I don't know I think it is around eleven here." Lynn could hear music in the background as Owen rattled bottles or glasses.

"What is that sound?" she could hear him moving around with his phone.

"Oh nothing, I just tripped on a couple of beer bottles."

"Have you been drinking? You sound like you are drunk." Owen stifled a giggle as he replied,

"No, I have only had a couple beers. I just wanted to talk to you. I missed your voice." Lynn felt mildly annoyed with him.

"Where are you?"

"I am staying at my favorite home away from home." confused Lynn pressed him for more information.

"Where is that?"

"The Lethbridge Inn; I stay here sometimes when I don't want to drive all the way back to the reserve." shaking her head Lynn was still confused.

"You stay in a hotel in Lethbridge instead of staying at your place? Doesn't that get expensive?" she could hear Owen laugh as he responded.

"No, I like staying here sometimes. I don't want to talk about it anymore. I called you to tell you how much I miss you. I haven't told you this before but I love you. I should have said it sooner. I love you and hope you still have feelings for me." Lynn felt mildly surprised and delighted at the same time. Finally, Owen had returned her feelings.

"I miss you and love you too Owen. I wish I was there with you right now." Lynn ached to feel Owen hold her and kiss her.

"Good it makes me very happy that you feel the same about me. I can't talk for much longer my cell phone battery is about to die on me. I will let you go back to sleep. It must be late out in Ontario." Lynn felt saddened, she had so much to say and he was hanging up already.

"Okay, I guess it is late. Will you call me later this week?"

"Sure, good night"

"Good night Owen, I will dream of you." Lynn hung up her cell phone and slide back under her blankets. She sighed as she tried to settle back into sleep. Owen loved her. Maybe he had a drinking problem but she had such strong feelings for him it was getting difficult for her to care anymore.

It was a couple of weeks when Owen called her again. Lynn was already asleep and had trouble waking up as her phone rang beside her bed. She was still groggy when she finally managed to find the phone and answer it.

"Hello?" she mumbled into the receiver with her eyes still closed.

"Hi, it's Owen. Did I wake you?" Lynn rolled onto her back and opened her eyes.

"Yeah, but that's okay. I love hearing from you."

"Oh sorry, I was just thinking about you and wanted to hear your voice. Is that needy?" Owen asked in a drunken voice; slurring the end of his sentence.

"No, I don't think it is needy. I am always thinking of you so it is nice to know you are thinking about me." she said gently.

"Oh good. I was worried you would think I was being weak and needy." Owen laughed as he answered her.

"Owen, something happened a couple of weeks ago that I want to ask you about. Were you at the hotel in Lethbridge last week, you know the one where we met?" she could hear hesitation in his voice when he answered her.

"I don't know, maybe. Why?"

"Because I had this strange vision where I seemed to be seeing the indoor garden at the hotel through your eyes. Were you thinking about me?" Owen didn't answer her right away. He seemed to be considering how to answer her,

"Maybe. I can't remember right now. I was at the hotel a week or two ago." He seemed reluctant to talk about the incident. He sounded very uncomfortable with their conversation.

"I don't want to talk about it right now. I called you because I wanted to tell you how much I care about you. I don't tell you often enough how I feel about you." Lynn ached to hear those words from him so she dropped the subject. She really didn't need him to tell her, she knew what had happened. They both did.

"You're right. I like talking about this much better." She sighed as she snuggled under the covers and listened to Owen pour out his feelings for her over the phone. She didn't care if he was drunk. At least he was finally opening up to her.

CHAPTER SEVEN

One Love

By early November everyone in the office was talking about the upcoming staff training in Kananaskis, Alberta. The email had gone around advising everyone that it would be held the first week of December and it was mandatory for everyone to attend. All staff for the department in the Prairie Provinces and the Northwest Territories would be flying out for four days of workshops and training. Lynn was not very excited about the prospect of travelling again. She had been doing so much travelling for the past year. But she made her arrangements for a sitter to come into the house to look after the kids while she was away. Her mother had moved back to BC earlier that year and she had found a very reliable retired lady to stay with her children when she was out of town. She decided that she would email Owen and let him know she was going to be in Calgary for the week. When she asked him if he remembered her birthday he sounded surprised that it was in late September.

"I remembered that your birthday is in early November Owen. It is coming up in a couple of days."

"I am impressed that you remembered Lynn. You don't have to do anything special for my birthday."

"No problem, I will send you the same thing you sent me. Oh, wait a minute. You didn't send me anything. Well I guess that makes it easy doesn't?

Owen laughed as he replied; "Boy you sure can be hard on me when you want to be can't you?"

Lynn just shook her head. "Why is it so hard for you to remember small things like my birthday or Thanksgiving?"

"I don't know. I guess they are not important to me."

"Well they are important to me. It would mean a lot to me if you remembered, even if you were to just call me."

Owen sounded mildly annoyed when he answered, "Okay, I will try to remember; you know I don't have email access on the reserve so I will try to call you next time."

Sounding slightly happier Lynn continued, "I am supposed to come out for a week long workshop with my entire office in early December. Are you interested in getting together on the weekend before or after my training? I can arrange to fly out earlier or stay for an extra day or two before I have to fly back."

Owen sounded interested when he replied, "Sure, I can drive up from Lethbridge on Saturday and pick you up at the Calgary airport. We can visit for the weekend and then I can drop you off in Kananaskis on Sunday night."

"Great, I will book my flights so I arrive early in the afternoon on Saturday before my training session and I will fly back with everyone else on the Friday afternoon. Have a nice birthday next week. I am looking forward to seeing you soon. Bye."

"Thank you Lynn, so am I. Good Bye." There, she thought as she hung up. Two can play that game. Instead of waiting for Owen to end the conversation she deliberately ended it. Let him see how it feels to have someone else control the conversation. Sitting back in her office chair Lynn debated whether or not to tell anyone else in the office that she was flying out early to see Owen. She was not completely convinced that he would follow through with their plans. He had been getting into a pattern of calling her every four or five weeks and their conversations were normally not more than ten to fifteen minutes long. I will book my flights but make sure I can change them at the last minute if he backs out, she decided. That way I will be covered just in case our plans fall through.

The week before Lynn was scheduled to fly out to Calgary she called Owen at his office.

"Owen Proudfeather please." the school receptionist replied,

"I am sorry; he is out for the day in meetings. Can I take a message?" frowning, Lynn agreed to leave a message,

"Sure, please ask him to call Lynn Thompson back. He has my number."

"Alright, thank you." Lynn interrupted the receptionist before she could hang up,

"Sorry, when do you expect Mr. Proudfeather back?" she could hear the receptionist check her schedule as she replied,

"He is supposed to be in his office tomorrow morning."

"Okay, thanks very much. I will try him back then." Lynn hung up the phone and sat looking out her window. Well, nothing I can do about it now. But I would feel much better if I talked to him at least once before I am supposed to fly out. Just to be sure. I wish he would get a bloody home phone. I hate trying to reach him at his office all of the time. It is really annoying. The next morning Lynn tried to reach him at his office again. He still was not in. So she left him another message. This went on for the remainder of the week. She was supposed to fly out on Saturday morning and she still hadn't been able to connect with Owen. Friday afternoon while Lynn was on her way home from work her cell phone rang,

"Hi Lynn, its Owen." Lynn sighed with relief.

Hi Owen, I was starting to wonder if I was going to hear from you."

He laughed as replied, "I have been really busy this week with meetings. I just got a chance to check my messages and call you back now. So are you still planning to come out tomorrow?"

Lynn smiled as she answered; "Yes, I am. That is why I was calling you. I wanted to give you my flight information and make sure you can still meet me at the airport."

"Sure, just let me get a pen and I will write it down. What time did you say you were landing in Calgary?"

"I should be there at eleven fifteen your time. I will be on flight one twenty one with Air Canada."

"Okay, I am going out for a couple of drinks with my friend the janitor at the school but I will be there to pick you up."

"Are you sure you will not be too hung over to drive the two hours from Lethbridge to Calgary first thing in the morning?"

Owen laughed and said, "No, I will be fine. I will be at the airport at eleven to pick you up. Okay? I have to go now; my friend is standing in the doorway waiting for me. See you tomorrow."

"Okay, bye." hanging up Lynn felt mildly uncomfortable. Owen said he would be there, but it sounded like he was not making her a priority, again. She decided it was too late to try and change her plans so she would fly out the next morning and wait for him to pick her up at the Calgary airport.

Lynn dragged herself out of bed early and waited for the airport shuttle bus to pull up in her driveway.

"This had better be worth it." she muttered as she hauled her suitcases out to the driveway. The shuttle bus driver greeted her as he put her suitcases in the back of the minivan,

"Good morning Lynn. It is unusual for you to travel on a Saturday; especially so early in the morning."

"I know this is not my favourite time to travel. But I am going to Calgary today so if I leave first thing in the morning I will have the whole day when I get there."

The driver nodded and said, "That makes sense." they drove the highway to the airport as Lynn tried to wake up and nodded as she listened to the driver talk about his business and the city politics. She was not really interested that early in the morning but she tried to feign some interest out of politeness. They pulled up in front of the Sudbury airport and the driver got out and helped her with her suitcases.

"Have a nice trip. I will be here to meet you next Friday night. I have your flight number." Lynn nodded as she dug in her purse,

"Do you want me to pay you now?"

"No, you can pay me for both trips when I pick you up."

"Okay, thanks very much, see you next Sunday."

As Lynn pushed her luggage cart through the automated doors she was pleasantly surprised to see no one else in line at the check in counter. No one else is crazy enough to travel this early on the weekend she thought. Lynn checked one of her bags and pulled the other along behind her as she made her way to the security gate. I think I will just try and get some sleep on this flight she decided while sipping her cup of green tea. I can always try and nap during my flight out of Toronto as well.

Once the plane landed in Toronto Lynn made her way to the second boarding gate and waited. She was too tired to even to get a Starbuck's chai. The flight to Calgary was quick. Lynn slept most of the way; waking up only once to eat her bagel that she had brought on board with her. When she landed in Calgary she claimed her baggage and walked to the front entrance of the airport. She looked everywhere for Owen; not finding him she decided to sit down near the front entrance and wait. An hour went by and still no sign of him. She had tried his cell phone a couple of times. It had gone to voice mail every time. Lynn left him a voice message before hanging up with a sigh.

"Hi Owen its Lynn; I am still waiting at the Calgary Airport. Call me when you get in and I can meet you out front." getting worried Lynn went for a walk through the airport while she tried to figure out what had happened. Did he get into a car accident on the way up from Lethbridge? Or was he still drunk and passed out somewhere in Lethbridge? Most likely he was still drunk or passed out somewhere.

Lynn waited for almost three hours before she decided to try and call her girlfriend Maggie Jeffery. If she was around that weekend then she might be able to stay at her place for the night before renting a car to drive up to Kananaskis. Maggie didn't answer her phone, even though Lynn felt stupid doing it, she left her a message and hoped she would call her back. After another hour of waiting and no return call from Maggie on her cell phone Lynn decided to find a hotel room and stay the night near the airport. She could rent a car tomorrow and decide what to do then. Cursing Owen under her breath she started dialing the hotels on the directory in the airport. When she found one that had a room for a reasonable rate she booked it and requested they send the airport shuttle.

Feeling angry and confused Lynn checked into her hotel and ordered room service. She hadn't eaten for hours. She had been too upset to eat earlier. Lynn sat in her hotel room and contemplated her options. She could just forget about Owen and try to enjoy her stay in Calgary; although she had been there many times before and was not really interested in doing any shopping. She was hoping Maggie would call her back. It was still early enough they could go out and catch a movie. Lynn waited for another two hours, no phone call from Owen or Maggie. Frustrated and concerned she decided to try and call the hospitals in Calgary and Lethbridge to see if Owen had been in an accident. She called every hospital in both cities and there was no record of an Owen Proudfeather being admitted anywhere. In desperation Lynn called the phone number Owen had given her for his mother. He had begged her to call her and talk to her one night; explaining that it was really important to him that his mother like her. Owen was very close to his mother who was already well into her eighties. In fact his best friend Jeff always teased Owen and called him a "momma's boy" whenever Lynn brought up Owen's mother. Lynn was not comfortable with the idea and the next time she spoke to him he had agreed with her. It could wait until she had a chance to meet her in person. While the phone rang Lynn tried to figure out what to say to her. She did not want to alarm her, but she was concerned and still upset that he had left her standing at the airport without even calling her. Mrs. Proudfeather answered in a thin, wavering voice;

"Hello?" Lynn took a deep breath and started to introduce herself,

"Hello, Mrs. Proudfeather? This is Lynn Thompson; Owen's friend."

"Who?" Lynn tried again, speaking slowly,

"Owen's friend, Lynn. The lady from Ontario." Lynn could hear recognition in her voice.

"Oh yes, Owen's lady friend from Ontario. Hello, how are you?"

"Fine thank you. I am in Calgary right now. I flew out this morning. Owen was supposed to meet me at the airport a couple of hours ago. He hasn't shown up or called me. I am getting a little worried."

Mrs. Proudfeather sounded surprised when she answered, "Oh dear that does not sound like Owen. He is usually very good about those kinds of things. He is not here right now. I don't know where he is. I can ask his brothers to see if they can find him."

Lynn felt some relief as she replied, "Thank you, I would really appreciate that. I would feel better if I knew that he was okay."

"Of course dear, I understand. Did you say you flew out all this way to see him?" Lynn nodded as she answered,

"Yes, I have training on Monday but I came out early to spend some time with him. I will understand if something happened. I just wish he had called me to let me know."

"Well, we will try and find him. I can't promise anything but I will be sure to tell him you are looking for him if I speak to him."

"Thank you very much Mrs. Proudfeather. I really appreciate your help."

"Okay, good bye now. It was nice to finally get to speak to you."

"Good bye. It was nice to speak to you too." Lynn hung up the phone and decided to take a walk around the block and get some fresh air. She was still feeling angry and frustrated with Owen. This had to be the worst thing he had ever done to her. The worst thing anyone had ever done to her, come to think of it. Lynn walked back into the hotel lobby and decided that she had to do something. So she did the only thing she could think of. She rented a small car and decided to drive out to Lethbridge to see if she could find Owen on her own. She knew which hotel he liked to stay in when he went into town so she decided to call and see if he had a room booked there for the weekend.

"Good evening, the Lethbridge Inn. Mike speaking, how may I direct your call?" Lynn felt nervous when she asked,

"Is there an Owen Proudfeather checked in this evening?" The young man on the other end of the line paused a moment as he checked the hotel guest registry.

"No madam, there does not seem to be anyone by that name checked in." Disappointed and relieved she decided to see if he knew anything about Owen's whereabouts,

"Would you know if he stayed in the hotel yesterday?" sounding mildly annoyed by the question he paused again as he checked.

"No, I am sorry. He did not stay with us last night either. Is there anything else I can do for you madam?" Lynn nodded as she replied,

"Yes, I would like to book a room for this evening. I am driving down from Calgary so I will be arriving in a couple of hours. Do you need a credit card number to hold the room?"

"Certainly madam, I can take that number from you now. All we have left is a queen smoking room. Will that be acceptable?" Lynn sighed as she replied,

"Yes, I guess so. I am a non smoker. How strong does the room smell?" Mike answered in a pleasant and well rehearsed tone, "Our rooms are professionally cleaned on a regular basis. I can assure you there is very little residue from any previous guest that may have been smoking in the room."

"That's fine. I will take the room."

"Certainly madam, what is your name?"

"My name is Lynn Thompson" she could hear a smile in the young man's voice as he continued,

"Very good, your reservation has been confirmed."

"Thank you. I will see you later this evening."

"Thank you Ms. Thompson, we look forward to seeing you this evening." Lynn hung up and picked up her bags. She was feeling better already. She loved Lethbridge and if she could not find Owen at least she could visit the park where she had experienced her first sweat lodge. There was something about that place that still had a hold on her. It was as if she had become bonded to it during the sweat lodge ceremony. Whatever it was she always felt it beckoning her gently, like an insistent lover calling her name quietly from the other room. If nothing else she looked forward to spending some time at Indian Battle Park; just to centre and get some focus on what was happening with Owen.

Lynn drove to Lethbridge and sang along to the radio. It took her mind off of Owen and helped her concentrate. It had been a long day and she was starting to feel tired. It was late when she pulled into Lethbridge and she was not sure exactly how to find the hotel. She knew the address but she was not that familiar with the town. The fact that it was divided by the river made it harder for her to figure out which side had the business section. She drove around for about a half hour until she found the right street and pulled into the hotel parking lot. Lynn was starting to feel exhausted, but she felt calmer knowing that she was staying in the hotel Owen was most likely to choose if he did come to Lethbridge. Something about that made her feel better. She liked knowing Owen had stayed there before, it made her feel closer to him. As she walked into the lobby she was greeted by the same person that had booked her reservation earlier.

"Good evening, welcome to the Lethbridge Inn. How may I help you?" Lynn glanced at his name tag and said,

"Hi Mike. Lynn Thompson, I have a reservation you booked for me earlier." he smiled as he said,

"Ah, yes, hello Ms. Thompson. I have everything ready for you. Please sign here and would you like one or two room keys?"

"One will be fine. Is there a restaurant or bar in the hotel?" she asked as she looked around the small lobby.

"Yes, we have a restaurant that opens at six am for breakfast and there is a lounge downstairs that is open until two am. Is there anything else I can do for you?"

Lynn smiled quickly at him and said, "No thanks. Have a nice evening." and she walked through the lobby towards the elevators. Once in her room Lynn was surprised at how big it was. It smelled faintly of stale cigarette smoke, but it was tolerable. Lynn washed up quickly and decided to go downstairs and check out the lounge.

The lounge was located in the basement of the hotel and it was small, dark and nearly empty. There were a couple of slot machines in the corner by the entrance and a small bar that had a couple of televisions playing with the sound turned off. Lynn noticed there were two young ladies working the bar and they had turned up the stereo system. The only other people in the bar were a couple of older men that looked like regulars. They sat quietly in a poorly lit corner nursing their beer; idly watching Lynn as she crossed the room. Lynn sat down on a bar stool and smiled at the young lady dressed in tight jeans and a low cut tee shirt as she asked for her order,

"Blueberry tea please." The young woman looked confused for a moment and then asked,

"Do you mean blueberry flavoured tea or the drink with Grand Marnier and Amaretto?" Lynn nodded at the second,

"I meant the drink with Grand Marnier and Amaretto. Do you serve it with a cinnamon stick on the side?"

"Yes, I think so. I can make sure I put one in your drink if you like." Lynn smiled again as she said,

"Thanks that would be great." the young woman walked to the other end of the bar and checked her hot water supply.

"It looks like I will have to go to the kitchen to get more hot water." she glanced in Lynn's direction and said, "It will just take a couple more minutes." Lynn nodded and continued watching the television. The other young woman at the bar was wearing a short leopard print skirt and seemed bored as she flipped through the compact discs behind the bar. She found one that interested her and she decided to replace the compact disc that was already playing. As the other bartender walked back into the room with a thermos of hot water for Lynn's drink she called out across the room,

"Check this out. This is the song I was telling you about." Both woman paused as the first song started playing. Lynn had never heard it before but she was captivated by the voice of the woman singing. The words of the song gripped her as she listened to her sing "One love, one need in the night. One love, one love, get to share it. Leaves you darling, if you don't care for it." My God, that sounds like she is describing the relationship I have with Owen. The song couldn't be more accurate. Lynn sat and listened mesmerized by the lyrics; feeling every line piercing her very soul. The two other women at the bar stood and listened with the same captivated expression on their faces. When the song ended they looked at each other as both said,

"Play that again." Lynn's waitress walked over and handed her the blueberry tea she ordered while humming along to the lyrics of the song.

"You don't mind if we listen to that song again do you?" she asked. Lynn shook her head and said,

"No, go ahead. I liked it too." smiling she turned around and walked back to the bar still humming along with the song. Lynn waited for the waitress to come back to ask her if she wanted another drink and she said,

"Who sang that song? The one we listened to a couple of minutes ago?" the young woman paused for a moment and then said,

"Oh, you mean Mary J. Blige and *One.* I think she sings it with U2. It's a great song isn't?" Lynn nodded and agreed with her,

"Yes, it is very good. I wouldn't mind picking up the cd." Lynn hesitated for a moment before deciding to ask her another question. "Would you remember if a gentlemen in his forties with black hair and is about six foot five ever comes into the bar?" the waitress looked down at Lynn and thought about it before responding,

"Do you mean a big guy with a funny sense of humour? He comes in her every couple of weeks." encouraged Lynn continued,

"Yes, he is funny, especially when he is drinking. He is usually very polite and wears a suit a lot of the time." The waitress seemed to recognize his description,

"Yes, that sounds like him. I don't know what his name is though. He is a regular around here."

"Do you know if he has been here this weekend?" the waitress shook her head as she replied,

"No, I haven't seen him this week. Come to think of it I haven't seen him for the last couple of weeks." Lynn couldn't help feeling a little disappointed. At least he had been there in the past but it sounded like he hadn't been there for awhile.

"Would you like anything else?"

"No thanks. I am good. Thanks for your help." sitting back Lynn tried to console herself with the thought that Owen had been there recently. That helped a little. She just wished he was there with her now.

Lynn finished up her drink and decided to go back to her hotel room and get some rest. She had had a long day. Standing up and dropping a twenty dollar bill on the table she waved in the direction of the waitresses and walked out of the bar. She walked up the stairs into the lobby. As she passed the front desk she nodded and smiled at Mike as he looked up from behind the hotel's computer.

"Good night. Oh, can you please set up a wakeup call for me at nine am?"

"Not a problem. Have a nice evening Ms. Thompson." Lynn walked back to the elevator to her room.

She was up before the wakeup call in the morning. She was anxious to get going that morning and do some sightseeing in the town. She had had a restless night. She kept dreaming about Owen and wondering where he was. Sighing, Lynn rolled out of bed and staggered over to the bathroom mirror. Where are you Owen? Don't you know how much my heart is breaking? She dropped her head as she leaned into the sink and fought the urge to cry. He didn't deserve to have her cry over him. Shaking off her feelings Lynn walked back into her room and dressed. She decided to walk down the three flights of stairs to the lobby and into the restaurant. She was greeted by one of the wait staff,

"Seating for one?"

"Yes please. Can I sit near the window?"

"Certainly, follow me please." Lynn sat down at the small table beside the window and looked out on the parking lot. There were only a few cars parked in front of the hotel. She sighed as she picked up her menu and tried to find a light breakfast. The waitress, a bored looking older woman came by to take Lynn's order,

"Can I get you something to drink while you are deciding on your order?"

"Sure, can I have a glass of orange juice and cup of green tea?"

"Okay, did you want to order now or do you need a few more minutes?"

"I think will have scrambled eggs and brown toast." After the waitress left the table Lynn pulled out the local newspaper she had picked up in the lobby. Flipping through the paper she looked for any local art shows. She didn't find any listing for art shows and nothing else jumped out at her. Lynn waited until the waitress came back with her orange juice and green tea.

"Are there any art galleries in Lethbridge?" she asked. The older woman thought for a moment before she answered,

"Yes, we have a small art gallery downtown. I think it is still open although it is late in the season."

"Great, thanks, I will check it out." Lynn's mood lifted as she planned her day. If she couldn't find Owen then she was going to enjoy Lethbridge for the day at the very least. Lynn finished up her breakfast and paid her bill. She walked out into the lobby and paid for her hotel room.

"I will drop off the room key after I bring my bags down."

"Not a problem. Thank you for staying with us." Lynn smiled briefly at the desk clerk and went up stairs to retrieve her bags. As she walked past the lobby desk on her way out of the hotel she paused and dropped off the room key. Pausing for a moment she decided to try her luck one more time.

"Kim, right?" the young lady looked up from the lobby desk.

"Yes, how can I help you?"

"Have you ever checked an Owen Proudfeather into the hotel?" she tilted her head to the right as she thought about the name for a moment.

"Yes, I think so. Why?"

"Well, I was just wondering if you recall the last time you saw him here."

"It would have to be a couple of weeks now. I haven't seen him for awhile."

"Okay, I was just wondering. Thanks,"

"Sure no problem; have a nice afternoon." Lynn smiled back at the young lady and walked out of the hotel. The sun was bright and made her squint. It had to be above zero but the wind was blowing so hard it felt much colder. The wind never stopped blowing in Lethbridge. That was one thing Lynn remembered about the place. Wind all the time and the dust. Still there was something about the place she couldn't put her finger on. She loved Lethbridge, even if she didn't love the wind. She struggled with her suitcases as she jammed it in the trunk of the rental car and jumped in as quickly as possible. She pulled out of the parking lot glancing at the map she had picked up in the hotel lobby. She decided to try and find the hotel she had stayed at the first time she had been in Lethbridge. It couldn't be that hard. Lethbridge was a small town. The only problem was the Old man River. It divided the town almost in half. She remembered a shopping mall across the street from the hotel she stayed at the first time she was in Lethbridge and what seemed to be the downtown core behind it. So she decided to try and cross the river and check out the other side of town. As Lynn drove through Lethbridge she kept hearing the same song play over and over again in her head. The one she had heard the night before in the bar. The lyrics haunted her as she sang them over and over again,

"You say one love, one life. It's one need in the night." she decided that when she found the mall she would make a quick trip in to look for a music store. She knew the name of the artist and the song. She was sure she could find the cd it came from. About fifteen minutes later Lynn pulled into the parking lot of a shopping mall after passing the hotel she remembered staying in over a year ago. Seeing it brought back memories of the time she spent with Owen and the sweat lodge. As Lynn walked through the mall she could have sworn she saw Owen at least twice. But every time she got close to the person they turned out to be too young or too short.

"My mind is playing tricks on me." she muttered as she tried to focus on looking for a music store. As she walked into the music store she scanned the racks of cds looking for a label under Mary J. Blige. Finding it she picked up the cd and found *One* in the list of songs on the back. Smiling she walked back to the sales counter and paid for the cd without even paying attention to the cost. It didn't matter. She had to have that song. She couldn't get it out of her head. Lynn decided to get something to eat at the food court before driving through the downtown core. She was really starting to crave a chai but she was not sure if there was a Starbucks in Lethbridge. She found a sushi place in the food court and bought some California rolls and a bottle of water. While she ate by herself in the corner of the food court she watched the locals coming and going in the mall. So many of the men reminded her of Owen; there were a lot of tall native men that were built the same way. She could tell he was from around there. Lynn finished up her lunch quickly and walked back to her rental car. She got in and decided to drive around until she found the art gallery or a Starbucks. Whatever one came first. As she drove down the middle of the downtown core she noticed a small sign that said "Lethbridge Art Gallery". She parked the car on the street and walked up to the small doorway. The gallery was locked up and had a handwritten sign taped to the window beside the door. "We will reopen May 1, 2006. See you then. Thank you for your patronage, Lethbridge Art Gallery".

"Damn. That is too bad." Lynn muttered as she peered in the window. She couldn't see much so she turned around and walked back to her car. Well I guess I could drive down to Indian Battle Park and take a short walk around. I could use the exercise anyways. As Lynn drove back the way she came she noticed Chapters behind another building facing the parking lot for a large pet store chain. So she decided to go through the green light instead of taking a right hand turn. Glancing around quickly she changed lanes and pulled into the parking lot. Sure enough the Chapters had a Starbucks sign on the side of the building.

"Great signage; you think they would try to advertise in the direction of the road." Lynn muttered as she shook her head and pulled into a parking space. It didn't matter. She had found a Starbucks. Lethbridge just kept getting better and better. She ordered the largest chai possible and walked back to the car. She sipped her chai as she drove back to the hotel she remembered from her last trip and pulled into the parking lot behind it. It overlooked the river valley below and had a great view of Indian Battle Park; the whole area for that matter. Lynn sat in her car with the motor running as she sipped her chai and listened to *One* play. Every time it finished she would hit the back button and play it again, singing along with the lyrics at the top of her voice.

"One love, one need in the night. One love, one love, get to share it. Leaves you darling, if you don't care for it." she didn't care if anyone heard her. The wind was howling so loud along the ridge they would never be able to hear her anyways. The lyrics just seemed to pierce her right to her heart. They expressed exactly how she felt about Owen. He was her one true love. He was the only man that looked into her soul when he looked into her eyes. Her whole body loved him, right down to her inner core.

After she finished her chai tea she decided to drive down to the park and take a short walk around and clear her head. The wind was still blowing pretty hard but she was dressed warm enough she could manage a short walk before starting to freeze. Lynn had brought her digital camera with her and she decided she would try and get some photos of the Old Man River and the park. She would love to draw or paint the area one day. Lynn pulled out of the parking lot and turned left to take the road down into the valley and Indian Battle Park. She parked close to where she remembered their bus stopping and got out of the car. The wind hit her full force and took her breath away. Her hair whipped her face and flew straight up from her head as the wind pulled it every direction. She pushed her hair out of her eyes and groped for her hood behind her head. She pulled it up and held it close to her neck with one hand while pushing her hair into her hood with the other. She dug in her front pockets and pulled out her gloves. She slipped them on and with a look of determination she started walking towards the gravel pathway that led down to the river.

Lynn could feel the familiar rush of energy as she stepped onto the path. She frowned slightly as she remembered the vision she had had the last time she visited this place. She didn't care to repeat the experience so she decided to refrain from touching the rocks or trees. The likelihood of it happening again was remote anyways. She could not control when it happened and it never seemed to happen the same way twice. The memory still haunted her; she could still hear the screams echoing in her dreams some nights. She could still see the vision of women clutching their children to their chest as they ran past her, through her, clearly terrified of something or someone chasing them. She could still smell the smoke and hear the sound of men fighting and dying all around her. She wondered if she had glimpsed the battle between the two tribes that Owen and Jeff had told her about after their experience in the sweat lodge the year before. Shaking her head to clear her thoughts Lynn muttered under her breath,

"It doesn't matter. It's not important right now. Some gift more like a curse." Someday it was going to drive her over the edge of sanity.

Lynn paused for a moment as she took in the surroundings and the flow of energy swirling around her. Her pace quickened as she got nearer the river. She could see the brush giving way to gravel shoals and as she stepped out onto the banks of the river she noticed that the water was much lower than it had been during the summer. Lynn stood there for a few moments, just taking in the sound of the river and the feel of the wind in her face and rocks beneath her feet. Glancing around she decided to try and find a small stone or two to take back with her. She bent down and started sorting through the stones until she found a couple that appealed to her. One was grey with bits of other coloured stones mixed throughout and the other was a smooth black stone that felt comfortable in her palm. Lynn slipped them into her right side jacket pocket and pulled her camera out of her left pocket. She took a couple of quick photos of the river and the trestle bridge that ran over head. She turned back towards the trail she had come in on and walked back into the brush looking for the clearing that the sweat lodge had occupied.

She walked around for another ten minutes and could not tell where the clearing had been. It all looked the same to her. So she decided to get back on the path and follow it to the other side of the park. It was not a very big park so it did not take long for her to walk the entire length of it. There was a wooden staircase at one end of the park that led up to a small observation post at the top of the hill. The wind was getting stronger and Lynn was starting to feel the cold so she decided to head back to her car and warm up.

Once inside her car she turned over the engine and cranked the heat up. She rubbed her hands together until they felt warmer and then she pulled off her gloves. She reached into her pocket and pulled out the two stones she had picked up on the river bed and rolled them around in her palms; first one then the other. Contemplating the stones and looking out the car window she sat quietly for a few moments just listening to the wind and thinking about Owen. She wondered where he was and why he still hadn't called her. She pulled her cell phone out of her side pocket of her jacket and checked to see if it was on. The batter was low and needed to be charged. So she pulled out the car charger and plugged it in.

"Damn you Owen, why don't you call me? You know I am looking for you. I am getting so tired of this game. " Closing her eyes, Lynn tried to forget everything for a few moments and relax. She knew she needed to do something to hang onto her sanity. Owen and his crazy behaviour were going to drive her over the edge if she let it. Breathing deeply Lynn tried to envision a blank screen as she repeated her mantra over and over again. "Om" The resonance in her voice soothed her as she slowly relaxed and released all of the anger and pain she was feeling. Lynn prayed to Mother Earth to receive her negative energy as she released it through her feet and then began pulling the positive light towards her from the heavens. Feeling better she decided it was time to head back towards Calgary and returned the rental car. She had until that evening to check in at her business conference in Kananaskis and she was not sure what she was going to do until then. Her whole weekend was supposed to be spent with Owen.

Lynn put the car into reverse and pulled out of the parking lot. Checking the map, she turned north and began driving towards the highway that would take her back to Calgary. About twenty minutes north of Lethbridge Lynn came up to the highway exit that took her to Owen's reserve. Wishing she knew his address she kept driving towards Calgary. As she drove past the turn off to the reserve she began to wonder if he would show up at the elementary school. He wouldn't miss work as well, would he?

Deciding to take a chance Lynn pulled off at the next exit and turned the car around. She knew which school he was the principal of so if he came into work today she should be able to find him. As Lynn drove past the oil rigs in the fields she remembered the last time she had been on the reserve. It had been during the tour offered by the Native Self Governance Workshop where she had met Owen. That seemed like such a long time ago now. Lynn found the school by memory and pulled into the parking lot as she looked around for Owen's vehicle. She couldn't see it, but it was close to noon. He may have gone somewhere for lunch or perhaps he was still on in his way in to work. Lynn dug out her day timer and found the phone number for the school. The school secretary answered the phone in a pleasant voice,

"Good morning, First Nation's Elementary School. How may I help you?"

Lynn smiled as she responded, "Good morning, Owen Proudfeather please."

"Oh, I am sorry but he is not in this morning."

"Okay, do you know when you will be expecting him?"

The secretary hesitated for a moment before answering. "No, I am not sure if he will be in this afternoon. Why don't you try again after lunch?"

Feeling mildly disappointed Lynn nodded as she said, "Sure, I will try back in an hour or so. Thanks very much." hanging up her cell phone Lynn sighed and looked around the parking lot. There was not a lot to see or do on the reserve. So she decided to sit in her car and wait. She had stopped to pick up some chicken fingers and fries on her way out of Lethbridge so she pulled the Styrofoam container out of the plastic bag and opened it up. The fries were getting cold so she picked at them and covered them in ketchup to try and make them more palatable. She managed to eat about half of them when a couple of stray dogs went wandering past her vehicle.

Lynn paused while she watched them running around the parking lot sniffing anything that looked like it might be a source of food. Just then two teenagers from the reserve walked past her vehicle. They hardly noticed her sitting in her car because they were so busy keeping an eye on the stray dogs. She watched as they walked across the parking lot and behind the elementary school.

It had been almost an hour and there had been no sign of Owen at the school. Lynn was getting bored and stiff sitting in her car. She tried to take a quick nap in the driver's seat but she wasn't able to sleep. She hadn't really slept in days. The lack of sleep was starting to affect her. Not only was she tired she was getting to the point of being over tired and strung out. Sitting up in the driver's seat Lynn pulled out her cell phone and called the school again.

"Good morning, I mean afternoon, First Nation's Elementary School."

"Hi, is Owen Proudfeather in yet?"

"No, I am sorry he isn't in yet. He should be in soon. Would you like to leave a message?"

"No, that is okay. I will try back later this afternoon. Thanks."

"Okay, good bye."

"Good bye." Lynn hung up her cell feeling the familiar rush of anger and frustration. Damn him, what the hell is going on anyways? No one seems to know where he is or what he is doing. Glancing at the clock on the dashboard of the car Lynn decided it was time to give up and drive back to Calgary. She still had to turn in the rental car and meet the resort shuttle at the airport. This was a total waste of my time; I should have never believed Owen when he said he would meet me at the airport. Lynn started up the car and pulled out of the school parking lot. She listened to her new cd as she drove back to Calgary, still fuming over the fact that Owen had stood her up for the entire weekend. Listening to the lyrics of *One* as it played again Lynn couldn't help feeling as if Mary J. Blige was peering into her very soul as she managed to describe her own feelings of anguish and frustration with her so called relationship with Owen. "You say one love, one life, its one need in the night. One love get to share it, Leaves you darling, if you don't care for it". That about summed up her feelings. She loved Owen and she was certain he knew it. It seemed to her that he was using her feelings for him to manipulate her.

"I am going to give him hell when I find that man. He can't do this to me and think he is going to get away with it!" Lynn exclaimed as she drove as fast as she could back up the highway. No one made a fool out of her like this. It was not acceptable. But deep down she knew whatever lame excuse he came up with she would eventually forgive him. God she hated herself at that moment.

Lynn pulled into the Calgary airport and returned her rental car. As the attendant handed her the receipt for her rental agreement she frowned. What a waste of money. There was no way to recover that cost, worst yet she had not planned on the expense. So it was coming straight out of her pocket. She was grateful that she had the money to pay for it. Being stranded in Calgary all weekend with no way to pay for anything would have been much worse.

"Thank you for your business, we hope you enjoyed your stay in Calgary madam." Nodding Lynn smiled weakly in reply and pulled her suitcases towards her as she turned to walk towards the arrival level. She pulled her suitcases along behind her on their wheels as she looked for the sign for the guest arrival lobby. She was supposed to meet the guide there to board the shuttle bus for the resort. Feeling lost Lynn decided to stop and ask directions at the information desk.

"Just down the hall to the first set of elevators and up to the third floor. There will be a sign that says Kananaskis Resort Shuttle. You can't miss it when you get off the elevator." Lynn smiled at the young woman and said,

"Okay, thanks very much." The young lady just glanced up from her desk and smiled in reply. Lynn pulled her suitcases along behind her as walked towards the elevators. She pushed the call button and waited for it to arrive. Standing in the airport again, after Owen had left her stranded there two days before felt strange. Lynn turned and surveyed the floor. It was bustling with people coming and going, looking for their luggage and meeting their loved ones as they waited for them beside the luggage carousel. Lynn watched as a young man met his girlfriend or wife at the luggage carousel and picked her up in his arms, kissing her as he lowered her back to the floor. They made it look so easy. She wondered if they knew how lucky they were to have one another. Feeling lonely and bitter Lynn turned back to the elevator doors. She willed them to open; wanting to be alone with her pain for just a few moments. The elevator doors opened and to her relief there was no else on the elevator. She stepped on quickly and pressed the button to close the doors. Dropping her guard Lynn covered her eyes and took a deep breath as she fought the urge to sob uncontrollably. Damn him, I don't want to keep on feeling like this. Standing up straight, Lynn took another deep breath and pulled herself together as the elevator doors opened.

As Lynn stepped off the elevator two older men pushed past her as they walked onto the elevator. Lynn ignored their presence as she stiffened her resolve and looked up and down the hallway for the Kananaskis Resort sign. Seeing it she turned to her left and walked towards the open door beside the sign. As Lynn walked into the shabby lobby she could see a few people scattered around the room sitting in lounge chairs and on an old couch. There was a television on in the corner that no one seemed to be watching and the room had the faint odour of cigarette smoke; even though there were no smoking signs posted on the walls. Lynn wasn't sure who was coordinating the shuttle bus service but she was pretty sure it was one of the staff members she knew from the Burlington office. As she stood there looking for someone she would recognize Scott Morey walked through the other doorway and stopped as he noticed Lynn standing in the middle of the room.

"Well nice of your to join us Lynn, I was wondering if you were going to show up soon. We only have one more shuttle bus heading out to the resort."

"Hey Scott, nice to see you too; I thought there were shuttle buses running until late tonight."

"Nope, don't know who told you that. The last one is at nine thirty tonight. If you miss that one then you are one your own."

Laughing, Lynn said, "Well I guess then I got here just in time. Do you know if there will be anything to eat at the resort when we get there?"

"No, not tonight; there will be breakfast in the morning but if you are hungry you should probably get something to eat while you are waiting for the shuttle. You have about half an hour before we leave."

"Okay, thanks. Can I leave my suitcases here while I go back down to find something?"

"Sure, no problem, no one else is up here except staff attending the conference."

"Great, back in a few minutes. Don't leave without me!"

Shaking his silver haired head and smiling Scott replied, "Can't promise that!"

Lynn just faked a smile and walked away. Scott could be such a jerk sometimes. He was so sarcastic. She knew it was only a form of self-defence. His ex-wife had left him with their two children and ran off with a younger man. As much as she empathized with him; he still got on her nerves.

She could only find a Tim Horton's that served food so she bought herself a sandwich and a drink and took the elevator back to the guest lobby. Scott was sitting in the middle of the room at a long table with a list of all of the employees that were scheduled to attend the conference. Glancing up as she walked back into the room he commented on the list,

"It looks like there are only three other people other than yourself that have not arrived. They have about fifteen more minutes and then we are leaving with or without them."

"Oh, how far is the resort from here anyways?"

"It is a good hour's drive and it will be hard to find in the dark if you do not know where you are going. If they miss the shuttle tonight their best bet would be to stay in Calgary for the night and rent a car to drive out tomorrow morning when it will be easier to see the signs for the exit."

"Well, they may show up yet. Their flight might be delayed." shrugging Scott got up and walked back out of the room. Lynn sat down to finish eating her supper when she noticed another woman sitting in the corner of the room. She was familiar but Lynn couldn't place her. The grey haired heavyset woman was glancing at Lynn over her novel that she was reading. Finishing her meal Lynn smiled at the woman and decided to strike up a conversation with her.

"Hi, I am from the Sudbury Office in Ontario. Which office are you from?" looking up from her paperback novel the woman smiled and replied,

"Hi, I am from the Iqaluit office in Nunavut. You look familiar, have we met somewhere else before?"

Lynn laughed and smiled as she responded, "You know I had the same feeling. We must have, I just can't remember where." they both paused until the older woman blurted out;

"I remember, the Native Self Governance Workshop in Lethbridge! That's where I met you."

"Oh my goodness, I remember now. That's right; we were both at the workshop. Wow that was over a year ago. Susan Whitson right, how are you doing?"

"Very well thank you. I am still working on consultation with the Inuit in the north. That is why I took the workshop originally. How are you doing?"

"Good, I am still doing the same job. I love it though so no real complaints. I am looking forward to the conference. It will be great to see some of the staff from the offices out west that I haven't seen in a long time." Susan nodded and smiled as she returned to reading her novel. She looked tired from the trip. It normally took two flights to get from the eastern arctic to Alberta. Lynn decided not to disturb her and tried to close her eyes and rest for a few minutes before Scott returned to round them up to board the shuttle bus.

Just as Lynn closed her eyes she could hear two voices sounding rushed and heading down the hallway towards the room she was waiting in. As the two young men burst through the doorway nearest her with suitcases in tow she opened her eyes.

"Hi, is this the right place to catch the shuttle to Kananaskis?" the one man asked as Lynn looked up at him.

"Yes, we should be boarding soon. Scott Morey has the list of employees so you should let him know you are here." looking around the room they answered,

"Okay, where is he?"

Shrugging Lynn replied, "I don't know where he went, but he should be back any minute." as Lynn finished her sentence Scott walked through the second door in the room and stopped as he noticed the two new arrivals.

"Hey, would you two be Garry Woodbury and Ted Smith?"

"Yes, our flight was delayed out of Winnipeg and we just got here."

With a hint of sarcasm he replied, "Good timing, we were just about to start boarding the bus. Follow me everyone." with that Scott walked out of the door without looking back.

The two men that had just arrived looked at each other and turned to Lynn as they muttered,

"Is he always like that?"

Lynn just smiled as she replied, "Yeah, pretty much. Don't take it personally. He treats everyone the same way." shaking their heads the two men followed the group out the doorway and back onto the elevator. Everyone piled onto the charter bus that was idling outside waiting for them. Lynn was grateful that it was already running and the heater was on. December nights could get pretty cold in Calgary. She deliberately chose a seat near the back away from the other passengers. She wanted to sit alone so she could try and get a nap in while they drove out to the resort. She was starting to feel the lack of sleep catching up to her. Lynn dozed as they drove through the night. She could hear the faint voices of the staff sitting up at the front of the bus. Their conversation didn't interest her. She was still feeling angry and frustrated with Owen and did not really want to have to make any more small talk if she didn't have to.

Lynn piled off the bus with the rest of the passengers after they stopped in front of the resort. She couldn't see much in the darkness and she was too tired to really care. Lynn knew she was sharing a room with Judy St. Amour so when she checked in she asked for her room number and picked up a room key. Judy wasn't in the room when Lynn let herself in so she picked the bed that looked as if it wasn't claimed and unpacked for the night. She heard the door open just as she settled in to a long dreamless sleep.

"Hi Lynn, are you still awake?" Judy whispered as she walked into the room. Lynn muttered a reply as she drifted off.

"Yes, I am really tired. Talk in the morning, okay?" Judy she sat down on her bed to take off her high heel shoes.

"Sure, no problem, see you in the morning. Bonne nuit."

Lynn didn't hear anything until their wake up call woke her from a deep sleep. She started awake as she heard Judy answer the phone. Lying in bed for a moment Lynn felt rested and for a brief moment pleasure at just being alive. Until everything rushed back; swallowing her bitterness Lynn rolled over and pulled out her ear plugs.

"Good morning Lynn." forcing a smile as she sat up and pushed back her blankets Lynn replied,

"Good morning Judy. How was your flight?"

"Good thanks. That was the first time I ever flew but it went really well. Carrie and Nancy took care of me during the flight. How was your weekend? You were supposed to meet up with Owen weren't you?"

Lynn just shook her head and grunted, "Not very well actually. He never showed up at the airport so I spent the weekend alone."

"Oh Lynn that is terrible; do you know if something happened to him?"

"I don't know. I tried calling his family. They didn't know where he was either. He didn't show up to work yesterday either. So I have no idea. I hope he has a good explanation otherwise he is a dead man."

"No kidding, I would be pretty angry if someone did that to me!" Judy said emphatically. Lynn believed her. Judy had a fiery temper.

"Well, I have my cell phone with me and he knows how to reach me. Somehow I doubt that I will hear from him anytime soon." trying to shrug off her feelings Lynn headed to the bathroom.

"Do you mind if I take a shower. I feel gross from travelling all day yesterday."

"Sure, go ahead. I had a shower last night. I am just going to dress and go downstairs to get some breakfast. I will meet you down there, okay?"

"Okay, see you downstairs." Lynn could hear the door close as Judy let herself out of the room. She stood in the shower under the hot water, letting it run down her back as she sobbed quietly. Tears flowed down her face as she slide to the bottom of the tub and hunched over her knees. The hot water washed over her as her sobs grow louder and her tears streamed down her face. Ten minutes later drained and no longer able to cry Lynn stood up and reached for the soap sitting on the edge of the bath tub. She finished showering and turned off the water. As she towel dried off Lynn looked at her reflection in the mirror. She was pretty, tall and successful. There was no reason why someone couldn't love her. She had so much to offer, why couldn't Owen return her feelings? What was wrong with her? Lynn knew it wasn't her fault that Owen was behaving like an idiot. She just couldn't help feeling hurt and rejected. She attempted a half hearted smile as she looked at herself in the mirror and said out loud,

"Pull yourself together lady, we have a busy day ahead of us and this isn't the time to fall apart."

Lynn dressed and finished her hair and makeup as quickly as she could. She knew it was close to nine already and breakfast was going to be finished shortly. She was going to have to hurry if she wanted something to eat before the welcome speeches started.

Once Lynn got downstairs she found the breakfast buffet and picked through what was left before sitting at the table designated for the staff from her office. Carrie Madison, Wayne Bradley and Judy smiled and greeted her as she sat down with them. Most had finished their breakfasts and were nursing their first or second cup of coffee. It was going to be a long day and Lynn was not looking forward to it at all. In fact she wished she were somewhere else, anywhere else where she could be alone.

The next couple of days were just a blur. Lynn could hardly remember the workshops or lectures she had attended. None of it mattered to her. Owen still hadn't called her and she was starting to feel obsessed with finding out where he was. She decided to call his mother again; it had been three days and she hoped his mother had heard something. Mrs. Proudfeather answered the phone after Lynn let it ring over ten times.

"Hello?"

"Hello Mrs. Proudfeather, how are you?" Lynn hesitated she did not like bothering her; she was a frail sounding eighty something year old.

"Fine, fine...I am doing well. Thank you and you dear? Have you heard from Owen?" Lynn shook her head and sighed as she replied.

"No, I haven't. I am still concerned about him. I wish I knew that he was alright."

"Oh I am sorry dear, but he has not called me or his brothers either. I am not sure where he is. I am sure that he is fine. He will call when he gets the chance."

Frowning, Lynn replied, "I hope so. Well thank you for your time Mrs. Proudfeather. I leave on Sunday so if you hear from Owen before then please have him call me at this number or my cell phone."

Lynn could hear her smile as she responded, "I will dear. You take care."

"Thank you, you too." Lynn hung up and dropped her head into her hands as she sat on the edge of her bed and tried to calm herself. She took a deep breath and tried to clear her mind. This was getting her nowhere and she was stressing herself out trying to find him. So she decided to try and do something else to take her mind off Owen; Judy, Carrie and Nancy Ellis were planning a drive out to Canmore to check out the town and scenery that afternoon so she decided to go along. Nancy worked at their office part time as an administrative assistant. She was tiny but fierce. Lynn had learned years ago to never cross Nancy. You only did that once. She was the self-appointed organizer of the group. They didn't do anything as a group unless they cleared it with Nancy first. Judy came through the hotel room door as Lynn was changing her clothes.

"Hey Lynn, are you planning on coming with us to check out Canmore?"

"Yes, I was just getting ready to go. Are you guys almost ready to leave?"

"Yes, we are all meeting downstairs in about fifteen minutes. Do you want to go down together?"

Lynn finished putting on her shoes and picked up her purse. "Okay, let's go. Oh, wait a minute. I forgot my camera." Judy hesitated at the door as Lynn rummaged through her suitcase for her camera. Brandishing it with a flourish she placed it in her purse and walked back to the hotel room door as she said,

"Okay, now I am ready to go." Judy opened the door and held it open for Lynn as she walked through.

"I brought my camera too," she said to Lynn as they walked down the hallway. "I really want to get some photos of the Rocky Mountains. I am really looking forward to seeing them up close."

"You are in for a real treat," Lynn commented as they continued down the corridor. "The Rockies are spectacular around here. You will be able to get some fantastic photos. " she smiled at Judy's enthusiasm. It was nice to see the mountains through some else's eyes for the first time. Carrie and Nancy were waiting for them in the lobby. Lynn hadn't had a Starbuck's chai in days and she was really hoping she could find one in Canmore. Nancy and Carrie were in agreement, they needed a Starbucks fix as well. Judy shook her head as they walked out to their rental car.

"You guys are crazy. Timmy's is the best. I don't know why you spend so much money on Starbucks and their expensive coffee."

"Coffee! Oh Judy, you don't know what you are missing. Chai and coffee are two very different things."

"That's okay, I will stick with my Timmy's." Nancy and Carrie both laughed as they opened the car doors and everyone piled into the car.

"You should try a chai Judy. I will buy it for you if you want one." Nancy said from the driver's seat. "I got Carrie and Lynn hooked on chai. I am sure I can convert you too."

Judy just laughed and shook her head. "No thanks!" Nancy backed the car out of the resort parking lot.

"We have about a half an hour drive to Canmore, but we should have some pretty good views of the Rockies all the way. Make sure you have your camera out Judy. Did you bring your camera Carrie?"

"No, I didn't bring it. But Judy said she would email me her photos when we are back in the office."

"Okay, well, what do you guys want to do first in Canmore? That is after we look for a Starbucks or Timmy's."

"I wouldn't mind doing a little bit of shopping if that works for the rest of you. There are a couple of blocks of pretty touristy shops and I am sure there is at least one chocolate place." Lynn suggested.

"Oh I would love to get some handmade chocolate. I am in for that!" Carrie cooed. "We can always count on you to find the best places for chocolate Lynn."

"No kidding, weren't you the one to find that handmade chocolate place in Kagawong on Manitoulin Island?" Nancy added from the front of the car. "It doesn't surprise me that you would know where the best place in Canmore is too." the group laughed as Lynn just shrugged and replied,

"I guess I just have a gift. Now if I could only use it to help humanity." everyone just shook their head and smiled as Carrie teased, "If anyone could find a way it would be you Lynn!" Judy interrupted the joking with a squeal of delight.

"Look at that view! Oh my God the mountains are more beautiful than I imagined." puzzled, Lynn leaned forward to ask Judy,

"Didn't you see them on the way into the resort on Monday Judy?" turning briefly to answer Lynn, Judy replied over her shoulder,

"No, we drove in after dark so I really did not see much of anything." Carrie interrupted Judy with,

"Quick Judy take a picture of that mountain!" startled Judy spun around to look out the front car window and line up a shot of the mountain that was looming over the highway.

"Can you slow down at all Nancy? I am not sure I can get the whole mountain in the shot." Nancy slowed down the car and pulled over onto the shoulder.

"How is that?"

"Perfect, I can get a couple of great shots now!" Carrie and Judy jumped out of the car as they exclaimed,

"Wow, unbelievable. I never thought they would be so big. I can't believe how high they are!" Nancy and Lynn sat in the car and smiled at each other. They were enjoying the moment with Carrie and Judy. They waited patiently while the two women stood on the shoulder of the highway and stared up at the mountains in awe. Lynn smiled as she watched them. Carrie stood nearly half a head taller than petite Judy. But both looked like little children standing on the gravel shoulder of the highway gaping at the scenery. After a few moments they shook off the spell that the mountains seemed to have cast over them and turned back to the two other women waiting for them in the car. They opened up the passenger side doors and jumped back in the car.

"Okay, have you two taken enough photos for now?" Nancy asked breezily in her best effort to imitate a tour guide as she put the car in drive. Both Carrie and Judy smiled and replied,

"Yes, for now."

"Great, let's get to Canmore and get something to eat. I am starving!" Lynn interjected as Nancy pulled back onto the highway. "Is anyone up for some sushi?"

"We already decided that we were going to find a Japanese restaurant so you are in luck!" Nancy answered without looking back at Lynn. "Carrie and I wanted sushi and Judy said she would try and find something else to eat on the menu."

"Yes, as long as it is cooked!" Judy added, "I am not eating any raw fish. " The other three women in the car laughed as Judy made a face and stuck out her tongue.

"Yuck, I feel sick just at the thought of eating something raw!"

"Don't worry Judy; most Japanese restaurants have lots of cooked food on the menu. Sushi is just one option." Nancy explained patiently. Judy looked relieved and leaned back in her seat as she looked out the passenger window at the looming mountain range and muttered,

"Great I hope we get there soon. I really need a smoke. Being the only smoker in the group sucks sometimes."

Lynn closed her eyes and dosed off for a few moments while she dreamt of Owen and the taste of his kiss. She knew she was only torturing herself but she couldn't help it. No matter what, she had it bad for him and she knew that she would see him again, eventually.

CHAPTER EIGHT

Addiction

Lynn half expected to see Owen in the airport on Sunday morning as she waited to board her flight. He seemed to be standing around every corner or walking past her every few moments. Lynn shook her head and tried to think about her kids and what she needed to do when she got home. It was only a couple of weeks until Christmas and she had lots to do before then. It was going to be a rough holiday for her. There would be no family for them to share Christmas with and Lynn was worried that she was going to become depressed. She hated Christmas at the best of times so this was going to be really difficult. She was determined to try and do as much as possible for her kids' sake. They were very excited about the holidays, even though they would not be seeing their father or grandparents this year. Lynn hated the fact that there was no one to invite over for Christmas dinner. It always made the holidays seem that much more special to have Christmas dinner with family and friends. This year it would be just her and the kids. She would still make a big turkey dinner with homemade cranberry sauce and stuffing. The kids expected it, besides it helped keep her mind off her feelings having to plan the meal and get all of the shopping done.

The boarding announcement roused Lynn from her musing and she picked up her carry-on luggage and waited in line to board. Flying was becoming as mundane as taking a bus or elevator; she found it boring and tiresome. Carrie, Nancy and Judy had flown home the day before. Lynn wondered how their flight had gone. Both Carrie and Judy seemed much more relaxed about the flight back home. Both had never flown before or seen the mountains before. They both had had a very interesting week. Lynn hadn't flown home with them on Saturday because she had arranged to stay with her single girlfriend Maggie Jeffery and they had planned an afternoon of skiing at Lake Louise before Lynn flew back to Ontario. The weather had been beautiful and they managed to get in about three hours of downhill skiing before the ski hill closed. Lynn had stayed with Maggie on Saturday night and they hung out together late into the night catching up and gossiping about the politics in their offices and who was dating whom. Lynn caught a cab on Sunday for the airport and as Maggie walked her downstairs to the front door of her apartment building she hugged Lynn and said,

"Promise me you will try and forget about Owen, he is no good for you Lynn. He seems to only bring you grief. You don't need someone like that in your life." Lynn hugged Maggie back and smiled as she replied quietly,

"I know, you are right; I will try too. Take care." Lynn waved as she walked out the front doors and hopped into the waiting cab. She really meant what she had said. Owen was bad for her, she knew that. At times she felt like she was addicted to Owen, or was it how he made her feel that she was addicted too? She wasn't sure. But she was getting resigned to the fact that she did not seem to have any way out. She was hooked and she could not stop needing to see him. Even after what he had done to her. Lynn leaned her head against the passenger window of the cab as she looked out at the passing traffic.

Was this how love was supposed to feel? Or was this something else; something much darker than love.

The second flight from Toronto to Sudbury was as uneventful as the first. Lynn was back home by early evening and even though she was exhausted from the two hour time difference she was happy to see her kids. Lynn had to work for a couple of weeks before both she and the kids had holidays. She was grateful to be busy. It helped her keep her mind off Owen. She and Carrie decided to buy him a greeting card and send it to him with a couple of brochures from Alcoholics' Anonymous. It was the only explanation for his behaviour. He had to be so busy getting drunk and passing out that he had totally forgotten about Lynn. They giggled like school girls while Lynn signed the card, "Sorry I missed you." Carrie folded up the brochures they had printed off the internet from the AA website and stuffed them in the envelope. Lynn wrote Owen's name across the front of the envelope after sealing it along with the words "Confidential, do not open." She put the smaller envelope into a large envelope and addressed it to the elementary school where he worked. She didn't have his home address because he had never given it to her. Lynn dropped it off at the post office on the way home that evening. She smiled as she dropped it into the mail box. Enjoy Owen, this is the least I can do after what you did to me. She felt a little better the next day and decided to put him behind her, no matter what it took.

When she got into the office Lynn made a straight line for Carrie's office. She walked in and sat down on her extra chair and announced, "I have decided that I need an Owenectomy. " Carrie interrupted her with the question,

"A what?" Lynn smiled as she explained,

"An Owenectomy. You know an operation that removes the part of me that is addicted to Owen. That is the only way that I can think of that will end this crazy relationship I have with this man." she paused as she let Carrie absorb what she had just said,

"So what do you think? Does it sound like a great idea or what?" Carrie just shook her head in disbelief and pushed her office chair back from her desk as she said,

"Well if it works for you Lynn, then I think it is a good idea. Just where do you get an Owenectomy anyways?"

Frowning Lynn hesitated for a moment before responding, "Well I haven't quite worked that part out yet, but I am sure it'll come to me. I think this is the best idea I have had yet." Lynn stood up and added, "I am sure that it is not that hard to find some way to get it done. I'll let you know when I figure it out." Carrie just laughed and waved her hand vaguely in her direction as Lynn turned and walked out of her office. She paused in the doorway as she glanced back and added "You know you should probably water those poor plants. They look half dead." Carrie just grinned at Lynn. "Nah, that would be too much work. Besides I like the half dead look ." Lynn shook her head at the assortment of dead or dying plants Carrie had scattered throughout her office. "Okay, whatever works!" and walked away. She smiled quietly and had a slight bounce in her step as she walked back to her office. This was going to be great week. She could just feel it.

Months flew by and Lynn thought less and less about Owen. Work had gotten stressful as there had been a change in the minister that was responsible for her department. The new minister had announced that he would be cutting positions and streamlining the department. Everyone had begun to worry about their job security. The day finally came when the minister's office announced that the Officer positions in Northern Ontario would be cut. Lynn's job was one of the targeted positions. She knew it was inevitable. The writing had been on the wall for almost a year now. She just was not certain what she was going to do. Most likely she would be offered a position somewhere else in the country. The department would not just let her go. Still she did not relish the idea of moving her kids to another province and starting over again. It had taken them years to become settled in the community they lived in now. To make matters worse the divorce had been dragging on for over a year and she was no closer to getting it finalized. Her ex-husband had been hounding her to stop the divorce proceedings and move back to BC with the kids. He had joined the Navy and was certain the military would move them and cover most of the costs. The way things were going with her job it was starting to look like a viable option.

Lynn scheduled a meeting with her lawyer to discuss the progress of the divorce proceedings. Elizabeth Banks was a force to be reckoned with. She was an older woman with a full set of snow white hair she always wore loosely swept back with a large clip. It seemed that she always had a big cigar smouldering between her teeth. The first time Lynn met her she asked Lynn if she minded if smoked. When Lynn looked confused she remarked, "Doesn't matter, I'm going to smoke whether you like it or not." Lynn just shrugged in reply and tried to find a place to sit in the cramped, smoky office.

"Just put those files on the other chair." Elizabeth directed as she waved her cigar vaguely in the direction of the chair. "Have a seat." Lynn sat down and unzipped her work jacket. It was very warm in the small office. Elizabeth noticed Lynn's sidearm on her duty belt and pointed her cigar at it. "I don't like those things in my office. Don't wear it next time." Lynn glanced down; she was so used to wearing her sidearm she sometimes forgot to mention it before entering someone's office.

"Sure, no problem; I am sorry I should have asked before wearing it here. I came straight from work."

"That's alright; just don't let it happen again." And with that Lynn met Elizabeth. She liked her. The woman did not take any guff from anyone and Lynn respected that. She just hoped that her attitude would help her get through the divorce as quickly and as painlessly as possible. Although it certainly hadn't seemed that way for the past year; she had insisted on writing letter after letter to her ex-husband and his lawyer. Every letter cost Lynn another five hundred dollars and didn't seem to get her any closer to being divorced.

"Well what brings you here today?" was Elizabeth's greeting as Lynn walked into her office.

"Hello Elizabeth, how are things?"

"Same as usual, nothing new." she replied while lighting up a fresh cigar.

"I wanted to see you today to discuss my case. Has my ex's lawyer sent you the signed affidavit that we mailed out to them?"

"Nope, I haven't heard or seen anything. " Lynn expected as much. He seemed to be dragging the whole thing out as much as possible.

"I have been talking to my ex husband and he has asked me to consider moving out to Victoria, BC with the kids. He wants to reconcile and he is certain the military will pay for our move."

Elizabeth looked shocked as she lowered her cigar into the overfull ashtray on her desk. "You aren't really considering his offer are you? Considering his past behaviour I would say you are taking an awful risk. You could end up without a job, without a place to live and stranded in BC. Have you considered that?"

Lynn sat back in her chair and thought about what Elizabeth had just said. It was true; she could end up losing everything. She just didn't feel like she had many options left. Her job was disappearing and she had no one left in Ontario. Her mother had moved back to BC before Christmas. They were all alone out here. It would be nice to be closer to both her family and the ex's family. Lynn nodded her agreement to Elizabeth's comments but she was certain this was the best option for all of them.

"I've thought about it and I think it is the best thing I can do for the kids and I. We'll be closer to family and I will be able to get a transfer through work. I'm sure we will be okay."

Elizabeth just shook her head and relit her cigar. After taking a drag she exhaled slowly and replied, "Alright, if that is what you have decided. But mark my words if you come back and tell me I was right I'm going to say I told you so." Lynn laughed as she stood up and extended her right hand out to Elizabeth.

"You are on. If this back fires I'll be back. Maybe just put aside my file for now. I'm planning to leave by the end of May or early June. We have a lot of arrangements to make before we move. I will pay you what I owe you out of the sale of the house. The market has really improved so we should do well on the sale. " Elizabeth waved her cigar in reply as she answered the phone. Lynn shook her head and walked down the stairs and back out onto the street. She really hoped she was making the right decision. She just didn't know what else to do.

The next couple of months flew by with the quick sale of their farm house. The property had more than doubled in the three years they had owned it so Lynn was able to pay off all of their debts and still have about ten thousand left over. Work was getting hectic. Spring was always a very busy time for them. Lynn was spending long hours working in the field. She hardly had enough time to get enough sleep and take care of the kids, let alone think about anything else. The possession date for the house had been the second week of June. She wanted to get as close to the end of the school year as possible for the kid's sake. They had arranged to ship both of their horses out to BC in an effort to help her oldest daughter, Olivia make an easier transition. That alone was going to cost them over three thousand dollars. But she figured it was worth it if it kept Olivia from acting out. Sixteen was a difficult age and she was worried that the move would be too much for her to deal with. With less than a week before the move Lynn had finalized all of the arrangements and only had to wait for the movers to show up and do the packing. She was grateful she didn't have to pack everything herself. That would make a world of difference.

Lynn had one more day of work before she was on unpaid leave of absence and as she drove into the office her cell phone rang. The number on the display looked like it was from Alberta. She couldn't think of anyone out there she was expecting a call from so she answered it with a quizzical "Hello?"

"Lynn, this is Owen how are you?" Lynn nearly dropped the cell phone in shock.

"Owen, I recognized your voice. How are you?" Owen laughed as he replied,

"I'm good. I am having lunch with my good friend Jeff and we thought we would give you a call."

"Well, this certainly is a surprise. I am driving back to the office right now but can I call you back in ten minutes?"

"Sure, I will be waiting to hear from you." Lynn hung up her cell and put it down on the passenger seat. She felt confused and delighted at the same time. It had been almost six months since the last time they spoke. She had just finally come to terms with letting him go and now he was back in her life again. Damn it. She really wasn't sure what to do. Just don't call him back. He will get the message and leave you alone. Lynn knew this wasn't realistic. She couldn't resist calling him back. His voice was like a drug to her.

She pulled into her office parking lot and as she got out of her work truck she locked the doors and put her cell phone in her jacket pocket. She walked briskly into her office and only waved at Judy as she passed her desk. Shutting her office door she sat down and took a deep breath. Her hand trembled as she pulled her cell phone out of her pocket and found Owen's phone number on the display. She dialed it on her office phone and sat back while it rang. Her heart was beating harder with every ring. He answered on the fourth ring and sounded delighted to hear her voice.

"Hi Lynn, I am glad you called me back." she smiled at the sound of his voice. It was as big and deep as she remembered.

"Hi Owen, I was pretty surprised to hear from you. To be honest I had given up on ever hearing from you again." Owen let out another big laugh. "I know; I just didn't want to call you until I was sure you wouldn't be mad at me anymore." Lynn shook her head in frustration. She wasn't mad anymore. It just wasn't worth the effort. But she wasn't about to let him off the hook that easily.

"Well it worked. I am not mad at you anymore. But I still want to know what happened to you. Why didn't you meet me at the airport?" Owen sounded distant, uncomfortable when he replied,

"I just couldn't do it. I had something else to do."

"That's it? You couldn't call me and let me know that you couldn't make it?"

"I should have called you. That was wrong of me."

"I'd say." Sighing, Lynn changed the subject. She didn't want to start an argument with him.

"So how are things, are you still working as the school principal?" she could hear him smile as he replied,

"Everything is going well. I am finishing up this year as the principal and it looks like the school board will be offering me a contract for next year."

"That's great."

"And you Lynn, how are things going for you?" she hesitated for just a moment before answering him; uncertain of how much she wanted to tell him.

"Okay, this is actually my last day at work. I am moving to Victoria with the kids. We leave in a couple of days." he sounded surprised when he responded,

"Moving to Victoria? Wow that is sudden. I hope it is a good move for you."

"So do I. My job is being phased out here and I do not have any family in Ontario anymore. I think it would be better for us to live near our family and I will get a transfer to a position on Vancouver Island eventually."

"Well good for you. Victoria is beautiful. I love that city. And that would mean you are actually closer to Alberta." Lynn smiled at the last comment. He was still interested; even if he didn't want to come out and say it.

"Yes, I would be closer to Alberta. Would that make a difference?"

"Oh I don't know. Maybe it would mean we could see each other more than once or twice a year." As much as Lynn had to admit she liked the idea of seeing Owen again, she knew that it was unlikely that it would happen.

"I am moving out to BC to be closer to my ex-husband Owen. He has arranged for the military to move us out there and we are talking about trying to work out a way to share custody of the kids. He is going to try and help us get settled." This was not exactly the truth and Lynn cringed as she heard herself say it. She wanted Owen in her life so badly, but she needed the stability her ex and her family offered. Owen certainly wasn't offering her any kind of support or stability.

"Well, I am glad that I called you today. It sounds like I may not have found you if I waited any longer."

"You are right. I am turning in my cell phone at the end of the week and my home phone will be disconnected at the same time. You called just in the nick of time."

"Okay, well be sure to call me once you get settled in Victoria. Have a safe trip and I will be looking forward to hearing from you." With that he hung up. Lynn sat in silence as she felt the rush of emotion flood over her. She still loved Owen; she knew that would never change. But he kept disappointing her and showing her that she could not trust him. So as much as she wanted to have a real relationship with him; it was becoming pretty obvious that the likelihood of that happening was pretty remote. Oh well, she always did like a challenge.

The flight out to Victoria was long and uneventful. The kids were restless and nervous the whole flight out. They were anxious to see their father and their new home. Lynn only felt the pit of her stomach drop to the floor when she saw Steve standing in front of the arrival gate waiting for them. She knew then it really was over between them. It was too late though, she was committed to trying to make things work between them and there was no going back.

Steve gave her a half hearted smile over the kid's heads while he bent down and hugged them.

"Hi, how was the flight?" he asked as he have her a quick hug and picked up the kid's carry-on luggage.

Lynn shrugged and replied, "Okay, long and tiring mostly." he nodded and turned towards the luggage carousels to find their flight number.

"It looks like your luggage will be showing up on carousel number three." he said as he walked towards the group of people standing around the nearest carousel. "I will get your luggage while you get a cart, okay?" Lynn nodded and took the kids with her as she went looking for a luggage cart. Lynn stopped and turned back towards Steve remembering they also had to claim their dog, Sam. They had brought him with them as well. "We need to go claim Sam at the luggage counter too Steve." He waved at her in acknowledgement from the other side of the luggage carousel. Sighing with resignation she pulled a cart towards her from the long line of stacked luggage carts and started pushing it towards the luggage counter. This was going to be harder than she thought. Not only was she unhappy to be back with Steve, he didn't look very thrilled about the prospect of being back with her either.

As they loaded up their truck Steve looked over at Lynn and said, "The military base housing is not ready yet. They said it would be another week before we can move in. I found us a motel room close to the base that we can stay in until it is ready." Lynn was tired and feeling annoyed she responded,

"Okay, is it big enough for all of us?"

"Yes, there are two double beds and a pullout couch. It also has a small kitchen unit so we can make most of our own meals. The military will only pay for the motel room not our meals." Lynn nodded and sighed. Great this was going to be a long week stuck in a motel room with three bored kids and one large, shaggy black dog.

"I hope that it has a pool at least."

"Yes it does. I made sure of that. I know how much the kids love to swim." Lynn attempted a weak smile and said,

"Good, I am glad you thought of it. The motel is okay with dogs?" Steve nodded as he answered her,

"Yup I checked. They said it is fine as long as we don't let him make too much noise." Lynn felt uncomfortable and awkward being alone with Steve after being apart for almost a year. She leaned against the passenger window being careful to put as much space between them as possible. She tried to make out the buildings as they drove past. It was already dark so Lynn could not see much as they drove to the motel. There would be lots of time to check it out once they were settled. She did not have a job lined up yet and she was going to try and enjoy her summer.

"Did I mention to you that I am taking two correspondence courses with Laurentian University? I am still working on finishing my law degree. " Steve looked over at her across the truck and said,

"Yes, you did. I was thinking we could pick up a computer and printer for you this week from the money we made from the sale of the house so you could do your assignments."

"Thanks, that is a great idea. Our old computer is so slow and out of date I was having trouble with it. Besides, it won't be showing up until the end of the week when the moving truck gets here."

"I thought of that. So I figured we could pick one up tomorrow if you want."

Lynn nodded, "Sure that sounds like a great idea." well at least if nothing else she would have a new computer to do her assignments on and be able to submit them on time.

"Here we are." Steve announced as they pulled into a clean looking two storey motel. It is not the most expensive place in town but it is clean and the rooms seem nice."

"I'm sure it will be fine." Lynn agreed as they went around back to the parking lot and parked close to their room.

"We are on the second floor we will have to carry our luggage up the stairs." Steve said as he jumped out of the cab and reached into the bed of the pickup for their suitcases. "I'll carry up the heavier ones and you guys can carry up your smaller bags. The dog can stay in the back of the truck in his crate for now okay?"

"Okay you guys you heard your dad, pick up your back packs and carry-on bags and start heading up the stairs." The kids groaned as they struggled out of the truck and groped around for their belongings before trudging up the stairs. Olivia being the oldest and self appointed spokesperson for the three of them announced,

"We are all tired mom and we don't want to carry our luggage up the stairs." Lynn nodded and said,

"I realize that, we are all tired and no one wants to carry luggage up the stairs. But if we all pitch in it will get done much faster and then we can go to bed, alright?" still grumbling the three kids continued up the stairs with Steve encouraging them as he followed them up with a suitcase in each hand.

"It is the last room after the stairs. I think the number is two thirty five. I am not sure though, just give me a minute to find the key." everyone stopped in the hallway while Steve fished around in his pockets for the key.

"I must have left it in the truck. You guys wait here while I go back downstairs and look for it. I will be right back." they just nodded and dropped their bags on the floor while he trotted down the stairs and back to the truck. A few moments later he raced back up the stairs, taking two at a time while flourishing the key.

"Found it. I left it in my jacket pocket. It is two thirty eight. I will open the door for you guys and you can start bringing everything into the room while I bring up the rest of the suitcases."

Exhausted, they picked up their bags and started trudging back down the hallway to room two thirty eight. Lynn was so tired she could hardly focus any longer. All she wanted to do was get into the hotel room and crash for the night. She was certain the kids felt the same way. When they got into the room she was shocked at how small the room was. Once they pulled the couch out for the kids to sleep on there was not going to be very much room for them to move around.

"Okay you guys drop all of your bags on that bed and find your pyjamas and toothbrushes while I make up the couch." Steve arrived with the last of the suitcases and as he shut the door he sounded out of breath as he commented,

"You guys sure brought a lot of luggage with you. Did you leave anything behind for the movers?" Lynn and the kids only nodded and tried to act like they found his comment amusing.

"We brought everything with us we figured we would need for the first week or two. Except for the stuff that was too big or heavy to bring on the plane."

"I can tell." he replied with a snort; ignoring him Lynn went back to making up the bed on the couch. When she finished she crossed the room into the cramped bathroom to check on the kids' progress with brushing their teeth.

"Okay you guys finish up and let's get to bed. Who wants to sleep on the couch?" Olivia was the first to respond.

"I am the oldest and I am not going to sleep on the couch. Eric and Marissa can have it and I'll sleep on the bed." the two younger kids did not seem too impressed with suggestion but Lynn decided for tonight to give it a try.

"Okay you two can share the couch tonight and we can switch everyone around tomorrow night. We are going to be here for at least a week so there will be plenty of time to get a turn sleeping on the bed." grumbling and complaining the two youngest crossed the room and climbed into the pull out bed.

"I want to sleep in the big bed tomorrow night." Marissa stated as she pulled the blankets up to her chin and struggled with her brother over how much room each got on the bed. "This bed is too small and Eric is going to kick me or roll on me all night long."

"Each of you stay on your own side." Lynn said as she put a pillow between them. "There, you should both have enough room now." she turned out the lights in the room and said,

"Good night you guys; get some sleep. We can go swimming tomorrow if you behave." but there was no answer from either bed, they were already sound asleep. Lynn was dreading going to bed. She did not look forward to sleeping with Steve. In fact she did not want anyone else touching her besides Owen. So she changed quickly into a pair of pyjamas that were baggy and revealed nothing. She lay quietly facing the wall as she heard Steve return from the bathroom and slide under the covers beside her.

He whispered "Good night."

Lynn answered him "Good Night." and closed her eyes. Her last thought was of Owen as she drifted off to sleep.

The next morning everyone was slow to get up. It had been a late night and Lynn as well as the kids were feeling the effects of jet lag. Steve was the first up and he made himself a cup of coffee as he waited for the rest of the family to wake up. Lynn could hear him talking to Marissa in the living room while he made her a bowl of cereal. Eric was not far behind so Lynn decided it was time to drag herself out of bed to get some breakfast.

"Good morning sleepy head." Steve teased as he pulled out more bowls and spoons for cereal. "I only bought cereal for everyone to eat this morning. I figured we could pick up more groceries today."

Nodding, Lynn reached for the box and poured some flakes in her bowl. "Did you remember to buy soya milk too?" she asked when she noticed only two percent milk on the table.

"Yes, I did remember." opening the fridge he pulled out a carton of vanilla soy milk for her and Eric.

"Thanks. " she said while pouring it on Eric's cereal and then her own. "So do you think we could go and check out some computers today? I have an assignment due in a week and I need to get started."

"Sure, there is a mall close to us. We can pick up the groceries on the way back." the rest of the week was spent much the same. Lynn and Steve shopped around for a couple of days until they found a new desktop computer and printer. The rest of the time the kids swam in the pool at the motel or Lynn took the kids and Sam, their large border collie cross to a nearby beach to play for a couple of hours. Steve only had the one week off so he had to report to duty for a few days before they were ready to move into their military housing. Steve had taken them for a drive to show them the housing complex that was full of military families. It surprised Lynn to see how big the complex was. It was the size of a large subdivision. The elementary school was right in the complex so the kids could walk to school and attend classes with other children from military families. She hoped that would make it a little easier for them when he his ship was sent back out to sea on another patrol.

"I already picked up the keys so we can go check the house out today and start making arrangements for the phone to be hooked up. " Steve explained to Lynn as they drove into the dead end street where their new home waited for them. Lynn tried to look excited when she replied,

"Sure, that sounds good. I would like to see the house and if there is any garden space. It is so much warmer here I should be able to start a garden now even though it is getting a little late into the season." Steve nodded as he pointed towards a large two storey home that was sitting empty. They pulled into the driveway and the kids and Sam jumped out of the truck full of excitement. They ran around to the small back yard and then back to the driveway while their large black shaggy dog followed them barking enthusiastically and wagging his long fringed tail. Lynn stood surveying the small, neglected flower bed in front of the house. It looked like something had been eating all of the shrubbery and flowers that were struggling to grow. She wondered what had been eating them, insects or something larger. She was wrenched from her thoughts by the sound of the kids squealing and shouting as they ran past her and onto the road. It was a very quiet road but it still made Lynn nervous. The memory of attending the funeral for a co-worker's two year old daughter after she was run over by her neighbour while playing on her street was still vivid, even if it had been a couple of years ago.

"Come on you guys, stay in the yard. You know I don't like you playing on the street." she watched as they ran back onto the front yard and started chasing each other on the grass. It was not long before the children next door noticed them and came running over to join in the chase. Smiling, Lynn turned back to contemplating the neglected flower bed. It looked like it just needed watering; the summers were so hot and dry in Victoria. Steve walked out the front door as he picked up the mail that was overflowing the mail box beside the front door.

"It looks like the mail is still being delivered for the last residents." he commented while leafing through the mail. "I guess we can just mark it return to sender once we have moved in." Lynn nodded vaguely as she glanced up from the garden.

"Sure, that is probably the best thing to do."

"Did you want to see the rest of the house?" Steve asked as he walked over to where Lynn was crouched.

"Okay, were the movers supposed to show up tomorrow or the day after?" standing up Lynn dusted off her hands and looked up at Steve. "It would be nice to get settled before you have to get back to duty."

Steve shrugged, "My commanding officer said I could take the next couple of days off as special leave to help with the unpacking. But after that I have to return to duty. Steve seemed to find his last comment amusing, as he smiled smugly at Lynn while saying, "I hope the movers show up sooner than later or you will be left to do most of the unpacking yourself." Lynn was not amused and only frowned at him as she walked towards the front door. Doesn't surprise me jerk; was her only thought. They walked through the small house together discussing who should get which bedroom and where to put their furniture. They both agreed that Eric would get the smallest bedroom; he never played in his room he always was outside playing.

"I am sure the movers will set up the beds for you and put the furniture where we want it." Steve said as they walked back downstairs. "So even if I am not home to help with all of the unpacking you will only have to deal with the boxes."

"That will still be a lot of work." Lynn frowned at the thought of unpacking the entire household on her own. "You are sure you can't get any more time off to help?"

"Nope, I have taken all of my leave and they won't advance me anymore." Steve seemed happy about this fact and he wasn't trying very hard to hide it.

"Okay, I will deal with it." Lynn sighed and walked back outside. "The rooms are pretty small; it is going to be crowded once the furniture arrives."

"I know, but this is one of the larger houses." Steve said as he followed her out of the door. "At least we get a break on the rent."

"I guess I do like the idea of the kids going to school with other kids from military families."

"Yes, I think it will be good for them too. Apparently they have special programs for the kids when we ship out. It is supposed to help them deal with our being gone for a couple of months at a time."

"I hope so." Lynn said as she walked back towards the truck. "We should go check on the horses. You haven't shown us where you boarded them yet."

"Okay, come on you guys we are going to go see the horses now." the kids cheered as they ran back to the truck. "Hooray, can we go riding today?"

Lynn shook her head, "No, our tack hasn't shown up yet. Besides we have lots to do before we can play with the horses." Olivia was the most excited about seeing the horses. They were hers really. Lynn had bought them for her and had made sure they kept them when they moved. She knew how hard it was to be sixteen and move away from all of your friends. She was hoping keeping the horses would help Olivia adjust to the move and keep her out of trouble. As they drove out to the stables Steve said,

"I haven't paid all of the boarding fees for the horses. We owe them about six hundred dollars for the last month. I was planning on using the money from the sale of the house to cover the cost." Lynn turned to Steve in shock.

"You mean we owe them six hundred dollars already? How much a month is going to cost to board the horses?"

"About six hundred a month, I couldn't find anything else cheaper."

"Oh my God, we can't afford that over the long run. We are going to have to find somewhere else cheaper or we are going to have to sell one of the horses."

Steve nodded, "I know. I figured I would wait until you got here to discuss it. Olivia may have to give up one of her horses." Overhearing their conversation Olivia interrupted,

"I don't want to sell either one of my horses! That's not fair. You make me move out here and then you make me sell my horse. I hate you both." Lynn turned around to look at Olivia,

"Olivia you don't mean that. We will try and figure something out but if we can't find somewhere cheaper to board the horses we will have to do something. I am sorry." Olivia sat back in angry silence. She had been against the move from the start and she was not about to make it any easier. Lynn was worried. Olivia had never been so angry and defiant. If they did not handle things carefully with her she was worried that Olivia would escalate her defiant behaviour and start getting finding other ways to act out her anger.

"Let's go see Meadow and Skittles, you can spend some time with them today grooming them and doing some groundwork with them. They have their basic tack with them so you'll have their lead lines and halters at least. We can stop along the way if we pass a tack shop and pick up a couple of things for them as well. Okay?" Olivia seemed calmer at the idea and settled down after nodding her agreement. Lynn turned back to face the front of the truck as she thought; this is not going to be easy.

They spent the afternoon hanging out at the stables getting to know the owner and the other boarders. Olivia managed to work both Meadow and Skittles in the round pen for about half an hour each. By the end of the day everyone was tired and happy. The youngest kids had spent the afternoon running around the stables playing with a couple of other younger children that were there while their parents or older siblings worked with their own horse. Driving back home Steve and Lynn decided to take the kids out for supper. Lynn was tired of trying to cook meals in the tiny motel kitchenette.

"This should be our last night in the motel. The movers should be showing up tomorrow. We can call the number the agent gave us to confirm their arrival." Lynn said as they walked into the restaurant.

Steve mumbled his agreement as he followed her through the doors. Lynn was already getting tired of Steve and his annoying personality traits. Mumbling was one of his most annoying traits. As they ate their dinner the kids talked and squirmed while Lynn ignored most of the conversation. She couldn't help feeling like she was living someone else's life. None of this felt right to her.

The next morning Lynn called the contact number for the movers and confirmed they were on their way to their new home. They arranged to meet them there by noon. Everyone was excited and as they packed up their suitcases Steve paid for the room and started loading the truck. As they all got into the truck Steve said to Lynn,

"I will drop you guys off at the house and then I have to report to my Commanding Officer." Lynn just nodded and sighed with resignation,

"Sure, whatever." Steve and Lynn drove in silence while the three children played and talked amongst themselves. When they arrived at the house Steve and Lynn unloaded the suitcases while the kids ran through the empty house and into the backyard. As Steve dropped the last suitcase onto the driveway he hopped back into the driver's seat of the truck and said through the window,

"Okay, have fun and I will see you later." Lynn stood in the driveway and watched him back the truck out and pull away. He didn't even glance back as he drove off. Lynn just shook her head and started carrying the suitcases into the house. She had just finished dragging the last of the big suitcases in through the front door when she heard a large truck pull up in front of the house. A young man wearing coveralls jumped down out of the cab of the truck and walked up to the front door carrying a clip board and a pen. He went to knock on the screen door as Lynn opened the door and said,

"Hello, you must be the movers." The young man looked mildly startled as he responded,

"Yes we are. Would you mind if we backed the truck into the driveway? "Lynn waved vaguely in his direction as she replied,

"Sure, I will make sure the kids stay out of the way." he walked back towards the truck and gestured to the driver to back it into the driveway. Lynn opened the front screen door and stepped out onto the walk way.

"You guys come over here and stay with me while the truck backs up." The three children ran back to stand beside Lynn while watching the large tractor trailer back into the driveway.

"Wow that sure is a big truck. Is all of our stuff in there?" Eric asked while looking back up at Lynn.

"Yes, but while the movers are bringing it into the house I want you guys to stay out of the way."

The three children answered in unison, "Okay."

It took the movers a couple of hours to unload the truck and carry all of the furniture and boxes into the house. Lynn was exhausted when they left. She stood in the centre of the living room surrounded by boxes piled almost as high as her head and surveyed the mess. It was going to take her weeks to unpack and sort it all out. She did not even know where to begin. It was getting late and Lynn realized that it was almost time for dinner. The kids were going to be hungry and looking for something to eat soon so she decided to order in pizza. It was a couple of hours later before Steve finally reappeared. He mumbled something about having to stay late to catch up on work. Lynn didn't really care so she did not press the issue. It had been almost two weeks and they still hadn't had sex.

Lynn had stopped even wondering if Steve wanted to make love. Their marriage had always been this way so why would it change now? Besides, she wasn't entirely sure she wanted him to touch her. It was almost a relief that he hadn't even brought it up. She still longed for Owen even though she knew that it was probably impossible they would ever be together again.

The next morning Steve left early and when Lynn struggled out of bed she staggered downstairs into the sea of moving boxes. The thought of trying to organize what seemed an over whelming mess was depressing so she decided to make some tea and have her breakfast before trying to tackle what seemed like the impossible. The kids started to show up one by one as they woke up and Lynn fed them breakfast before turning them lose on the neighbourhood. It was easier for her to let them go outside and play while she unpacked the kitchen and living room. She would get them to help with their bedrooms later in the afternoon. The phone had only been hooked up that morning but it was already ringing. Olivia had called her boyfriend in Sudbury and the two of them were making plans for him to come out to stay with them indefinitely. It was his parents on the phone and his step mother sounded frantic.

"Peter left last night on the Greyhound bus. He said he was moving to Victoria to be with Olivia and there was nothing we could do to stop him. We are very worried about him; he still has to finish high school. But he told us he is going to get a full time job out there and work." Lynn listened and smiled faintly.

"Don't worry about Peter. I will keep an eye on him and he can stay here and sleep on the couch. I will make sure things are not inviting enough for him to stay any longer than the summer. He will want to come home by the end of August. I'm certain once he and Olivia see each every day all day they'll both get tired of each other's company." Lynn knew that Peter and Olivia were not that compatible and once they spent every waking moment together they would soon figure it out. The worst thing they could do was fight them on the matter and end up making them even more determined to be together. His step mother still sounded very concerned when she replied,

"Are you sure? He is such a good kid I wouldn't want anything to happen to him. I am afraid they'll do something silly like run off and get married." Lynn laughed. She knew Olivia was too much of a princess to agree to running off with no money to elope.

"I don't think you have to worry about that! Olivia would never agree to anything like that. I say we let them have what they want and they'll figure it out on their own. I promise that I won't let them get married or pregnant. " that was the last thing Lynn wanted for her daughter. She was not about to let her do something she might regret for the rest of her life.

"It'll be fine. I will help Peter get a job nearby and I'll make sure he stays in touch with you. What else can we do?" she was not prepared to argue with a hormonal six foot four teenage boy. Besides, Peter Anderson was a good kid so she wouldn't mind him being in the house. She could always use the extra help unpacking. A couple of days later Peter arrived in Victoria and Lynn arranged for Steve to pick him up with the truck and drop him off at the house after work. She was not used to only having one vehicle and she was getting frustrated with Steve using the truck every day and staying out late almost every night. So she decided to discuss her feelings with him the next day when he got home from work.

Lynn waited up for Steve until past midnight. She tried working on her law assignment for awhile but she was getting too tired. She had picked up a new game for the computer when they bought it and she had been playing it ever since. She opened up Zuma and started playing while she waited for Steve. Sometime around two in the morning he finally pulled into the driveway. Lynn could hear him try to open the back door as quietly as possible as he padded softly through the kitchen. Lynn watched Steve until he stopped in the dining room when he finally noticed Lynn sitting patiently waiting for him in front of the computer.

"Hello." he said as he tried to fake a quick smile. He started to walk past Lynn when she said,

"Hello, you are home awfully late. I can't imagine work keeping you this late so do you mind sharing with me where you have been?" Steve turned back to look at her and glanced away.

"Out, I went out with some of the guys I work with." Lynn was not sure she believed him. He had been acting distant and secretive, even for Steve.

"Hmm, you know I want to believe you. After all I just gave up my job and dragged three kids, two horses and one dog halfway across Canada to be here with you. But it is starting to look to me like you don't really want to be with us." hearing herself say what she had been thinking made Lynn's heart sink. This was starting to look like it was a bad idea. She watched Steve standing in the living room doorway and stared down at the floor for a few moments while he digested what she had just said. Lynn dreaded hearing what he was going to say.

"You are right. I don't think I want to be married anymore. I met someone else and I am in love with her." that was more than what she expected to hear. His words resounded like a shockwave through the room. Lynn started to feel like the room was spinning as she sat with a look of shock and disbelief on her face. She watched Steve shift his weight from foot to foot as he became uncomfortable with the silence in the room. He had braced himself for Lynn's verbal assault and instead all he had received was cold silence. Lynn took a slow ragged breath as she tried to collect her thoughts. So many things were flying around in her head at the same time.

"Bastard! How could you?" Was the first thing that she said as tears welled up in her eyes. "Don't you think it would have been a hell of a lot smarter to tell me this before we moved out here?!" she was starting to struggle with her rising temper. All she could think of now was hurting him. Damn where was her sidearm when she really needed it? Gritting her teeth Lynn stood up and glared at Steve as she hissed,

"You are so God damn lucky I had to leave my gun at work when I left; because if I had it here with me now you would be dead." Steve looked uncomfortable and tried to calm Lynn with the worst lie she had ever heard,

"It is not my fault. I only met her two weeks ago and we just fell for each other right away." Lynn shook her head and took a step closer to Steve.

"Do you really expect me to believe that? What the hell were you doing calling me and telling me that you wanted us to move out here so we could be a family while all the time you were screwing some other chick?" Steve looked sheepish as he shrugged his shoulders and seemed unable to explain his actions. Lynn stood and stared in disbelief for a moment or two until it finally struck her; he had been lying to her to get her to move out to BC with the kids. He didn't want her, he wanted the kids.

"You never really meant what you said, did you? You just wanted me to believe that we were going to try again when all along you were just planning to get the kids closer to you. To hell with me! Right?"

Steve nodded and started to get the strangest look on his face. It seemed to Lynn that he looked proud of what he had accomplished. He had tricked her into giving up everything and moving out to Victoria just so he could see his kids once in awhile. He really didn't care about her or her life. He wasn't interested.

"Well, it looks like it worked. You are here and I am closer to the kids. There isn't much you can do about it either." Steve said smugly and smiled at her. Lynn could not believe that she had allowed herself to be conned by him like this. She had wanted her family to be stable and happy so badly that she had ignored all the warning signs; even when they were staring her in the face.

"You think so? Well I am telling you right now. I will not take this from you. We will be leaving as soon as I can make the arrangements for us to go. I will not stay here without a job or a place to live!"

Steve shrugged and said, "You can stay here. I won't tell the military that I am not living with you."

Lynn only shook her head, "Yah, right. As if you would pay the rent for this house every month and the rent on something else. I can't trust you. Besides, I need a job to support us and I have not even gotten one interview yet." Steve turned and started to walk up stairs.

"I am tired and I want to go to bed now. We can talk about this later." Lynn could not believe he would actually think that after lying to her and sneaking around with another woman that she was going to go to bed and sleep with him.

"Where the hell do you think you are going?" Lynn demanded as she watched him walk towards the stairs.

"Upstairs to bed. Why?" Lynn just shook her head and tried to control her temper as she said,

"There is no way that you will be spending another night in this house. I don't care where you sleep but it won't be here and it sure as hell won't be with me. "Steve stopped in his tracks and turned back to look at Lynn,

"Where am I supposed to sleep?"

"I strongly suggest that you go ask your little girlfriend that question because it is no longer my problem. " Steve started to get angry as he realized that Lynn was no longer going to play along with him. This frightened Lynn momentarily. Steve was taller than her and in extremely good physical shape. He had passed the military physical tests with such high marks that he was exempted from ever having to take them again. He had a very lean, muscular build and if he wanted to hurt her he could with very little effort. Even though she was scared of Steve she was not going to back down. She had put up with enough. He had cheated on her and lied to her one too many times. Lynn pointed to the front door and said with as much determination as she could muster,

"Get out, now. You can come back tomorrow to get the rest of your belongings. I will not put up with your lying and cheating any longer." Steve shook his head and stood in the middle of the living room while he considered his options. Lynn knew he wanted to hit her, she could see it in his eyes. He glared at her while he clenched his fists and growled,

"I can't stay with my girlfriend. Her roommates won't let me." this response shocked Lynn, he had already tried to move out. Damn she was blind sometimes. Lynn shook her head and shrugged.

"Either you leave now or I call the police. I do not want you in this house any longer." Steve looked like he was about to lunge at her but changed his mind.

"I will be back tomorrow to get my stuff." he said as he walked towards the front door. He slammed it closed behind him and Lynn walked over to lock the dead bolt. Her hands were shaking as she reached out to turn the bolt. Fighting back tears Lynn walked upstairs and went into the bathroom to wash her face. She changed into her pyjamas and curled up under the blankets; she pulled the covers over her head and buried her face in her pillow as she finally allowed herself to sob.

Morning came and as her room filled with sunlight Lynn rolled over and pulled her covers closer. She was too depressed to get out of bed. She felt like the floor had been yanked out from under her feet and she was in a free fall. Nothing mattered and nothing made sense any more. Lynn stayed in bed for most of the day, alternating between sleeping and crying. Whenever any of the kids came to her door she would just yell at them to go do something and leave her alone. Olivia and Peter had come home after Steve had left last night so they were not aware of the argument that had happened. Olivia was confused by Lynn's behaviour and when Lynn finally did get up in the late afternoon she confronted her mother.

"What is wrong with you mom? Why are sleeping all day and acting so depressed?" Lynn felt too broken and disappointed in herself and Steve to do anything so she mumbled something about not feeling well while shaking her head and looking at the floor. She was sliding into a severe depression and did not seem to be able to help herself. All Lynn could think about was calling Owen. Maybe that would make her feel better. Their phone had a long distance plan so she waited until that evening to call him. Her heart skipped a beat as the phone rang. Owen did not answer and it went to his voice mail.

"Oki, this is Owen. Please leave me a message." Lynn sighed and hung up the phone. It had made her feel a little better just hearing his voice. She still had no idea what she was going to do but she did not have to figure that out right then and there. While she was lying on the couch contemplating her options she heard Steve pull into the driveway with the truck. The kids went running out the front door to see him while she sat on the couch. She was not looking forward to this and she knew it was not going to be easy. She stood up as he walked through the front door and grunted in her direction. He started to walk past her to towards the kitchen while saying,

"Is there anything left over from dinner? I am hungry." Lynn had not expected to hear that from him and there was no way she was going to feed him.

"No, there are no leftovers from dinner. I suggest you go ask your girlfriend to feed you." Steve spun around to glare at her and said,

"I paid for the rent on this house and half the money left over from the sale of the house is mine." Lynn was determined not to make anything easy for him. He didn't deserve it.

"Yes, but after we paid all the bills and bought the computer and the new washing machine there is only a couple thousand left over. I have to buy myself a vehicle if you are going to keep the truck so I am going to have to use some of it for a down payment on a car and pay for the insurance. "Steve didn't seem impressed by her answer but decided not to argue the point with her.

"Fine," he grunted, "but I still want my share." Lynn just nodded and said,

"Whatever, your stuff is upstairs. I suggest you pack it up and take it with you."

"I have dirty laundry that I need to wash." Lynn shook her head.

"Not here. You gave up that right when you decided to leave us for another woman." Steve looked furious as he stomped up the stairs and began packing all of his belongings in his suitcase.

"I can't believe how unreasonable you are being. " Lynn stood in the bedroom doorway watching him pack and leaned against the door frame.

"Me? Unreasonable? Really, you should have thought about that before you decided to lie to me and trick me into moving here." The kids were becoming upset with the argument between their parents so Peter and Olivia took them outside. Lynn was embarrassed that they had to see what they had deteriorated into. She recalled vaguely for a moment that once a very long time ago she had loved Steve; so much in fact that she could barely stand to be away from him. Now she could barely stand the sight of him. Steve stood up from his packing and clenched his fists.

"You stupid bitch, I would not have to trick you if you were more reasonable to deal with." Lynn was confused by his answer.

"What do you mean by that?"

"All you had to do was agree to live closer to me so I could see my kids." Lynn laughed in disbelief.

"Steve since we have been here you have hardly spent any time with your children. You leave early in the morning and you come home long after they are in bed. In fact they have been asking me when they are going to get to spend some time with you. The argument was beginning to heat up and both Steve and Lynn were yelling,

"Just get out. I don't want to look at you anymore." Steve stood up and reached over to grab Lynn by the arm.

"What if I don't want to leave? This is my house. I am paying for it. Maybe you should be the one to leave!" Lynn reached down to break Steve's grip on her arm and pushed him away from her.

"Let go of me and get the hell out. If you don't leave I am going to call the cops right now. If that happened the military police will show up and you will be disciplined by your commanding officer." Steve clenched his fists again and looked as if he was going to take a swing at Lynn.

"Bitch. I am going right now and I won't be back. You had better find somewhere else to live because I am not going to keep paying your rent." Lynn stepped back from the bed room door way to allow Steve to pass her in the hallway. She glared at him as he walked past her and down the stairway. Lynn was starting to shake again as she walked into the bed room and picked up the cordless phone. She knew it was not over until he actually left. She followed Steve down the stairs and watched as he started towards the front door. He turned to look up at her standing on the stairway and said,

"You were never that pretty, I don't know why I would have ever married you." Lynn did not even bother to respond to his petty comment. She chose to ignore it and replied,

"I think you should leave your key for the house. I do not want you showing up here uninvited." Steve snorted with laughter,

"I don't think so." and walked out the front door. The kids came running up to their father confused by what was happening. He stopped and hugged them both before loading his suitcases in the truck and leaving. Olivia and Peter both came back into the house looking worried and confused.

"Are you alright mom? What just happened?" Lynn fought back her tears and nodded.

"I am okay. Steve is not going to live with us anymore. He has met someone else." She felt tears welling up in eyes and could not fight them back anymore. Olivia wrapped her arms around her and hugged her.

"It's okay mom. He was no good for us anyways. We are better off without him." Lynn nodded and tried to swallow her tears,

"I know, but it still hurts." Peter looked uncomfortable as stood in the living room shifting his weight from foot to foot, waiting for someone to explain to him what was happening. Olivia looked over at him and said,

"Come on Peter, I will explain it to you later." They left and Lynn found herself standing alone in the living room wondering what the hell she was doing with her life. She was startled to hear a knock at the back door and tried to pull herself together as she walked through the kitchen to answer the door. Her next door neighbour was standing on the back step looking awkward and unsure of what to say.

"Hi Lynn, my wife sent me over to ask if we could borrow your uh, mop. Ours is broken." Lynn tried to smile as she said,

"Sure, just a minute while I get it for you." her neighbour took a step into the house and glanced around nervously,

"Uh, are you okay? Do you need anything?" Lynn handed him the mop and said,

"I'm fine. Thanks for asking." her neighbour smiled at her and thanked her as he took the mop. Lynn slowly closed the back door behind him and leaned against it for a moment. It was nice to know her neighbours were concerned about her well being. She had suspected from the beginning that he knew something that he wasn't telling her. He had trained with Steve and he seemed to know a lot about what Steve had been doing for the past twelve months. She found it hard to believe that he didn't know Steve was dating other woman. Lynn decided at that moment that she was not going to be a victim. She was going to do whatever it took to fix her and the kids' lives. Remembering that they had received a welcome package from the military when they moved in she started digging through all of the paperwork in her desk. Finding a phone list for military contacts Lynn decided that she would make some phone calls tomorrow first thing.

The chaplain's office set up an appointment for Lynn for the next day after she briefly explained her situation. They also provided her with contact information for the counselling services offered to all military personnel and their spouses. Lynn flushed with embarrassment as she explained her situation to the emergency counsellor on the phone.

"We moved out here to be with my husband and we have only been here a couple of weeks when he told me that he is in love with another woman and he does not want to be married any longer." The counsellor listened quietly and then paused before saying,

"When you say "we" who are you referring to?" Lynn sighed and tried to stay calm as she clarified,

"Myself and my three children."

"Okay, I understand. So what are you planning on doing now?"

"I have made an appointment to see the chaplain tomorrow to discuss my options with him and I would like to make an appointment to see you as soon as possible." The counsellor paused and Lynn could hear her flipping through what sounded like an appointment book.

"I can get you in next Wednesday afternoon at one. Does that work?" Lynn was disappointed that it would take almost a week to get into to see her but she agreed,

"Yes, that works for me. Do you have anything sooner?"

"No, but if we have any cancellations I will put you on the short notice list."

"Okay, thank you."

"You are welcome. I will give you our crisis line phone number just in case you need any help before I see you."

"Okay, go ahead."

"The number is one eight hundred crisis one. That is a twenty four hour line. Take care Lynn and we will talk on Wednesday."

"Thank you." Lynn hung up and she felt like crying. Talking about her situation with someone else, however briefly had brought up all of her feelings again. Lynn was determined not to let her anger and pain take over her day so she got ready to take the kids out for a walk to the beach for the afternoon. They spent the next couple of hours playing on the small beach near their home; throwing sticks into the tidal pool for the dog to fetch and collecting rocks and seashells. The kids went swimming in the tidal pools and waded around looking for sea urchins and sand dollars. When it was time to go back home Lynn was in a better mood and the kids were exhausted from playing in the sun all afternoon. They walked back through the trails to their house and Lynn started dinner on the barbeque in the backyard. Steve appeared while she was still cooking on the barbeque and the kids ran out into the yard to greet him. Lynn was not happy about his appearance and did not expect anything good would come from it. He was most likely there to try and con her into giving him something or doing something for him. After greeting the kids Steve strolled over to Lynn,

"Hi there, barbequing huh?" Lynn nodded and without looking up from the grill she said,

"Hi Steve, what do you want?" Steve tried to feign a smile as he stood close to the barbeque and squinted down at Lynn.

"Oh nothing, I just came by to see the kids and I was hoping to do a load of laundry while I am here." Lynn shook her head. It figured. He would not have come all the way over just to see his kids.

"Nope, I told you the other day that there is nothing here for you. Go ask your girlfriend to do your laundry." Steve looked like he was starting to get frustrated with her but he seemed determined to try and charm her into giving him what he wanted.

"Oh come on Lynn, I am not asking that much. Besides you know I am living in the camper on the back of the truck and I don't have anywhere to do my laundry."

"How about a laundry mat?"

"Those places are expensive and I don't have the money. It is only my sheets and a couple pairs of pants and a couple of shirts. Only one load of laundry." Now Lynn's curiosity was peaked. Why did he need to wash his sheets already?

"Why do you need to wash your sheets already?" Steve shifted his weight and looked like he did not want to answer the question.

"Cause they need it." Lynn stopped flipping the burgers on the grill and looked at Steve.

"So you were screwing some chick in the camper huh?" Steve looked her right in the eye and tried to fake another smile.

"No, I wouldn't do that. They just need washing." Lynn shook her head and said,

"Steve you are such a pig. Don't bother. I know exactly why you need to wash the sheets. And the answer is still no." Steve was about to argue the point with her when his cell phone rang. He pulled it out of the front pocket of his jeans and answered it in a sweet tone that Lynn had not heard in years.

"Hi, how are you?" She was pretty sure it was at least one of the women he was seeing. Steve turned away from her and took a couple of steps back up the driveway towards the truck while still talking.

"Oh I am almost done here; I was going to come by in an hour or two. Would that be okay?" he was still speaking in honeyed tones and sounded like he was going to start cooing with love. Lynn felt sick to the pit of her stomach. She was furious at the thought of Steve sleeping with this woman and cooing to her right in front of her. Blind with rage she dropped her metal spatula on the grill and charged at Steve yelling on the top of her lungs.

"You hang up the phone right now you bastard. How dare you talk to that whore you are cheating on me with right in front of me." Steve looked at her in disbelief as he tried to take a couple of steps further away from her. He tried to smooth over the situation with the woman on the phone by lying to her right in front of Lynn.

"Oh no, don't worry about that everything is fine. No, no there is nothing wrong. Don't worry about it." Lynn was on the verge of getting violent with Steve if he didn't hang up the phone. She couldn't stand anymore of his lying and cheating. Besides, the woman he was sleeping with probably didn't even know she and the kids existed so she figured she would make sure she knew what the truth was.

"Hang it up right now. You son of a bitch; there is no way I am going to stand here and watch you talk to that little whore right in front of me. I bet you haven't even told her you are married and have three kids." Steve sighed and made an excuse for hanging up the phone.

"There are you happy now? Do you have to be so rude?" Lynn shook her head in disbelief and walked back to the barbeque and the burning hamburger patties.

"Get out of here. I can't the sight of you. Go lie to someone else. I am tired of it." Steve hesitated as he looked like he was thinking about saying something else to her. Instead he just grunted in frustration and walked back to his truck. He jumped in and pulled out of the driveway without looking back or saying good bye to the kids. Still angry Lynn scraped all of the hamburgers off the grill and carried them inside as she called to the kids to come inside for dinner. They seemed confused by their father's behaviour and Lynn was not in the mood to explain anything to them so they ended up eating in silence as Lynn tried to calm down. That evening Lynn thought about trying to call Owen again. She had not been able to reach him and she wished she had someone to talk to. Still feeling angry from Steve's visit earlier she decided not to call him. She did not want to talk to him while she was still upset. Lynn cried herself to sleep again that night. Full of bitterness, anger and shame; she hated herself for letting Steve put her in this position. She had known that this was not a good idea right from the start yet she had agreed to it anyways. What the hell was wrong with her? Lynn drifted off to sleep well after midnight hoping tomorrow would be better.

The next day Lynn took the bus to the military base and met with the chaplain. He was a kind looking man in his late thirties or early forties. He seemed genuinely concerned as he sat down with her and asked Lynn to explain her situation for him. She felt uncomfortable and mildly embarrassed as she looked down at her lap and fought back her tears.

"Well, just over three weeks ago I moved here with our three children from northern Ontario. I sold our house, gave up my job and shipped two horses and a dog out here to be with my husband. About a week ago my husband told me that he was in love with another woman and he did not want to be married anymore." Lynn took a ragged breath as she continued, "I don't know what to do. I don't have a job and he took our only vehicle." The chaplain shook his head in sympathy and waited for her to finish.

"Unfortunately I can't tell you how many times I have heard this story. It is a real shame what has happened and I'll tell you that you are not the first woman to have this happen to them. Sometimes when the men are away from home for almost a year living as if they were single they get used to not having any responsibilities and once their families show up they do not want to accept their responsibilities any longer. I have actually had one fellow come to me the day after his family was moved here to ask me to send them back because he did not want a family any longer."

Lynn looked back down into her lap and twisted the Kleenex in her hands into a knot. She drew another ragged breath and tried to hold back her tears as she looked up at the Chaplain to ask,

"What do we do now? I am completely lost. I do not know what to do." the chaplain just shook his head gently and said,

"I am sorry to say you will have to move out of the military base housing. It is rented to your husband so you cannot stay if he is no longer living there. "Lynn looked distressed at this information and the chaplain quickly clarified.

"Don't worry, we won't throw you out. The military will give you up to six months to find somewhere else to live." Lynn nodded and looked back down at her lap.

"The rest you will have to figure out with your husband. If you wish to move back home he should pay for it. If the military has to pay for your move we will garnish his wages until his debt is paid off and then he will be released with a dishonourable discharge. You may want to explain that to him." Lynn nodded her head again and looked down at the Kleenex she had destroyed in her lap. The chaplain handed her the box of Kleenex and said;

"Here, there are plenty of them." Lynn attempted a weak smile as she took a couple more from the box.

"Have you contacted the emergency counselling service yet?"

"Yes, I called them yesterday and I set up an appointment with them for next week." The chaplain nodded and replied,

"Good, they'll be able to help you figure out your next move. I wish you all the best and I'm sorry that we had to meet under such trying circumstances." Lynn shook his hand and said,

"Thank you for your help." As she walked out of his office Lynn tried to pull herself together. This was not going to be resolved in a day. But she was determined to get her life back on track. At that moment a troop of naval seamen marched by in the same uniform that Steve wore. Lynn was consumed with rage as she watched them march past her. They all reminded her of Steve and what he had done to her. Lynn took a deep breath and waited for them to pass. I guess I still have a ways to go before I can let this go she thought as she walked back to the bus stop. The first thing I am going to do is find myself a car. She was fed up without having a vehicle. It was difficult and time consuming trying to get groceries or do any other errands. So she decided to start looking for a car the next day.

Lynn got up the next morning and told the kids she would be gone for a couple of hours while she went shopping for a car. She left Olivia and Peter in charge of the two youngest and told them she would be back in a couple of hours. She walked to the main street and started looking for car lots. It only took her a couple of hours of looking and she found a used car lot with a cute little four door sedan. It was relatively new and good on gas. Lynn filled out the credit application and went for a walk while they processed it. She found another used car lot across the street that had a used Toyota Corolla. Her in laws had always sworn by Toyota and Honda so she decided to give it a test drive. The kilometres were rather high; over one hundred thousand but her in laws had driven their Toyota well past three hundred and fifty kilometres so she figured it was worth the ten thousand the dealer was asking for it. When she talked to the finance person she found out it was the same dealership for both the cars she was interested in so they just called the dealer across the street to get all of her information. Lynn gave Steve a call on his cell phone.

"Hi Steve, remember my mentioning to you the other day that I was planning on buying a used car? Well I think I found the one I want to buy. Do you think you could come by and have a look at it with me? I am not sure what to check for before buying it." Lynn could tell Steve was trying to decide whether or not he wanted to help her. After a long pause he answered hesitantly.

"Okay, where are you right now?" Lynn smiled with relief when she answered him,

"I'm at the car lot on the main street by the house; the one closest to the Arby's at the bottom of the hill. How long before you think you can be here?" She felt a little anxious while asking him that question. She was uncomfortable asking him for his help but she didn't know what else to do.

"I just finished up at work; I can head over right now. I should be there in about twenty minutes or less."

"Great, thanks very much. I will wait here for you." Lynn hung up the office phone she had borrowed to call him and smiled up at the used car sales man.

"He should be here in the next twenty minutes or so. If you don't mind I would like him to take it for a test drive and have a look at it before I buy the vehicle." The middle aged sales man nodded and smiled,

"Sure thing; I will make sure there are dealer plates on the car and get you the keys. You can just wait here if you like." When Steve arrived he and Lynn took it for a short test drive and drove back to the house. They pulled into the driveway and got out to pop the hood. Steve had a quick look at the engine and the tires.

"It looks like it is in good shape. The tires still have quite a bit of rubber left on them and the engine sounds good. If you like the car it is a good buy. Toyota's are usually pretty reliable." Lynn nodded and they got back into the car to drive back to the dealership. Lynn signed the finance papers and wrote out a check for a thousand dollar down payment on the car. The province sent over an agent to issue her the insurance and plates for the vehicle while she was still at the dealership. After everything was finished Lynn thanked Steve for his help and he left. Lynn drove her new car home and when she pulled into the driveway the kids came running out of the house to inspect their new car. Feeling like celebrating her new found freedom Lynn and the kids drove to Dairy Queen for ice cream.

CHAPTER NINE

From the Ashes

Lynn and the kids had started to settle down into their new home and they were enjoying the hot, sunny weather. They took walks almost every day on one of the trails that ran through the military housing complex. Now that they had a vehicle they were also able to do some sightseeing in Victoria. Lynn had tried to focus on being happy with the small things everyday and to do something positive for her and the kids daily, no matter how small the gesture. It helped, along with the counselling she was getting weekly. The hardest part had been their first meeting when Lynn had to recount the gory details of her foolishly moving herself and her kids to Victoria only to find out Steve no longer wanted to be married.

"So where do you see yourself going now?" the counsellor asked as she and Lynn met for the weekly session. Lynn hesitated before answering. She had been wondering the same thing. Where to now? She had decided that the most logical answer to her dilemma was to go back to Ontario and her old job. Leaning forward in her chair Lynn replied.

"Back to Ontario I think. I held my old job open for a year under the spousal relocation clause in our collective agreement. I am going to call my old boss and ask him for my job back." the counsellor nodded,

"Okay, that sounds reasonable. Have you figured out how you are going to move yourself back to Sudbury?" Lynn shook her head and looked down at her lap. She felt the surge of tears welling up and took a deep breath as she fought to control her emotions.

"Have you talked to your ex about him paying for your move back?" The counsellor asked, trying to help her work through her emotions.

"No, I tried once and he refused to talk about it. He does not seem to feel that he is responsible for what he did. He keeps telling me it is my problem not his." The counsellor looked annoyed as she put down her pen and leaned forward to emphasize her point.

"We have gone over this before Lynn. You have to hold him accountable for his actions. That means insisting that he take responsibility for lying to you and manipulating you into moving out here under false pretences. So when you do speak to him about the move, make sure you tell him that he is responsible and he will pay for the move; one way or another." Lynn nodded as she dabbed at the tears in her eyes and looked up. She tried to harden her resolve as she said,

"You are right. I will talk to him about it again and I will make sure to stress that he is responsible for paying for our move back to Sudbury." The counsellor smiled briefly at her and then leaned back in her chair before continuing.

"Good, now have you given anymore thought to the question that I asked you last week?" Lynn looked slightly confused for a moment,

"Which one?" she replied with a slight smile.

"Why do you think you allowed Steve to do this to you?" Lynn frowned as she recalled their previous conversation. The question made her cringe. She hated looking at her own mistakes. Worse it made her feel foolish even childlike to talk about the reasons why she had allowed this to happen.

"I think I wanted to believe what he was telling me, even if I knew deep down that it was not true. I wanted everything to be okay. I wanted us to be a family again and love each other. I wanted someone to take care of us." She felt her emotions wash over her as she admitted out loud that she wanted to be loved and cared for. "Is that wrong?" she asked looking up at the counsellor.

"No, it is not wrong to want those things. I think I would be safe in saying most people want those things but we have to be careful who we ask to give them to us. Sometimes not everyone we love is worth trusting. That is something that they have to earn." Lynn nodded and looked back down at her lap. She knew that what she was saying was true. As much as she wanted Steve to be there for her and the kids he was not interested or capable of doing it. No matter what he told her. The counsellor brought her back to their conversation,

"Our time is almost up so I want you to work on your plans to move yourself and the kids back to Sudbury for next week. No matter what he tells you Steve is responsible for this and you must hold him accountable. Okay?" Lynn nodded and sighed.

"Okay, can we book our next appointment for next week?" The counsellor nodded and reached for her appointment book.

"How about next Wednesday at the same time?"

"Sure, sounds good. Can you please write that down on an appointment card for me? Otherwise I will not remember." The counsellor wrote down her time and date and handed her the card. She smiled at Lynn and said,

"Try to have a nice week Lynn. We will see you next Wednesday." Lynn smiled back at her and walked out of her office and down the narrow, twisty staircase. As she stepped out of the front door of the crisis centre she could feel the wave of hot air hit her. It had to be close to thirty. She still was not used to the dry heat that Victoria got during the summer. She actually missed the humidity that was normal for an Ontario summer.

That evening Steve showed up after dinner while Lynn cleaning up the kitchen. There were still boxes strewn about the house. She had stopped unpacking when she made the decision to move back to Sudbury. He looked mildly annoyed as he made his way through the dining room boxes to try and find a chair that was empty to sit on. Sighing he gave up and stood in the dining room doorway with his hands crammed into his pockets. Lynn hardly looked up from the dishes as he stood there watching her.

"So what can I do for?" she asked as she continued washing the dishes. Steve looked down, almost depressed as he replied,

"I am having a really bad day. My girlfriend just dumped me. I don't know what to do." Lynn stopped scrubbing and looked up.

"What?" she said with disbelief. This was rich. He dumps her for another woman and then expects her to feel sorry for him when she figures out that he was lying and cheating.

"I said I am really upset because my girlfriend just dumped me." going back to washing the dishes Lynn answered him,

"Oh I heard you. I just couldn't believe that you would show up here looking for sympathy from me."

"I didn't have anyone else that I could talk to about this." Lynn shook her head and she finished up with the dishes and dried her hands off on a tea towel. She placed it back on the handle of the stove and looked up at Steve.

"It sure sucks when you find out no one else wants to be involved in the middle of a divorce, doesn't it? Especially when you were lying to them in the first place." Steve looked like he was going to cry or yell at her. Lynn couldn't tell what he was going to do. Finally he answered her,

"Yes, it does. I really think I loved her. This really hurts." Lynn shook her head again and walked out into the living room.

"I don't want to hear about it. But while you're here I would like to talk about how you are going to pay for our move back to Sudbury." Steve looked at her and frowned.

"I already told you. I don't have any money and I can't pay for your move back to Ontario." Lynn sat down on their old plaid couch and looked up at him.

"I really don't care how you get the money but you will pay for the move. You are responsible for this mess and you will fix it." Steve stood in the doorway between the living room and dining room glaring at Lynn.

"I came over here hoping you would understand what I am feeling. But instead all you are doing is making more demands of me. I can't believe you sometimes." he said as he turned and walked out of the back door of the house. Lynn just sat on the couch and tried to get her anger under control. God she hated that man and she was going to be so happy once she was rid of him once and for all. She sat quietly and listened to the sound of the crickets calling in the warm night air. Lynn walked over to the open living room window and looked up at the full moon. She wondered if Owen was looking up at it too. Reaching for the phone she dialled his cell phone number and waited for him to answer.

"Hi" was all he said when he answered the phone. Lynn loved the sound of his voice.

"Hi, I was just thinking about you so I decided to give you a call." she could hear a smile in his voice as he responded,

"I know, I could feel you thinking about me." Lynn smiled. She knew that he was often aware of her thinking about him. She could often tell when he was thinking about her. Their connection was still strong even though they had not seen each other in almost a year.

"I was wondering if you had seen the moon tonight. It is beautiful." she could hear him get up and walk to the window as he looked outside he replied,

"You are right, it is beautiful tonight." Lynn sighed and sank back into the couch. Holding the phone as close to her as possible she said,

"I have been doing a lot of thinking and I have decided that things are not working out here so we are going to be moving back to Sudbury." she hesitated, waiting for him to say what she had been longing for him to say for over a year.

"Oh, that is too bad. You will be further away from me in Ontario. Are you sure that is what you want to do?" Lynn nodded and sat up as she rearranged the cushions behind her.

"Nothing else seems to be working. I can't even get an interview with my department or any other government department and we are going to run out of money in a couple of months so I have to do something."

"Aren't you still on the priority list for hiring with your spousal relocation clause?" Owen asked.

"Yes, but it does not seem to be helping me out at all. There just aren't that many federal jobs on the island and the provincial jobs that I have applied for I keep getting screened out. I am going to call my boss tomorrow and ask him to give me my old job back. At least then I can buy a house and get the kids back in their old school. They need some stability in their lives right now." She could hear Owen sigh before he answered her,

"Well it sounds like you have given this a lot of thought. You should do what you feel is best." Lynn couldn't help feeling a little disappointed. Deep down she was hoping that he would offer to come to her rescue and ask her to come live with him so he could take care of them. Instead it sounded like he was not going to offer her any help at all.

"Well I have to get going now. I will try and give you a call in a couple of days. Okay?" Lynn felt mildly panicked.

"No, don't go. I just called. Can't we talk a little longer?" Owen chuckled at her earnest request and said,

"No I have to meet a friend soon so I have to get going. We will talk again in a couple of days. Take care." With that he hung up and Lynn was left cradling the phone as she whispered,

"No, don't go." Fighting back tears of disappointment she put the phone down on the coffee table and lay on the couch as she looked up at the ceiling. It was becoming apparent to Lynn that no one was going to help her out of this mess. She was going to have to do it all by herself. Lynn got up from the couch and walked through the house as she checked the doors and windows. Steve still had his key so she didn't know why she bothered locking the doors. If he really wanted in during the night he would be able to let himself in. She shivered slightly at that thought. She had already had Olivia's father appear at the foot of her bed in the middle of the night while he was very drunk and high a long time ago. That experience had scared her enough to know she did not want a repeat of it with Steve. So she decided that she would go to the hardware store tomorrow and buy some deadbolts to put on both of the doors. At least then she would be able to sleep a little better.

In the morning Lynn got up before the kids and dug out her old day timer with all of her contact information for her job in Sudbury. This was not going to be easy for her. She was going to have to swallow her pride and ask her boss to give her old job back. She knew he was going to ask why she wanted to come back so soon and she cringed at the thought of trying to explain to him what had happened. She sat quietly nursing a cup of green tea while the phone rang. She got his voice mail so she left him a message asking him to call her back as soon as possible. Hanging up Lynn sighed. Well at least she had taken the first step to getting her life back in order. She knew that the next step would be to talk to Steve's parents. He wasn't being reasonable with her so she was going to have to ask them to intervene. That was not going to be easy. She did not have a close relationship with his parents. They were polite to her and they loved the children. But they never seemed too interested in getting to know her very well. In fact her mother in law had told her a few years ago that there was no point in trying to tell her anything because she would do what she wanted to do anyways. Lynn really didn't see a problem with that; considering the fact that her mother in law had said it when she was frustrated with Lynn for not listening to her daily advice. She dialled her in law's number and waited for the answering machine. She knew they had both probably left for work so she was planning on leaving them a message to call her back as soon as possible. The phone only rang twice before going to the machine so she left a brief message for them,

"Hi it's Lynn. Could you please call me back as soon as possible?" she hung up and finished her green tea. It was getting late in the morning and she decided to do some homework before the kids woke up. She noticed that Olivia's boyfriend was not sleeping on the couch when she went back into the living room. He must have snuck into her bedroom while she was busy on the phone. This seemed to have become a regular routine for the two of them. Lynn frowned slightly debating whether or not she wanted to do something about it or ignore it for the time being. Just then the phone rang and Lynn walked back to the dining room table to answer it.

"Hello?" she could hear the sound of a couple of chairs rustling and someone cough on the other end of the line. She realized she was on speaker phone. Just then her boss spoke up sounding as if he was at the bottom of a barrel.

"Hello Lynn its Brian and Rob calling. I got your message earlier and since we were both in the office for a meeting I thought I would call you back on the speaker phone. I hope you don't mind." Lynn did not feel she was in any position to complain so she just tried to feign a smile in her voice as she responded,

"No not at all. Hello Rob how are things in northern Ontario?" She could hear Rob's chair squeak as he leaned closer to the speaker phone.

"Hello Lynn. About the same; business as usual. How are things on the Island? You must be enjoying the nice weather out there."

Lynn couldn't help nodding and smiling. If nothing else at least she had nice weather every day.

"No complaints; sunny and warm. The reason I called you is because I wanted to discuss my coming back to my old position in Ontario. I know that under the spousal relocation clause there is a position held open for me; just not necessarily the same position." she could hear the silence on the other end as both of the men were surprised by her request. Brian spoke up after a moment or two.

"Well that is the last thing we expected to hear from you! We figured you would be happy to be back in BC. Sure, your position is still here I don't see why not. Can I ask why you want to come back so soon?" Lynn had been dreading this moment. She knew he would ask, any one would ask the same question. She drew a deep breath and recited the response she had been practising all morning.

"Things have not worked out here as planned. My husband has decided that he would like a divorce and I have not been able to find another position."

"Oh, I see. Certainly I don't see a problem with you coming back to the Sudbury office. But you have to understand that Fisheries and Oceans won't pay for your move. That would be your own responsibility." Lynn nodded she already knew that would be the case. She was just relieved to have her old job back.

"Not a problem. I expected as much. I will be trying to get everything arranged for us to be back in Sudbury by the first week of September." Brian sounded surprised.

"Well you have just under a month to do it. We will be looking forward to seeing you back in the office. I will have Judy draw up your paperwork for you to sign."

"That's wonderful. Thanks very much Brian I really appreciate this. I am hoping to fly back to Sudbury in about two weeks to find a house. I will drop by the office to sign everything then if that works for you."

"Sure, sounds good. See you then. Take care Lynn." She hung up the phone feeling a wave of relief wash over her. At least she had a job to go back to. Now she if she could figure out a way to buy another house. She had a good relationship with the manager of her old credit union in Sudbury. Maybe if she talked to him when she got back to Sudbury he could help her work something out. It was worth a try.

She was worried about the cost of the flight back to Sudbury so she had been checking into her air miles. She barely had enough to get her on a late night flight to Regina, Saskatchewan where she would have a layover for ten hours before her second flight to Toronto where she would have to change planes for her last flight into Sudbury. The trip back was just about as bad. There was no way she could afford a hotel room and restaurants for a week so she was going to have to find someone to stay with while she was in Sudbury. She had been in touch with Carrie Madison and Judy St. Amour by email for the past couple of weeks. They had been trying to offer her as much support as possible. When she emailed that she was planning a trip back to Sudbury they immediately offered her a place to stay and help with her house hunting. Things were beginning to come together. It seemed to be much easier and quicker to get their move back to Sudbury arranged than any other option so she must be on the right track. The only piece of the puzzle left was the cost of the movers. She still had not been able to figure out how she was going to get that done. Her in laws had not returned her call. She had tried calling them again a second time and leaving them a longer message. They still hadn't called her back. She knew they were talking to Steve, God knows what he was telling them. She was sure he forgot to mention his new girlfriend. Lynn decided that she had waited long enough for her in laws to get back to her so after dinner she tried again. This time her father in law answered.

"Hello?" His strong British accent always made it hard for Lynn to understand what he was saying, even after eight years.

"Hi Grant, it is Lynn. I have been trying to reach you the past couple of days. Did you get my messages?"

"Yes we did Lynn. We haven't had a chance to call you back." Lynn decided not to press the issue.

"Sure, I understand. I wanted to talk to you about Steve. He has asked me for a divorce and we have to move out of this house. The military has given us a couple of months to find another place but Steve is refusing to pay for the move. I spoke to the military and they have told me that if he won't pay for the move they will. But they will garnish his wages until he has paid off the debt and then he will be released with a dishonourable discharge. I am hoping you can help us. Otherwise I have no other choice than to ask the military to pay for the move." There was a long pause as her father in law digested what she had just said. He sighed and finally responded with,

"Okay, can you give us until tomorrow to talk to discuss with him what we are going to do and then we will get back to you. " Lynn nodded, this was about as good as she could expect from them.

"Alright, I can expect a call back from you tomorrow evening then?"

"Yes, after we have talked to Steve."

"Okay, thanks very much." Hanging up the phone Lynn couldn't help but hope they would work something out with him. If Steve was unemployed things would only be worse for them. She needed him to pay child support.

The next evening both her in laws were on the line when they called her back. Her mother in law greeted her and chatted about nothing in particular for a few moments before Grant interrupted her with,

"We spoke to Steve last night and we will pay for your move back to Sudbury. I will book the movers once you have a date for me." Lynn felt relieved and disappointed at the same time. She was grateful to have their help but disappointed in Steve for failing to live up to his responsibilities. She hoped his parents would see it that way too.

"Okay, thanks very much. I will have to fly back to Sudbury on my air miles to find a house. I will be trying to take possession of it by the first of September. I am not sure I will be able find one that quickly. If not then I will try for September fifteenth." Lynn could hear her mother in law sigh.

"You do know Lynn that you are welcome to live in our downstairs suite if you want to stay in BC and keep looking for a job." Lynn couldn't help but smile at this offer. That would make her mother in law ecstatic. She would have total control over Lynn and the kids. She could keep track of her every move and give her orders daily. They did live in their downstairs suite when they first got married and it was a disaster. The woman had no concept of personal space or privacy. She would walk into their home unannounced whenever she felt like it day or night. She would even walk into their bedroom first thing in the morning without knocking. Lynn only wished that they were having sex when she did. That might have taught her to at least knock first.

"Oh thanks very much Madeline but I would rather get back to work as soon as possible and give the kids some stability by putting them back into their old schools. I appreciate the offer though." She hoped that was diplomatic enough to keep them from feeling insulted. She knew they wanted the kids to be closer to them. They had objected when she first took her transfer to Ontario.

"Okay, well the offer is there if you change your mind." That was not going to happen. Lynn was determined to go back to her old life. There was no way she was going to live on welfare in her in laws' basement.

"I understand and thanks very much. I will call you when I get back from Sudbury to give you the date for the movers." Lynn hung up and let out a sigh of relief. Things were coming together. All she had to do now was concentrate on writing the final exam for her law course on Monday afternoon and then get ready to fly back to Sudbury. She only had the weekend to study for her exam but she was certain that would be enough.

Friday night and she was home alone with the kids and nothing to do but study. For the first time in the past week she had the chance to sit down and relax for a few moments. She couldn't help but feel a little lonely. She reached for the phone knowing that she shouldn't but she dialled Owen's number anyways. Holding her breath she listened to his cell phone ring on the other end. It went to his voice mail after a couple of rings. Disappointed she hung up the phone and went back to staring at her homework. Owen hadn't called her back this week like he had promised he would. That really didn't surprise her. He rarely did call when he said he would. She had come to expect it of him. The weekend wore on and Lynn tried to focus on studying for her exam. She was fairly confident that she would do well on the exam but she wanted to be sure. There was no way she was going to allow Steve and this disaster to cause her to fail.

It was late Sunday afternoon when Owen finally called. Lynn answered the phone and was surprised to hear his voice.

"Hi Lynn. I just wanted to call to let you know that I hadn't forgotten about you. I just spent the weekend with my mother. She was getting a Governor's Award and I wanted to attend."

"Hi Owen nice to hear from you. I was wondering where you were this weekend. How did things go with your mother?" She could hear the pride in his voice as he answered.

"Very well thank you. It was a very nice ceremony and my mother was very happy." Lynn smiled,

"That sounds wonderful. Please tell your mother that I said congratulations."

"I will." Lynn missed talking to him and she had so much to tell him from the past week's events.

"I have been very busy this week and I have finally made most of my travel arrangements to fly back to Sudbury next week."

"That's good. Have you written your final exam yet?" Owen asked. His tone had changed but Lynn couldn't figure out what was going on with him.

"No, I write it on Monday afternoon. I have been studying on and off all weekend. I think I am almost ready for it."

"Good, why don't you call me after you write your exam to let me know how you did?" Lynn liked that idea. It made her feel like he cared.

"Sure, I will do that." she hesitated for a moment and then added, "Is everything okay Owen? Something seems wrong." She still didn't know what it was but it was she had an unsettling feeling growing in the pit of her stomach.

"No, there is nothing wrong." Lynn didn't believe him. The feeling she had was overwhelming her, making her feel like she was going to choke on the heavy, dark air that surrounded her.

"Are you sure Owen. I have this awful feeling something is wrong and I can't shake it. Are you okay? Is everything okay with us?" Owen repeated his earlier response and he sounded insistent,

"No, there is nothing wrong." I have to get ready for a long drive tomorrow. I have a meeting with a Chief and council and I have to pack yet. Make sure you call me tomorrow night, okay?" Lynn nodded with resignation and replied,

"Okay, I will. Have a good trip. Bye."

"Good bye." Lynn hung up. She still couldn't shake the feeling that something was wrong; very wrong. The feeling hung over her all day. After dinner Lynn sat down to study again and decided to focus on her course and ignore the feeling that kept nagging at her. She got up early the next morning and made sure the kids had something to eat before she left to write her exam. She had arranged for the military base to set up a room and invigilator for her so she drove to the naval base and walked to the building that had been assigned for her to use. She took three hours to write the exam and she was exhausted when she finished. But she felt good about it. She had answered all of the essay questions in full and had not had any problem understanding any of the multiple choice questions. Her cell phone vibrated in her pocket as she walked back to her car. It was a text message from a phone number she didn't recognize.

It read "Leave Dr. Proudfeather alone. We have three children and we are trying to work on our marriage." Lynn stopped dead in her tracks. She read the text message again and shook her head in disbelief. This had to be a joke. Owen wasn't married. He had told her he wasn't married. Feeling confused and angry, Lynn decided to send a text message back to the anonymous person. "Who is this? Owen is not married." she didn't have to wait for long for an answer. "This is his wife. Men lie. We have been married for three years." Lynn felt like she had been punched in the stomach. This was not making any sense. Had the past three years been a total lie? She had been talking to Owen and seeing him for three years and he had assured her more than once there was no one in his life, especially not a wife. Could it be possible that he had played her all this time? Lynn's hands shook with rage as she texted a response back to Owen's wife. "I am so sorry. I didn't know." She didn't wait for a response to her last message. She dialled Owen's cell phone and tried to calm down as the phone rang. It went to his voice mail like it usually did. Lynn drew a ragged breath before leaving her message. "Owen this is Lynn. I just got a very disturbing text message from someone claiming to be your wife. I need you to call me and explain how that is possible." Lynn hung up her cell phone and dropped in into her purse. She was still shaking with rage and shame. Her cell phone rang about fifteen minutes later. It was Owen and he sounded worried.

"Hi." was all he said as she answered the phone.

"Hi, did you get my voice message Owen?"

"Yes I did. It is just a misunderstanding. I can explain."

"Okay go ahead I am listening."

"I am married, technically. We have been having problems and agreed to a trial separation." Lynn felt stunned. He was married and had been lying to her about it for three years. God, could things get any worse?

"So let me get this right. You have been married for the past three years that we have been talking and seeing each other. So every time I specifically asked you if you were married or had anyone in your life you lied to me?" Lynn could hear him sigh before he answered her,

"Yes, I suppose I did."

"You suppose?" Lynn could feel her temper rising. "You suppose? That is the best you can do? What the hell happened to I lied to you and made you into the other woman. What happened to I am sorry?" Lynn paused as she waited for Owen to apologize or at the very least acknowledge what he had done was wrong. Owen only sounded impatient with her as he responded.

"There is no need to be overly dramatic. I was in the process of separating from my wife and was planning on getting a divorce." Lynn was filled with disbelief as she realized that Owen was not even remorseful for lying to her.

"Did you marry that woman after I met you Owen?" Lynn was only met with silence on the other end of the phone.

"Jesus Christ you did didn't you!" Lynn's heart sank as the full impact of the truth hit her.

"After all you put me through because I wasn't divorced when we met. All the bullshit you fed me about it being morally wrong to see me because I was still married. You were married the whole God damn time! What makes it worse is that you married her after you met me!"

"I might have. What does it matter?" Owen's tone had changed,

"What does it matter?" Lynn felt as if his words were driving a stake into her heart. Fighting back tears she managed to say,

"I can not and will not be the other woman. I obviously can't believe a word you say. I do not even know who you are. We are done." hanging up her cell phone Lynn stood in the middle of the parking lot in dumbfounded by what had just happened. As it sank in Lynn began to feel as if the ground was dropping away from her feet. This couldn't be happening, not right now. Her life had already fallen apart; this was just the final blow. She staggered to her car and leaned against the driver's side as she clutched her cell phone to her chest.

With that Owen was out of her life, again. Lynn stood in the parking lot leaning against her car. She dropped her head down into her arms on the hood and fought the urge to wail. The grief and anguish were overwhelming. Never in her life had she felt so much pain and shame from being lied to by someone she loved. Owen had turned her into something she despised; the other woman. Lynn eventually stood up and bit her lip while she dug in her purse for her keys. The pain helped to distract her from her grief. She managed to get into her car and drive home. She could not remember what route she took home or how long it took her to get there. Everything was a blur as she staggered into the house and upstairs to her bedroom. She locked the door and crawled between the wall and her bed pulling the covers down to wrap herself into a ball. She stayed curled up in a ball on the floor for a couple of hours before she heard her oldest daughter knocking on the bedroom door.

"Mom, are you going to get up soon to make dinner? It is already past five and we are getting hungry." Lynn could hardly focus on what she was saying and answered her from the floor,

"Just order a pizza. I will pay you back for it later."

"Okay, do you want any?" Lynn was not hungry. Food was the last thing she wanted right now.

"No. Just leave me alone."

Lynn wrapped herself even tighter in the quilt and curled up against the wall. She started to sob and couldn't stop. She cried until there were no more tears. She drifted off to sleep and dreamt of Owen's voice calling her from the darkness as she slipped into an abyss of loneliness and betrayal with no way out. Lynn spent the loneliest, darkest night of her life on the floor beside her bed. She drifted off into a light sleep for an hour or so before waking up again to her loss. Sobs wracked her body as she curled up on the floor trying to stop the pain that was crushing her chest. By the morning light Lynn was so exhausted she fell into a restless sleep for a few hours until the banging on her bedroom door woke her.

"Mom it's almost lunch time are you going to get up soon?" she heard through the door. Groggy with the lack of sleep and still grief stricken Lynn had lost the will to move.

"No, go away." was all she managed before she curled back up and tried to slip back into sleep where she could escape her pain. The next time Lynn woke up it was dark outside and the house was quiet. Struggling to her feet Lynn managed to stand up and make her way out of her bedroom and down the hallway to the bathroom. The kids were already in bed sound asleep. Olivia had put them to bed after making them spaghetti for dinner. Lynn stood in the bathroom with the door closed and looked into the mirror over the small sink. She held onto the edge of the sink for support as she peered into her red, swollen eyes. She reached up to touch the dark circles under her eyes and sighed. She couldn't bear to look at herself any longer and turned away from her reflection full of grief and self loathing. How could she let this hit her so hard? She knew she couldn't count on Owen for anything. He had never been there for her when she needed him in the past. That was part of the reason for her agreeing to move out to Victoria in the first place. Even though her heart was with Owen she hated him with an intensity she had never felt before. He had lied to her and turned her into the other woman. She could never trust him again. She could never trust any man ever again.

Lynn splashed some cold water on her face and brushed her teeth. Feeling drained and depressed she dragged the hair brush through her hair a few times before becoming exhausted. Giving up and not caring about her appearance Lynn left the bathroom and walked down the stairs to the living room and kitchen. She dug through the fridge until she found some leftovers to warm up in the microwave. Sitting alone at the dining room table Lynn forced down the leftover spaghetti. It tasted bland to her. Nothing seemed to have any colour or flavour. Finishing Lynn stood up and dumped her dirty dishes in the sink. She had a drink of water and walked back into the living room to sit down on the couch. Every movement was slow and difficult. She felt as if she were swimming through the air;

pushing her body to take every step, every breath. Lynn sat quietly in the dark feeling her heart beating and listening to her breath. She wondered if she stopped willing her heart to beat if it would just stop on its own. She was afraid to find out so she kept willing it to beat. She hated life at that moment but somewhere deep inside her there was still a small glimmer of hope; the will to live.

Lynn knew she had to do something to pull out of her depression; anything to make her feel like she was moving forward in a better direction. Picking up the phone she walked back into the dining room and sat down at the computer desk. She was going to find a flight back to Sudbury and book it with her air miles. At least she would feel like she had accomplished something that day. It took her the next couple of hours of searching flights on the internet and talking on the phone with a booking assistant before she finally managed to book a flight in one week from Victoria to Sudbury with a lay over in Saskatoon. It was the best she could manage on such short notice.

Feeling tired and slightly less depressed Lynn decided to go back to bed and try to get up during the morning the next day. As she slipped off to sleep Lynn said a silent prayer. Please God take my pain and help me to find a way to make our lives better. She welcomed the darkness and could feel it envelope her as she closed her eyes. The pain in her chest faded and she slide into a deep sleep with no memory of her dreams.

The next morning Lynn woke to the sound of her kids playing with the next door neighbours children in the front yard. The sun was already heating up the day even though it was only just past ten. Lynn lay in bed feeling rested and comfortable until the memory of the past two days began to flood back. Tears welled up in her eyes as she started to feel the same crushing pain in her chest and began to will her every breath. Lord be with me now. I need your strength to get through the day. I am not sure I can do this on my own. Lynn was not big on organized religion. It had failed to provide her with the support and comfort in the past when things had gone wrong in her life. But she did know deep in her heart that God was listening even if she couldn't always find him in church. Clinging on to her hope that her faith would get her through the day Lynn struggled out of bed and reached for her bathrobe. With grim determination she willed her feet down the hallway and into the bathroom. Leaning against the bathroom sink she looked at her reflection in the mirror. The swelling around her eyes had gone down and the black circles under them were smaller. She brushed her teeth and washed her face while trying to plan her day. It was going to be better today. She was determined to have a better day. She was not going to let any man destroy her life. No one deserved that much power over her. As much as she feared being alone; in that moment she decided being alone was better than allowing someone to destroy her life, their lives. She would focus on giving her children the best life that she could; a stable, secure life with a peaceful home and no more drama. Even if it meant she never had another relationship again.

Lynn ate her breakfast while she looked out the dining room window. Her two youngest children were running past the window while playing a game of chase with Sam, their border collie cross and the two children from next door. The dog was barking as it ran beside the children as the squealed with delight. She admired how well they were coping with all of the chaos that was going on in their lives. They knew something was wrong and that their father had left them. Yet they still managed to laugh and play. If they could do it then she could do it too. Lynn stood up and walked back into the kitchen. She washed the dishes that were piling up in the sink and then went back upstairs to get dressed. It was a nice day to take the kids and the dog for a walk down to the beach.

Stepping out into the warm air Lynn could feel the heat of the sun on her face. She loved the semi Mediterranean climate. She could hear the birds calling from the trees behind their house. The smell of the roses and lavender bush growing in the front yard delicately wrapped her in a feeling of warmth and comfort. Taking another deep breath she called the dog and kids.

"Come on you guys we are going to take a walk down to the beach." All three came running around the side of the house while barking and shouting happily,

"Bye you guys we are going for a walk with our mom right now. We will play with you later." Forcing a smile Lynn reached down and put the leash on Sam. Eric reached up and took her hand as they started to walk down the driveway.

"I love going for walks to the beach. It is so much fun to look for shells and rocks in the water. Do you think we will find some really good rocks today mom?" Lynn looked down at her son and she could feel her heart warm. Squeezing his hand she smiled and said,

"I am sure we will find some really good rocks today."

ONE LOVE

iUniverse books may be ordered through booksellers or by contacting:

iUniverse
1663 Liberty Drive
Bloomington, IN 47403
www.iuniverse.com
1-800-Authors (1-800-288-4677)

ISBN: 978-1-4917-3658-6 (sc)
ISBN: 978-1-4917-3660-9 (hc)
ISBN: 978-1-4917-3659-3 (e)

Printed in the United States of America.

iUniverse rev. date: 7/9/2014

CPSIA information can be obtained at www.ICGtesting.com
Printed in the USA
LVOW10s1742160914

404335LV00001B/157/P

9 781491 736586